More than Justice

Lou Briganti

ISBN-10: 0615522556
ISBN:-13: 978-0615522555 (Bigtrain Publishing)

DEDICATION

Many people have contributed time, experience, information, and inspiration in shaping this story, and I am grateful to all of them more than I can say. Writing is by definition a lonely business, and their friendship is a comfort and shield against that loneliness.

Family has been the center of civilization since our ancestors left Eden. My family has been the foundation for all the ways I have defined myself since puberty, when most of what I thought about was doing what one must do to start one. My daughters, Elena Phipps and Christiana Briganti-Dunn have been bright stars in my personal "Southern Cross" since their birth. Whatever else I do, right or wrong in this life, they are the all the proof I need of my success.

Having said that, I dedicate this book to one whose love, encouragement, and belief are gifts which no fledgling author should be without. She has seen me through more thin days than thick, carried on through more of her own sickness than health, and made my last 23 years more precious than gold. My wife Jackie is a new gift to me every morning I open my eyes. If readers like you enjoy this story and the ones that follow, you'll help me pay a small part of the debt that I owe her, while I work to repay the larger part, in which the only currency is love.

ACKNOWLEDGEMENTS

Sgt.Maj. James Phipps, USMC (Ret.) has served our country with valor, dedication, and old fashioned loyalty. What he accomplished as a Marine in Iraq, Kuwait, and Okinawa makes me proud to know him. Today, he serves other veterans through his work at the Veterans' Administration. My admiration extends beyond his military service, to his contributions to my daughter, Elena's happiness, and to his skillful parenting of two magnificent grandchildren. I am grateful to him for his time and 101 helpful suggestions.

Tyler Phipps has begun what I hope will be a successful career as a graphic artist and cover designer, with the design for this volume. At 17, he has begun to hone his skills and find his own life design – an exciting time!

Pete Hargrove, of Chevy Chase, Maryland, an international educator, helped with one of the most difficult challenges I faced in writing this book – writing love scenes. His approach took much of my hesitancy and discomfort out of the equation, by adding the truly helpful and gentle ingredient of humor.

Margie Ross, President of Regnery Publishing, Janie Gabbett, former Managing Editor of Reuters North America, and Lee Euler, Managing Partner of Online Publishing & Marketing, LLC: all are close friends and true, life's greatest treasures. All have read early drafts and both encouraged me and kicked my butt ever so gently. Many thanks. I WILL learn, honest!

Lou Briganti

All men want things.
Wealth, pleasure, freedom,
justice, knowledge,
wisdom, excitement,
sex, power.

Men want all these things.
Many want more all the time.
Most of them want more than
the next man gets.

Some men don't care
how they get them.

These are the romantics.
They still believe in a free
lunch.

Chapter One
The Rodent

Uniglobe Petroleum Americas Campus, Fairfax, Virginia
August 4, 3:45pm

Roger Toople popped his third antacid of the afternoon. He preferred Tums, despite the deluge of TV commercials for more powerful products that promised to end his suffering with only one pill a day. Acid indigestion was his assigned lot in life, and he accepted it as one of the many personal crosses he bore on his way to what he was sure was a sacrificial death.

His cubicle was a marvel of industry and dedication, at least to a workspace designer. Two computers, twelve file drawers, two storage cabinets, 14 linear feet of horizontal work surface, 12 of which were covered with neat stacks of bound and unbound documents. To Roger, it was an insult.

He rubbed his aching stomach, then his creased forehead. His mood was foul, for reasons way beyond the stress of Uniglobe annual budget season and its requirement for sixty-hour weeks for at least two months.

This year was worse than before. He'd been turned down for two level five positions he'd posted for in the past 90 days, as well as for a merit promotion from his current grade 4 accounting slot. His salary of $47,600 was almost embarrassing at the holiday parties at his wife Cassandra's law firm, Stirman, Haver & Mills, especially since he'd blurted it out in a cocktail fog last Christmas. (Hers was $750 large plus bonus and four weeks at the firm's time-shares in Colorado, the Caribbean, Hawaii, and Tahiti.)

Despite surviving seven of Uniglobe budget seasons, this year his dyspepsia was worse than ever. For Roger, the reason was simple. Money: the company's fortune, his lack of it, and his suspicions about where the company's was going.

Uniglobe had filed its last 10K, reporting $3.9 billion in profits for the quarter. Gas at the pump was on the rise, and might hit $4.00 if OPEC kept holding back on production. Level 4 accountants like Roger didn't have access to the service station in the basement of Building One, where even premium was only $0.99 a gallon, and that went to pay the salaries of the pump jockeys.

Roger had long nursed a suspicion that financial funny-business was afoot within Uniglobe.

Granted, $3.9 billion was a huge amount of profit for 90 days of business, but after seven years, and despite the fact that his job duties mired him in the most insignificant of accounting details, for Roger, it didn't add up at all.

He'd been looking everywhere he could look, quietly, almost casually at first, but lately with more persistence and better tools.

For three years, he'd taken night courses at a branch of the ITT Tech Schools, learning more about software and systems security – without notifying his employer or asking for tuition reimbursement.

He was nowhere near brilliant, but if his instructors had paid any attention, they might have agreed that he was highly, though quietly, motivated. He was no world class hacker yet, but breaking into his first two secure Uniglobe modules had given him a sense of possibility. Breaking in and then covering his tracks so thoroughly that his intrusion was knowable but untraceable -- that gave him more confidence.

A week ago Roger Toople finally stumbled into a "turn-the-corner" day, a life-changing day of discovery, a "keys-to-the-kingdom" day. He'd nearly stopped breathing then, and for five following days he'd become a serious rodent, burrowing quietly into the dirt and muck of corporate secrets never meant for the light of day.

Last night, he'd eaten almost nothing of his housekeeper's baked scrod, drank almost none of his wife's latest Chardonnay purchase. He'd barely listened to the daily litany of her legal exploits, and though he'd gone to bed early and alone, he'd slept for less than an hour. The rest of the night was a furious fantasy.

His discovery? Just what he'd expected, only more. Much more. At least three, and probably a few more of Uniglobe's executives were cooking the books, hiding profits behind bogus exploration and development expenditures, among others. He'd even learned that three of the subcontractors to whom the bogus expenses were being paid were shell companies, headquartered in the Caribbean and North Africa, and given what he could find, he doubted they did anything other than serve as the executives' private banks.

The scope of their piracy was so huge he found himself astounded, actually admiring their boldness. If his numbers were even close to correct, and if the three executives he'd identified were the only ones involved, each would leave the company one day with several billion. If one of them was the leader and thus took a leader's share, in a few more years his take could even approach Bill Gates' fortune, especially now that Uniglobe was engaged in the massive new European pipeline venture with all the political shenanigans that entailed. As a matter of fact, that pipeline appeared to be the centerpiece of their machinations.

Unless, of course, they got caught.

If his expeditions into the protected enclave of their private files were accurate, they'd been at it for almost thirty months. That they had covered their tracks with mountains of phonied up data and serious scientific jargon made their work all the more impressive.

These first days of Roger's excitement only made his indigestion worse. He could barely contain the roiling of his stomach and bowels, and even breathing became something of an effort. There had been no real excitement in his life until these last few days, and he wasn't prepared for it, or for the sudden and huge fear that came with it. That gave him sudden sweats and diarrhea – along with the embarrassment that usually accompanies it, a feeling with which he was much more familiar.

The misery made his treatment by the company feel all the more unfair, undeserved, and insulting. Still, he now held the magic lamp, and as he contemplated its genie, he found it nearly impossible to restrict himself to three wishes.

It was mostly at night that he thought about those. He hadn't slept well all week. He would have tossed and turned, except that he didn't relish waking his wife, who had enough reasons to be unhappy with him as it was. So he lay completely still on her $3,200 Tempurpedic foam mattress and let his mind devour the wishes like chocolates.

("First, there is a car. A new car, and no econobox like the Hyundai Accent I drive now. Something with serious power, speed, and class even greater than Cassandra's BMW -- perhaps a Mercedes AMG coupe with 550 horsepower or so. Hell, not even a new car, but a classic, a collector's six-figure jewel that others only buy to store away, and I'll actually drive it.)

("Then, there's my body. I'll get hair to cover the bare top I've suffered with for a dozen years, and some Botox or whatever they inject these days to give me a real Marlboro Man chin instead of the little receding thing that I've got now.)

("Next? Even though it might take months, I'll have both the money and time to work out and put muscle

on my narrow shoulders and turn the pillow below my
belt buckle into a chiseled triangular masterpiece.")

With the car, the hair, the body, sudden fame, and
serious cash of his own in his pocket, there would be
other benefits of course. He closed his eyes tighter and
considered a long string of women throwing themselves
at him. That was enough of a fantasy to raise a minor
tent pole beneath the covers, but Roger couldn't risk the
embarrassment of waking his wife by jiggling the bed
servicing himself, so he changed the dream.

It was enough that Cassandra Hastings would see
him differently. She had sweetly but firmly refused to
take his name when they'd married nine years ago,
explaining that it would cause unnecessary grief to her
10-year old daughter, Tara, by her first husband. "I
couldn't do that to her, Roger. I mean, for God's sake,
Tara Toople? Puhleeease!") Life with Cass could begin
again – on something like *his* terms.

As dawn announced the new day, however, he
found himself overwhelmed with fear. For one thing, if
he was to achieve his dreams as a whistleblower, he was
going to have to leave his office and the Uniglobe
campus with hard evidence.

That would not be easy. There were security
procedures, high tech surveillance, and random searches
in a paneled section of the lobby between the upper floor
elevators and the separate elevators to the garage. He
didn't want to think about getting caught trying to leave
with the evidence he'd now gathered.

But what flooded his stomach and esophagus with acid right now was a bigger question: what to do with his discovery – and his evidence?

He had never imagined himself as a whistleblower. Now, he was lost in a vortex of fantasy, seeing himself hailed as a hero, being interviewed by Matt Lauer, authoring a best-seller about his own exploits, making speeches about the failure of corporate integrity. The scenes of his new life flooded his mind so thoroughly he could barely see to shave and dress.

It was not his nature to get carried away in fantasies like that. He might dream of himself now and then as an action hero and a Don Juan, but wide awake, he knew himself as a small man of small achievements. Sure, he was fond of precision, procedure, and daily perfection. A leader he was not, but an introvert's introvert, a quintessential accountant, a man who bathed in details and ate digital printouts three times a day. Above all he found himself terribly, painfully lonely. Still…

Two days later he had screwed up all his courage for what he knew would be the most dangerous part of his hurried plan.

"Step One: Getting my precious data out of the building." Even before he would try to leave with these documents, he didn't really know everything he wanted to know about surveillance software that might be monitoring his own workstation activity. Then, downstairs, there was the security team in the lobby.

*("No one passes in or out of the building except
by going through them. They know me, and I doubt if I'm
someone they imagine would have the balls to do
anything as big as this. Still, it is what goes out that
seems to concern the security people most.")*

He would have to "tag" all the documents he
wanted and download them all at once with maximum
speed, then get them out immediately. Hard copies were
out of the question – he'd have to get them out on a
laptop or PDA of his own, though presently he didn't
own one. No CDs either. They were too easy to
confiscate and search. He'd have to store them on a
laptop hard drive, and even encode them somehow to
disguise them, if he could do it really quickly.

The more he thought about it the more frightened
he became.

When he finally settled on it, his plan was simple
enough, perhaps too simple, and far bolder than he felt.
Even as he prepared to execute it, he began to perspire,
though when he thought about it, the growing sweat
beads on his forehead might actually serve him well in
the "lobby act."

Chapter Two
Getting Out

August 12
12:16 pm

Roger held his breath as the elevator descended, a failed effort to stop his heart from racing. He was about to stop on his way out of the building to do something he'd never done before, make small talk with the two guards on dayshift.

They knew him by name, of course, and he'd read their first names enough times to remember Phil, the tall white one who must have played defensive line for some big-time football team and Baron, the black one who looked a lot like the latest TV pitchman for Allstate.

Phil was the younger one, more outgoing and friendly. Baron took himself very seriously, as if he had to live up to his name and his mother's royalty dreams.

"Going out to lunch today, eh Roger? Tired of the brown bag sandwich or ya got somethin' special goin' on. Which is it?" Phil asked.

Roger stopped, shook his head slowly, and did his best lame dog frown.

"No...well, not exactly. My wife wants me to buy a new laptop for our, well I mean her daughter, Tara,

who's in college. I'm going over to Circuit City, I guess. I'm not sure what to get."

It was precisely the opening Phil seemed always to be looking for – an opportunity to advise people – on virtually any topic – from his boundless expertise.

"Laptops, Roger? If your daughter's not a Mac person, and you know how those folks are, they drink green tea and drive Saabs, there's only one brand to get, man, Dell. Don't you agree, Baron?"

Baron didn't just speak. He intoned, his deep baritone almost auditioning for the lead in the next God film.

"I'd recommend Dell, not for feature content, but for reliability and service. Especially the Inspiron Mini-9s. It's one of their newest, and in my view, it's one of their best."

Roger brightened up his face, as if the weight of the world had just been lifted from him.

"Gee, thanks guys! That's a big help. I had no idea what to get, and my wife's a real you-know-what when I screw something up."

Both men chuckled at that. He knew they'd be talking about him for several minutes after he'd left, and when he came back 45 minutes later, he made it a point to stop, open the Circuit City bag, and show them the box with the new Mini-9 laptop.

"Boy, you guys were right. This seems like a great machine and the price wasn't bad, either. I really appreciate your help!"

He noted their smiles of satisfaction, as Phil clapped his shoulder, sympathetically. He knew they saw him as a dweeb bean counter and loser in life, and right now he hoped that would work in his favor later.

Back up in his office, he carefully opened the computer, so as not to mess up any of the packing material or box tabs. Once it was out, he inserted the CD on which he'd copied all the documents he'd discovered, thirty-four in all, and then saved them onto the machine's 16GB hard drive. He then replaced the CD in his desktop and deleted the priceless documents from it. Finally, he smashed the CD into very small pieces and distributed them in several trash cans, including one in the men's room on his floor.

After downloading the documents onto the machine's hard drive, he renamed each file with names of courses his step-daughter was taking at school, then carefully wiped the outside of the unit and repacked it in the foam packing and back into the box it had come in, taking care to place a new strip of wide tape over the box tab, just as it had come from the store. He then replaced it in the colorful Circuit City plastic bag.

He stayed in his cubicle for an extra fifteen minutes beyond his normal 5:30 quitting time, and as he prepared to leave, he made himself slightly more frumpled than usual, his collar button unbuttoned, his tie an inch or so to the left, and several of his longish, thinning hairs out of place. He even pulled his white shirt a couple of extra inches out of his trousers, making himself as unimpressive as possible.

Chapter Three
Uniglobe Campus

August 12, 5:44pm

When he emerged from the elevator on the lobby floor, Roger was immediately shocked, so severely he nearly dropped the Circuit City bag and fell over his own feet.

Phil and Baron, the lunchtime security guys, were gone, nowhere to be seen. The setup he'd worked so beautifully on his lunch hour was now pointless.

Jorge Acevedo and Uri Mosch were the lobby security team that evening, and they usually didn't show up until six. Roger very nearly turned around and went back up to his cubicle, his heart in his throat.

("For God's sake, breathe! You can do this. These guys know you, and you know them. They laugh at you even more than the day-shift. Just be your nerd self and say good night.")

Besides, he was pretty sure they were paid even less than he was, but that didn't stop them from feeling superior and more important than he was. As he neared their station, it started, like clockwork.

"Hey, Roger, how many beans you count today, eh? One hundred, two?" (Chuckle chuckle.)

He played along, dropping the corners of his mouth into a sullen pout.

"What you got there, Roger Dodger?" Uri was always the more attentive, the curious one.

"Oh, this?" (his mind raced furiously. He wasn't good at this and he felt new sweat beads form instantly.) *"My wife wanted a new mini... to uhh...to play 'Brain Age' on. She thinks it'll keep her brain young. I got it at lunch time -- last Thursday -- and I've been forgetting to bring it to her."*

That brought more laughter, especially from Jorge.

"Oh, Roger, baby, you can't go around forgetting these things for a big-time tough-guy wife like yours, man, she gonna do some serious whup-ass on you."

Still more laughter, but they made no attempts to search the bag. He started to move past them.

"Hold on, there, Roger. Maybe we should check your machine."

Heart in his throat, he fought his entire body just to keep it from jumping out of his own skin. He turned around and gave them his best attempt at a pleasant "sure, Uri."

He stepped over to their table and placed the bag down. Uri reached over and took the box out of the bag. Jorge joined him, reaching over and lifting the neatly packed and taped box.

"Haven't even opened it, hey Roger?"

"No. As I said, I've been forgetting it for three days."

Uri raised one eyebrow. "So Roger, where's the 'Brain Age' game? Did you forget that, too?"

Roger shook his head.

"No, she's already got that at home. She plays tennis with a group on Saturdays and one of the men in the group gave all of them copies."

"One of the **men** in the group?" Jorge asked, shaking his head with mock sadness.

"This isn't good, Roger Dodger. Not good at all, letting the little woman out to play with other boys, amigo, especially in those little tennis outfits with the little panties showing under the skirt. Occasion for sin, man, you know what I mean?"

Uri laughed out loud at that one, and in a moment of actual sympathy, stuffed the box back in the bag.

Roger Toople, grade four accountant, all 5'8" and 211 soft pounds of him, carried his beleaguered pout all the way out of the campus.

———————————

Step One. Done.

Step Two would be harder – especially for Roger and his suddenly overwhelming loneliness. What to do with his digital treasure trove?

He'd been thinking about almost nothing else for several days, and had gotten nowhere. It was too big for him to handle alone. But Roger was a man with very few friends, in fact none he could actually trust…

…except maybe Cassandra Hastings, known to him alone as Mrs. Roger Toople. He was half afraid of her response when he raised it with her, but in the absence of better ideas, he decided to rely on her vast network of connections in Washington, running to places far higher than he could ever reach.

That Cassandra Hastings was full of self-importance was an understatement. That she considered her husband a harmless rodent in a world of sharks and tigers was beyond question.

Still, for some reason, she had stayed for nine of her 47 years. Why? Maybe it was because Roger had done his best to get along with her daughter, who'd been extremely difficult pre-teen when he'd met her. Maybe she'd had enough of big-time Washington politicos like her first husband, who never stopped his search for the ultimate blow job. As far as that went, Roger had no doubt that she had "friends" in several other cities, and her frequent travel gave her all the opportunities she needed to enjoy their "companionship."

Despite all of that, he had worshipped the ground she walked on from the first time he'd met her, and would still forgive her anything and forego anything,

such as children of his own, for whom she had no desire
at all. In a court of law he'd have to admit that she'd
stayed with him for those nine whole years, and even
today, made no noises about leaving him. If he'd been a
bit less introverted and depressed, he'd have also
observed that a good number of their social acquaintances
were actually curious about him, wondering just what
Cass saw in him that kept them attached. Still, he had
admitted to himself many times, the whole thing just hurt.

He straightened himself up, retied his tie, and
combed his hair before opening the door of their Great
Falls home. They'd bought it more than seven years ago;
that is, she'd bought it, and it still felt like someone else's
place to him. The fact that his entire salary barely paid
the mortgage was only part of that.

"Hello, Cassandra. I—"

*"Shit, Roger, you're late! I've been waiting for
damn-near ever for you! I have news to tell you about the
plans the firm has for me. It's really exciting…"*

Forty minutes later, she took a breath, and he
spoke his next words.

*"Something has been happening to me at
Uniglobe the last few days, Cass, and…and I think I need
your help…"*

It took the next few minutes to convince her he
hadn't screwed up the Corporate Financial Statement and
gotten himself into big trouble. When he finally got it
out, however, he suddenly had her attention, something
that didn't exactly happen every day.

She demanded, of course, to see his documents. He opened the new Mini and called up his collection. She sat silently, scrolling through them rapidly, then began to mutter softly.

"Oh, my God! Holy shit! Son of a…! Jesus, Roger, this stuff is a goddamn Hiroshima bomb!"

"Yeah, I sort of thought so too. What do you think I should do?"

"Do? Do!? For Christ's sake, Roger! You damn well ought to buy some life insurance, for one thing!"

"Yeah, well, I mean, I was thinking about who I should give this stuff to…like the SEC or maybe the Department of Energy, or…who?"

Cassandra Hastings sat back on the sofa and looked up at him, her eyes wide as saucers. Her expression suggested that he'd just demonstrated the mental acuity of a Pop Tart.

Slowly, the expression changed, however, and it seemed to him that she was really impressed with the enormity of what he'd discovered. He began to hope, maybe, that he'd done something worthy of his high-powered wife's actual respect.

"So, uhh, what do you think?"

He had interrupted her thoughts. Not a good thing. She ignored the question and got up and walked past him to the brass and glass bar trolley in the corner of their Great Room. She poured herself three fingers of single malt and three cubes of ice, then returned, not to the sofa, but to a wing chair in another corner of the room, completely oblivious to him.

Roger just stood there, fixed as a stone, half hurt and half in hope. *("You might have asked me if I wanted a drink too....")*

Finally, several minutes and half of her scotch later, she fixed her gaze on him.

"What I think, Roger, darling, is that this is bigger, a very good bit bigger than the God-damned SEC and the Department of Energy. Jesus!"

Seventy percent hurt, thirty percent hopeful.

"OK, then where should I go?"

"Nowhere, just yet. I have some calls to make, and a meeting to convene with the partners tomorrow morning.. We may have some proactive damage control to do before you blow this horn, my dear.

"Then, when the firm is in the clear, you're going to call in sick to dear old Uniglobe, but insteat of going to the doctor....(he waited through a dramatic, but interminable pause…)

"...instead of going to the doctor..,I'm gong to get you your first ever, and probably only appointment...

"...at the White House,."

Chapter Four
1600 Pennsylvania Avenue

August 17, 4:42pm
The Visitor's Entrance

There were many things Roger Toople hated about his own body. Near the top of the list were his two or three million overactive sweat glands. Even though the Washington weather was only in the eighties, slightly cooler than normal for this time of year, Roger's collar was almost soaked through as he stood next to Cass at the Visitor's gate, while the guard scanned their drivers' licenses and checked for their names on the guest list.

He tried everything he could think of to chill himself down, but nothing much worked. Cass had already noticed and shook her head at him with a look very close to disgust.

"Calm down, sweetie. Nobody's going to have you for breakfast."

She said it in a voice that was as close to sweet as anything he'd heard in a long time. It gave him hope.

Five minutes later they were inside, and the building's air conditioning have him more hope. The suddenly chilled moisture of his clammy shirt was actually refreshing.

Cass recognized Pete Trakis, the Secret Service's senior man in the Presidential Detail.

Trakis had greeted them just inside double front doors of the north entrance, had carefully screened and tested Roger's laptop, and was now walking them toward the west wing and the Oval Office.

"Your first time here, folks?" he asked casually.

Roger nodded mutely, while Cass simply smiled as if the question had been directed to her alone.

"Heavens no, Pete! And I'm really hurt you don't remember the dance we shared at the President's dinner for the Queen last year."

Trakis blushed with embarrassment. *"Oh, of course I do... Mrs. Hastings! Of course I do! Who would forget that? I must be having a senior moment!"*

Roger felt his 5'8" become 5'7". He noticed, however, that the curious admixture of shame, embarrassment, self-loathing and anger began to help calm his sweat glands.

Roger Toople's 15 minutes of fame and glory actually lasted 28 minutes and 44 seconds.

He knew he'd never have gotten near the President of the entire United States in a million years but for Cass pulling strings as only she could. Despite his excitement, his presentation of the greatest whistle-blow in the history of America went without much of a hitch. At least he didn't melt into a warm puddle and his powerful wife kept her own counsel almost throughout.

As Roger laid out his accusations and supporting data, he watched the faces of the President and the Chief of Staff, though doing so forced him to move his head back and forth, as the Chief of Staff sat to his left and the President remained behind his massive desk. Cass wanted to smack him. (*"Keep your focus on the President, Roger, dear. You look like a god-damn bobble-head. Jesus!"*)

Both men seemed predisposed to dismiss Roger's presentation as "impossible" for the first few minutes. At about the 8-minute mark, however, his details began to score points. When he opened his laptop and began showing them the documents he'd stolen, the Chief of Staff began sharing hard glances with the President, who leaned forward in a new attitude of attention and focus.

By the 17-minute mark, Roger knew he had their attention, big-time, though he had the feeling that wheels were turning in both their heads, and he had no idea where those wheels were heading.

Still, when he was finishing the prepared part of his presentation, he was gratified by their response.

"My God, Mr. Toople, this is devastating, shocking material. I'm at a loss, sir. This is ten times, a hundred times worse than Larry, here, has led me to expect. When I think of the impact this is going to have..."

Larry Claymore merely nodded, though Roger thought something about his reddened face suggested that he resented Coleman Farr's statement, or at least that he was embarrassed by it.

"I'm sorry, Mr. President. I had no way of knowing that Mr. Toople's research had been so...so thorough. Mrs. Hastings 'request for this meeting was certainly urgent, but I had no idea..."

Coleman Farr waved his hand to dismiss Claymore, and Roger felt a moment of real sympathy.

"Never mind, Larry. Mr. Toople, this is simply too much to take in at one time. Obviously, we're going to have to get to work right away to learn more about what you've uncovered, and to bring some hard justice to what appear to be crimes of monstrous proportions. Because they are so monstrous, however, I'm sure you'll agree that even our national security requires that we keep this material totally, uhh, 'secure' until we're ready to move on it in a fully, uhh, coordinated way. You see where I'm going here?"

"Yes sir, Mr. President. I certainly do."

"So my next question is terribly important – may I call you Roger?"

"Of course you may, Mr. President." Roger sat up a little straighter and pulled his head back a half inch. His wife barely concealed a smile which Farr noticed, but Roger didn't.

"This set of documents, then, Roger. These are your only copies?"

"Yes, Mr. President. I have to admit I was plenty frightened just trying to get these out of the office."

Coleman Farr almost leaped out of his chair, came around his big desk, and reached for Roger's hand, pumping it so hard it made him feel like a sudden rock star.

"You'll let us keep your computer and take it from here, of course, and we'll bring the full weight of your government down on these corrupt bastards, won't we Larry?"

A tiny, tiny synapse in the back of Roger's head had connected with his left nostril, commanding it to sniff, and process the data collected by the sniff. It was a faint, almost imperceptible odor, suggesting a liverwurst sandwich that someone had hidden under the President's desk a week or two ago. It wouldn't do to try to eat it today.

As quickly as that whiff had arisen, however, it was overwhelmed by the perfume of President Farr's next words.

"I want you to know how greatly impressed we are with the courage you've shown and the enormous risks you've taken to bring this information to light. You're going to be quite overwhelmed by your own fame in the days and weeks to come, and let me tell you, the spotlight can make you a hero beyond your wildest

dreams, but it can also be quite harsh. Are you prepared for that?"

Roger started to reply, but Cass cut him off abruptly.

"Absolutely not, Mr. President. Roger is about as underprepared for what he's gotten into here as a man can be. But the partners of my firm and I are ready to hold his hand and keep him out of trouble every step of the way."

Farr smiled knowingly. *"Well that's certainly a blessing, Mrs. Hastings. You tell Dick Stirman and Avery Mills how much we'll need their help for Roger, here, but also tell 'em that they owe me big time when my library gets built at the end of my term, especially after I let 'em both imagine they could keep up with me last spring out at Augusta National before the Masters, ok?"*

The final minutes of their meeting were taken up with pleasantries, a bit of flirtation, and shop-talk between Cass and Coleman Farr – minutes in which Roger Toople felt himself simply evaporate in a puff of warm mist.

A final stern and patronizing demand to say absolutely nothing about Uniglobe to anyone unless he, Coleman Farr directed it, and Roger found himself alone with his wife on the pedestrian promenade that had once been the 1600 block of Pennsylvania Avenue.

───────────────

Fifteen minutes later they were in Cass's BMW
M5 heading west on the GW Parkway, toward the
American Legion Bridge and then north on I-270 toward
the home of the Hon. Richard Stirman, who had "invited"
(commanded) Roger to dinner.

Cass had decided to let Roger drive, something
she rarely did in her BMW, a small bone to a hungry dog.
She had successfully avoided contemplating how much
she despised her husband, and how often she showed it,
preferring to congratulate herself for her generosity in
marrying him. Occasionally, she recognized that he'd
been a kind and patient father figure for her daughter, and
she'd had to admit that his adoration of Cass herself had
been convenient, if not at all reciprocal.

Sexually, he was a willing servant, and apparently
satisfied with a minimum of her passion in bed –
something else to be thankful for. As to her other
liaisons, she could only attribute his lack of suspicion to a
benign brain tumor.

As he steered the car across the Key Bridge and
down onto the George Washington Parkway, she gave a
moment's thought to one other piece of good fortune. In
nine years she had never seen him angry.

That realization occurred to her at an ironic
moment, because it was precisely then that a great wave
of it rose in him.

In fact, he felt himself afloat in an eight-foot
dinghy in the climactic scene from "The Perfect Storm."
He had never before felt such waves of absolutely
oceanic rage. They washed over him again and again, so

violent that he found it impossible to focus the anger on any single target.

There was Cass, of course, who had made a nine-year hobby of belittling him. More than Cass, there was God, who clearly had made him the dipstick he was. Finally, because he was habitually honest, he looked at himself, a multi-dimensional and creatively complete failure who had somehow allowed God, Cass Hastings and a hundred others to shrink him to the size of a pea.

As he drove west on the GW, he began to accelerate beyond the 45, then 55mph speed limit. When he began passing other cars and moving back and forth along the two-lanes of westbound parkway, Cass took inevitable exception.

"Hey cowboy, slow your ass down! You're no Mario Andretti, you know, even in my car!"

It was the wrong thing to say. Roger didn't slow down. He took the curving, downhill ramp onto the American Legion Bridge at 65mph and pulled across three lanes of the bridge in one move, accelerating further as clouds turned the evening a sudden grey.

He steered onto 270 heading north through Bethesda and Rockville and on toward Darnestown to the massive Stirman mansion. By now he was really moving, passing car after car like they were standing still. Cass let him have it again.

"Jesus, H. Christ, Roger! Slow the fuck down! You got some kind of sudden death wish now that you're a national hero wannabe?"

Roger Toople glanced directly at his wife --
actually took his eyes off the road and gave her a look
long enough to really frighten her. The speedo now read
85. She started to open her mouth again, but when she
did, he stopped her – with words she'd never, ever heard
from him in the nine years of their marriage.

"Shut your foul mouth, Cass."

The oil tanker ahead of them had moved into `the
left lane – his lane. It was lumbering up a long grade,
doing barely 60, and it definitely wasn't supposed to be
using the left lane.

Roger was overtaking it way too fast, but there
was traffic to his right. At the last second he whipped the
wheel to the right and slid into a narrow opening ahead of
a Chevy Tahoe, its horn blaring. As he sped past the
tanker, he glimpsed the Uniglobe logo on its flank, which
only enraged him further. He slowed the BMW and hit
the button to lower his side window.

As he passed the tanker's cab he extended his left
arm out the window and flashed his third finger at its
driver, who immediately hit his air horn in answer. The
blast was deafening, and it drowned out Cass's scream.

Guido Callucci had driven tankers for Sunoco,
then Exxon, before the merger with Mobil, finally
moving over to Uniglobe. He'd seen everything on the
roads, shitheads of every description, most of whom
never got what they deserved.

Thirty-four years of experience behind the wheel
and a dozen safety seminars had kept Guido alive, but

they had done little to blunt the force of his temper. He didn't suffer road fools gladly, and when some had "gone asshole" on him, he often found a way to punish them, male or female, sometimes miles and long minutes later. The dipstick who had just swerved around him was stupid enough just to have done that, but flipping him the bird was over the line. Even though the BMW could outrun him any day of the week, for Guido it was pedal-to- the-metal time, and the big rig roared forward. He would have his justice.

Roger wanted nothing more than to scream himself, to let loose 49 years of simply being Roger Toople. Having swerved back into the left lane ahead of the tanker, his third finger still serving as the battle flag of this, his first rebellion, he hit the top of the rise a half mile north, accelerating past 85 mph again.

The sudden view of 200 cars and trucks inching along at a walking pace in front of him pulled another scream from Cass. There was no time and Roger had no driving skills that might have done any good, although the left shoulder was almost wide enough.

What he did was wrong, and he did that with a panicked violence that made things worse, despite the car's anti-lock brakes and stability control system.

Yanking the wheel to the left and hitting the brakes with all the strength in his left leg sent the car into a shuddering slide sideways. The BMW's front bumper bounced hard off the jersey wall before Cass's passenger door hit the rear of an aging Toyota Tercel and shortened it by at least a foot, sending it into a Ford Expedition, shortening its front end by another foot and barely damaging the big SUV.

The M5's front and side curtain airbags deployed on schedule and saved Roger and Cass from serious head injuries. The airbags also blinded them both to the view of the oncoming tanker which breasted the top of the rise going 65. It wouldn't have been a pretty sight, but as it was, they heard it coming.

Roger started his own scream, but in his final act he failed one more time. It was a pitiful half-squeak, a truly rodent thing, stopped cold by the crushing force of the big Peterbilt's front bumper and heavy diesel. The BMW's side door beam was woefully inadequate.

Guido was shocked at the sudden appearance of stopped traffic, when everything had been speed-limit or better up to this point on 270 northbound. It was one of the highway scenes he hoped never to see sitting in front of 8400 gallons of 91 octane 'lighter fluid.' He would have shaken his head, but the cords of muscle in his neck had gone rigid as he prepared for the impact. It would take over 400 feet to stop his rig from his current speed and there was nowhere near 400 feet of clear space ahead.

Nevertheless, he hit the Peterbilt's anti-lock brakes and prayed that the kingpin would hold. A second later he knew the trailer brakes weren't going to keep the trailer behind him. As it slid to the right, it clipped a little Toyota Yaris three-door which went under the tank's rear wheels, vaulting it into the air behind him. The kingpin didn't hold, and the tanker broke free, already ruptured behind him.

When he hit the BMW in front of him, the impact hurled him forward over the big wheel and through the windshield, suddenly wishing, for the first time, that he hadn't disengaged the shoulder belt sensor in order to start the truck and drive without using the thing. As he flew forward, his legs broken at the hip by the bottom of the big steering wheel, a wave of the gasoline washed forward out of the ruptured tank and over him, its smell flooding his nostrils. He felt himself shiver in its sudden cold.

He heard the sounds of the impact as the rig made wheeled coffins of the BMW and the little compact in front of it, and then what seemed like an eternity of milliseconds later, he heard the deafening boom of the explosion. With it, the cold gasoline became warmer than warm.

For a small eternity of seconds, Guido couldn't move or even scream, but he actually felt himself start to bubble and char from the inside out before the terrible need to inhale flaming gasoline finally stopped.

Chapter Five
Presidential Quarters

August 17
11:01 pm

Coleman Farr rarely went to bed before midnight, and rarely got more than five hours of sleep. His meeting with Roger Toople that afternoon, however, had excited him beyond anything in his administration in months, and by 10:15 he was exhausted.

The opportunity created by Toople's revelations was heaven-sent. By 8:05, after barely picking at his dinner, he'd retired to his office and mapped out a strategy to take full advantage of that opportunity. Mrs. Farr had expressed her usual concern that he was working himself too hard, but he ignored her, as usual.

By 9:45, he'd thought through dozens of permutations and variables. Basically, all were manageable, save one: Toople himself and his hot-shot attorney wife. He would have to figure out how to deal with them, but as he considered the alternatives available to him, he grew suddenly tired, and headed upstairs to the Farr bedroom suite.

Hitting the pillow at 9:52, he was asleep in minutes, but it didn't last long. At 10:55 he got up to pee, and decided to watch the 11:00 news on WRC, Washington's NBC channel. Its national news was disgustingly liberal, but its local anchors had more intelligence and personality than the others.

Settling himself in his favorite recliner he flipped on the big-screen set in the sitting room adjacent to the bedroom where his wife was fighting to get back to sleep despite his departure.

"Our lead story tonight is the tragic, and truly horrific accident this evening which claimed the lives of five people on I-270 during rush hour. Four cars and a Uniglobe gasoline tanker were involved, and the occupants of all four vehicles perished in the fiery crash...

Something vaguely telepathic nudged the President to pay attention.

"...witnesses attributed the accident to excess speed, aggressive driving, and an unexpected back-up caused by an earlier accident just minutes before. Debra Dornberg is on the scene, but we should warn you that some of the footage you're about to see is graphic and horrifying. Debra?"

"Thanks, Jim. Witnesses to this fiery holocaust say that a black BMW sedan had just swerved violently across two lanes to avoid crashing into the rear of the Uniglobe tanker, nearly hitting a Ford Expedition at speeds near 90 miles an hour. As the BMW overtook the tanker, its driver made a rude hand gesture aimed at the truck driver, which was driving illegally in the left-hand lane. At the top of this rise, less than a mile north of that event, the same driver's speeding sedan was suddenly confronted by nearly stopped traffic just ahead, and had

no time to stop. Seconds after his car went sideways into a compact Toyota, the tanker came over the top of the hill and slammed into the driver's door. What you see here is all that was left of the tanker and three other cars after firefighters extinguished the raging inferno created by thousands of gallons of gasoline.

"The truck driver, Guido Calluci, 62, of Odenton, Maryland, died, as did the sedan driver, his wife, and two people inside the small car originally struck by the BMW."

"Do you have anything on the identity of the dead yet Debra?"

"Yes, Jim. We've just learned that the BMW was driven by Roger Toople of Great Falls...

The President of the United States almost leapt from his chair, struggling to stifle a shout.

...with him was his wife, Cassandra Hastings, a well-known Washington attorney. Ironically, Jim, Mr. Toople was an employee of Uniglobe, as was the truck driver, though it's likely that neither knew it at the time of the accident."

Coleman Farr sat bolt upright, his eyes wide, barely breathing for nearly a minute. Finally he inhaled, smiled, and let out a deep sigh.

The First Lady rolled over in her bed at that moment, opened her eyes long enough to see the flickering light from the adjoining room and the mostly unintelligible murmur of the TV. She did, however, hear her husband, the leader of the entire free world, utter a half-whispered *"Thank you, Jesus! Thank you Lord! Thank you Jesus!"*

She made a mental note to ask him what inspired him to pray when they awoke the next day, and promptly went back to sleep for a third time.

_____

Larry Claymore picked up his beside phone, noting the time on the alarm clock base – 11:22pm. He didn't have to ask who it was.

"Yes, Mr. President?"

There was no greeting, and no apology for awakening him. *"Larry, what did you do with that computer from the Uniglobe guy this afternoon?"*

"Uhh, do with it, sir? Nothing...I..."

"Laarrry, wake up for Christ's sake. What the fuck did you do with it?"

Larry sat up and shook himself. *"I put it in my safe, sir."*

"You talk to anybody about it?"

Claymore kicked his brain into gear, thinking faster than it wanted to go just after the warmth of his pillow.

"No sir. No one." *("He wants this quiet. I wonder why? But it doesn't matter, as long as he gets what he wants....")*

"Did anyone see you taking the laptop out of my office, Larry?"

"No, Mr. President. Marion was not at her desk when I went by and I took it directly to my office and into my safe, sir."

Pete Trakis had been standing outside the President's office door, but Larry decided Pete didn't count.

"OK, then. I need your ass in at six. I want what's-his-name, the Uniglobe CEO in my office ASAP, and I <u>don't</u> want him on my schedule or coming in the front door, understood?"

"Uhh, well...yes, Mr. President."

The click of the broken phone connection served as a poor substitute for *"Thank you, Larry, and my apology for waking you at this hour."*

Try as he might to get back to sleep, that was the end of rest for Larry. His brain had been forcibly kicked into gear, and now would not let go of its own forward – or backward motion.

After speculating with little success about President Farr's plans for Roger Toople's laptop and the

Uniglobe CEO, other synapses fired and he was back seven years ago, an eternity that often felt like yesterday.

Chapter Six
K Street NW

November 7
Seven Years Earlier

It should have been insignificant. It should not
have been a rock dropped in a quiet pool, there should
have been no widening circles of ripples. It definitely
should not have been what the chaos theorists laughingly
call a "butterfly sneeze." It was a mere slip this
November morning, a less-than-perfect communication,
an unfortunate and probably unintended insult,
surrounded by arguably justifiable purposes.

Just four days after the voting, after Coleman Farr
had been congratulated by his Democratic opponent and
joyous Republicans in all 37 red states, there was still no
rest for the weary. The long campaign was over, but now
it was time to build the Farr White House team. The
Cabinet was already largely in place, but the White
House staff was not, and that crucial responsibility had
fallen to one Harvey Gross.

Harvey had been a close friend of the President-
elect for years, a college classmate and drinking buddy,
best man at his wedding, a confidant and golf partner
ever since. He was closer to the newest White House
resident than anyone on earth.

A fanatically clean-shaven multi-millionaire with a military officer's hard body and meticulous buzz cut, Gross was a student of all things politic, but a man with no ambition whatsoever to run for office. Even his electronics business no longer excited him much, and he'd relished taking the last year off to run the President-elect's campaign.

Harvey wielded more influence over Coleman Farr's staffing decisions than anyone else. Though he'd been a nominal number two in Farr's campaign team, insiders knew that number one, Arizona Senator Hank Skilling, was on top strictly, and solely, for the value of his name. Coleman Farr trusted Harvey Gross with his life, his wife, his fortune, and his good name. Harvey was proud of it, though he knew it wasn't because he was any kind of genius or world leader.

No, Harvey was a soldier. He'd never served in a uniform, never gone to war, but he might have been a Marine, so focused and devoted was he to serving and protecting his "commanding officer." He'd long understood that every successful President, especially in these times, needed a Harvey Gross.

He also recognized that while Coleman Farr was in the White House, and probably for years after, he would never socialize with the man in public, never play another round of golf with him, and never allow a photograph to be taken with him. Once his immediate staffing job was done, he would fade into the ether and hopefully be quickly -- and entirely -- forgotten. It was the only way he could continue to serve in his unique role.

On that November 7th, Harvey was running the
search for Farr's Chief of Staff. He sat in his borrowed K
Street office among half-finished cups of cold coffee
teetering atop call lists, printouts of eleventh-hour polls,
and assorted other campaign refuse and stared at the
resume of Lawrence Claymore, the top candidate for the
position.

This position was critical, and far more difficult
than it should have been. Farr had his own short list of
seven men he knew well and trusted implicitly, but none
of them could pass even the most superficial of
background checks.

On his wrist, the Rolex told him it was crunch
time. This decision couldn't wait.

Though he had hesitated longer than he'd meant
to, Gross had to admit that Claymore had all the
credentials and all the pedigrees. He had the brains, the
experience, the stamina, the confidence, intensity,
toughness, and chutzpah for the job.

Why had he hesitated? Probably nothing more
than the man's stature. Claymore stood all of 5'7" even in
his brogues. Gross had an instinctive, lifelong suspicion
of small men.

Still, three separate vettings had produced only a
Topeka shoplifting bust at age 11 (a whole box of Topps
baseball cards!) Aside from that, he'd come up so clean
he squeaked. He'd returned the baseball cards unopened,
apologized to the variety store owner, written and
delivered a school essay on the wages of crime, and been
grounded by his father for three months. The story even

gave him a little added credibility inside the Beltway in a perverse, but cute sort of aw-shucks, down-home, heartland kind of way.

The interview, completed less than an hour ago, had gone well enough, and Harvey was finally forced to admit he was satisfied. As he reviewed it one final time, he thought through the interview's final minutes.

For Harvey, those final minutes tackled what was for him, Issue One, the single item that would make or break any candidate for any job in the Farr Administration.

"Let's talk about loyalty, Larry. Loyalty and silence."

Claymore had raised one eyebrow, a questioning look that almost rang a little alarm bell in Harvey's brain.

"Those are two important values, Harvey. I believe loyalty is a must within any President's team, though I'm not certain where the President-elect intends to take 'silence.'"

Gross studied Claymore's face.

"Larry, with your experience, you know damn well that in any two-term administration the leader of this nation will have to make some decisions, take some actions that make the pissant liberals in this town call for his head on a pike. At those times, Coleman Farr will need to rely on your loyalty. At other times, to protect other actions he'll take, he'll need to rely just as surely on your silence...."

Larry raised both hands in response, but Gross ignored the gesture.

"...Let me finish, Larry. Are you one of those people who thinks he hasn't scaled the heights until he's written a god-damn memoir and gone on a book tour?"

Claymore felt his cheeks redden and his jaw tighten.

"No, Mr. Gross.... I am <u>not</u> one of those people."

Gross noted the cheeks and jaw, and waved the back of his hand, a gesture of dismissal, and a second not-exactly- intended insult.

"Don't get all tight-lipped and pouty with me here, Larry. This is not some casual side-issue we're talking about. Coleman Farr is exactly what this country needs in times like these: a leader with an understanding of the forces arrayed against us around the world, and the balls to keep America secure.

"He's a man who knows full well that our most dangerous enemies aren't in Teheran or Damascus, or even in Beijing or Moscow. They're in Manhattan, San Francisco and Hyannis Port, for God's sake.

"This administration is going to have some god-damned discipline, for the first time in maybe two centuries. There will be no leaks, Larry, none...and no fucking kiss-and-tell books. You, above all, are going to be responsible for seeing to that. Am I just perfectly clear?"

Lawrence Claymore would never forget that speech. Actually, he did forget most of the words, but he remembered the tone and the message beneath the message -- and how he'd felt about it.

The rest of the interview had gone well enough, despite the fact that in its final minutes he *was* rather tightlipped and pouty. Lawrence Claymore didn't suffer insults well at all.

Months later, he admitted to himself that he had never believed much in any President's ability to keep anything private -- even less, secret. The press, media, and the blogosphere were too invasive, too curious, and way too powerful, primarily because there were just too damn many of them. His own belief was that any politician with half a brain probably ought not to delude himself about keeping anything quiet for more than twenty minutes.

Six years later, he had learned a great deal about loyalty and silence working for Coleman Farr, to his own surprise.

He'd grown to respect the President, albeit from a distance. Coleman Farr had surely made a long list of decisions that were difficult, sometimes controversial, and often delicate. Carrying out those decisions had often required loyalty, both from his staff and from men and women on both sides of the aisle on Capitol Hill.

Other decisions had indeed required silence -- the kind of total, perfect silence that he'd thought impossible in this day and age.

Early on, there had been two exceptions – neither national security cases, but leaks of potentially embarrassing information. In both cases, the identity of the leaker remained secret, from the media and the country.

In both cases, Lawrence Claymore, Chief of Staff, received immediate phone calls, not in his office, but at his home, from an angry Harvey Gross. The first call was at 5:18 am.

"I want the name, Larry. Today. No delays, no bullshit. I want the name."

"I don't know it, Harvey, but I'm sure the President –"

"-- The President, nothing, Larry. He's no part of this. You were hired to run a tight ship and watch his back. Don't even bring this up with the President. Just find out who opened his or her god-damn mouth. Parker will help you. No one else. And no one else gets the name…except me. Understood?"

Jack Parker, US Secret Service, Presidential Detail, did help, in both cases. The first leaker turned out to be Dugan McMannis, a junior speech writer, who'd been working in the White House only a month, and was still in the foolish rush of his own rookie self-importance, as if he was the newest star on "West Wing."

He'd gone to the Hawk & Dove, drank three beers, and found himself elbow-to-elbow with Richard Carrack, the vaunted Times columnist and frequent NBC pundit. Here he was at 25, being pumped by a virtual media god thirty years his senior. It was delicious.

"So, Dugan, what's Coleman got you working on right now?"

He knew better than to answer the question. He'd gotten the loyalty and silence message several times during his interviews and orientation. But Carrack continued to press him until his blushing new sense of his own importance finally convinced him he could, and should at least give the man a clue or two, a tiny taste.

Claymore got the word from Parker later, when he was alone in the staff suite at nearly nine in the evening. He called Gross at his home in Tulsa.

"Thank you, Larry. Fire him. Now. Tonight. Clean out his desk and have Parker go to his home and lift his ID and White House pass. I'll take care of the rest."
"The rest?"

"Don't ask, Larry. Don't talk to the President about this either, now or ever. Just keep your mouth shut. Loyalty and silence, Larry."

Larry followed Gross's instructions.

An hour later, when Parker found McMannis at his home in Fairfax, Dugan didn't take the news well.

"You can't do this! I didn't do anything wrong! I'll go straight to the President. I'll --!"

Parker was 6'4", more than half a foot taller than McMannis and nearly 80 pounds heavier. He stepped into the younger man's personal space and forced the young man to look directly up at him and smell the Altoids that minted his warm breath.

When he spoke, his deep voice was soft, his cadence slow, and very, very personal.

"You'll be very, very quiet, is what you'll do, Dugan. A few weeks, a few months, you'll have another job, and you'll get on with your life. Above all, Dugan, you'll remember the assurances you gave about loyalty and silence, and you'll honor those assurances. Completely. Any questions?"

"Just one…What if I don't? What are you going to do about it? This is still America and as far as I know the Bill of Rights hasn't been repealed!"

Parker shook his head slowly, his face clouded with sudden sadness. He lowered his voice even further, almost whispering, but not quite.

"I'm not sure, Dugan, exactly what will happen first. But what will happen second…is that you will sincerely regret you ever asked that question."

Two days later McMannis's mother, Marian, 49, picked up Dugan's two year-old daughter, Penny, at pre-school and headed toward his home, where she would stay while his biologist wife was in Switzerland at a medical research conference.

The trip was only six blocks in length, but neither grandmother nor daughter made it home. Two dark-haired males approached her Ford sedan on foot from opposite sides at a stop light and climbed in simultaneously, pushing Marian to the center of the front seat. They had timed their approach so that they could move out immediately, the light having just turned green, and there was no scream or other commotion at the sight.

Grandmother and granddaughter were found dead three hours later.

By the time the bodies were discovered, both men were sitting in first class seats at 33,000 feet altitude, headed home to the mountains of Paraguay, where they would resume an interrupted residence and career, albeit $80,000 richer.

Dugan McMannis remembered Parker's last words, and got the message. Neither he nor his traumatized young wife said a thing about it, though local news reporters tried for a statement for weeks.

The second leak happened shortly thereafter, still in President Farr's first year in office. It followed a similar pattern.

Paula Phillipousis, a tiny, 67-year old white-haired widow, had served in various White House Administrative Assistant positions for 33 years, making her by far the senior employee in the Farr Administration.

A momentary spat with a new Assistant on the Vice President's staff, a woman young enough to be her granddaughter, left her outraged and seething.

Minutes later, a senior Washington Post columnist who knew her well, passed by her desk and offered a friendly greeting. A simple "how are things?" opened a minor flood of her anger, as well as her disdain for the young woman's work on the President's forthcoming State of the Union Address.

The columnist, who knew his job and his way around the White House, proceeded to "happen by" the younger woman's desk and scanned a draft of President Farr's planned statement supporting cuts in early childhood education subsidies.

It was a crude draft which would never have seen the light of day otherwise. The resulting Post column, though citing only "a reliable White House source," created an embarrassing distraction, especially when it was picked up and enlarged by the new anchor at CNN.

Lawrence Claymore received another call from Gross, and again followed his instructions to fire both women, and not to bother the President about it.

Paula's reminder to remain silent didn't even take a day to arrive. She received it, in fact, when she walked into her Potomac waterfront apartment on Maine Avenue that very evening, carrying a single cardboard box containing 33 years' worth of her White House personal effects.

Hanging from the venetian blind cord at her living room window was her twelve-year old white Persian cat, Shaba. It had died quite recently, its body still warm when she reached it. It was several hours later, still in shock and sorrow, that she found the note in a single email on her home computer. It was very short.

"Meow...me-. Loyalty and Silence, Paula."

Within seconds of her entering her access code and calling the email to her screen, a computer virus overwhelmed the hard drive and obliterated the email and all other stored documents.

Claymore never did learn about Philipoussis' cat. He'd shuddered at the earlier coincidence of McMannis's mother and daughter, but thought better of asking questions, and like all awful memories, that one faded rapidly, especially as Claymore's own work schedule filled his entire consciousness nearly twenty-four/seven.

Five years later, he had had few reminders about loyalty and silence, but needed none.

————————

Claymore had done his job as well as any man could, but while most men would have enjoyed the position's power and perks, to him their price was too high.

He had long felt that his relationship with Coleman Farr was a second dark cloud on his personal horizon, and an undeserved one at that.

Outwardly, the two men were entirely, determinedly "polite and correct" with each other in public. On the few occasions when it was just Farr and Claymore, it was never "Coleman and Lawrence." It was always "Mr. President" -- and "Larry."

Whenever Farr was pissed about something, which was way too regularly, it was "La-aaarry." He pronounced it with a broad "A" and a deliberate sing-song cadence that communicated his Presidential displeasure quite effectively.

Though he couldn't understand why, Claymore had long since got the message that he had never fully earned the President's respect and trust, and certainly not his friendship.

There had been only one conversation between the two men in which the President had seen fit to share anything like a "personal confidence" with him. He remembered it vividly.

Farr had just come through a long and bloody fight with Congressional Democrats in both houses on Capitol Hill over his national security and tax reduction initiatives early in his first term. He had won most of the battles in this war, but only after spilling gallons of blood and incurring a huge reservoir of permanent enmity on Capitol Hill.

Larry had congratulated Farr in a way that caused him to respond in a surprising fashion.

"It was certainly a long, tough fight, Mr. President, but it looks like you've gotten just about everything you wanted!"

"Shit, Larry, that's so fucking far from the truth I can hardly stand to think about it!"

"Really, sir? I'd have thought..."

"—Larry, for Christ's sake, wake up and smell the Goddamn coffee! What I <u>want</u>, you numbnuts, is to make just one decision without having to stroke 536 self-important Congressional asswipes from Honolulu to Hoboken.

"What I <u>want,</u> is enough money to buy even a month's worth of loyalty and obedience from a half-dozen legal geniuses in their long black Robes on the Court.

"What I <u>want</u> is to stop having to suck about a thousand dicks and cunts to get any single thing <u>done</u> in governing this country. And you know what? I'm never going to have that until I'm out and gone from this office. But by God, La-aarrrry, I'm gonna have it one day!"

That last condescending extension of his name echoed painfully, reminding him of the insults and high-handed treatment from Harvey Gross. Rather than fade with time, their memory burned through his stomach lining, requiring almost a dozen antacids a day.

So Lawrence Claymore found himself working to exhaustion, non-stop for nearly seven years, for a man who gave him little recognition, little praise, and no friendship.

He would never admit it to a soul, but it hurt. It
hurt so much, and for so long, that it burned a synapse in
his soul to a hard, crusty cinder. As such accumulated
hurts often do, his crusted synapse needed something to
help him justify his continued participation in the bad
dream his life had become. So, slowly, it gave birth to
his own private desire.

While that desire took on its own distinctive
shape, like Farr's, it would cost money. A very large
amount of money.

Chapter Seven
Cranberry Back Country, West Virginia

August 21

Petrarch Ptolemy Trachilius had fought perhaps 200 fights before the age of 10 – defending his name. He'd lost most of the first 50, but though the losses were painful, they toughened him up pretty fast. He won almost every one of the remaining 150, and by the time he was 12, kids in his neighborhood and school had learned how to pronounce Petrarch without making the slightest bit of fun of him.

When he enrolled at West Point in 1967, rather than endure another round of laughter among the older Cadets, he simply dispensed with his half-Greek, half-Italian father's burden of a name. He became Pete Trakis. Not Peter. Pete.

Twenty-five years later, in June, 1992, Colonel Trakis left the Army with more chest salad than the average grunt, but less idea about what to do next than the average 43-year old retiree.

Two years of wandering the backroads and small towns of a dozen western states in a nine-year old Corvette consumed his savings and retirement pay and satisfied his somewhat romantic desire to "discover America." When he came back to Washington DC at 45, he had nothing. No job, no prospects, no money except his paltry retirement pay, no family, and no idea what to do next. What he did have, however, was one friend.

Jack Markham had met Pete when both were assigned to help plan and conduct our disastrous Operation Eagle Claw in Iran in 1980. Markham was a Marine helicopter pilot, while Trakis was part of an Army Special Forces team that had infiltrated into Tehran prior to the mission. The rescue of 52 American captives held by the Iranians for over 400 days was to have been the high water mark of Jimmy Carter's otherwise ugly Presidency. Despite what seemed like bold and decisive planning, the mission had quickly disintegrated into perhaps the biggest failure in the history of US military operations.

Both men took the defeat very hard – and very personally. For Pete Trakis, it spelled the beginning of the end of his military life, while it had given Jack Markham new resolve to, stay in the Corps, learn, improve, and see to it that we didn't go there again.

Markham and Trakis became fast friends during that fiasco, but perhaps because it was such a disaster, they decided, without a word, to keep their friendship very private, and very quiet.

It was Markham who helped Pete Trakis get a Washington job, one that he'd never even imagined doing. Still, the Secret Service was perfect for him, and he'd risen faster than most. When Jack Parker retired a few months ago, Pete had become head of the Presidential Detail.

Today, as the two men hiked the trails and logging roads of the Monongahela National Forest, they retraced the mis-steps of Operation Eagle Claw for perhaps the hundredth time, but without the intense pain of fresh disgrace.

As usual, Jack Markham had told no one about his hiking companion – or even that he had one. For Pete Trakis, there was no one to tell. The two men had driven separately, heading west through the Virginia suburbs and into West Virginia along Route 55, stopping in Wardensville to pick up a few backpack items for their week-long hike.

The two men hiked silently into the mountains from the parking lot, moving rapidly in the late afternoon's failing light. Two hours later they had made nearly eight miles into the park and stopped to set up a pop tent in case it rained. Trakis gathered wood and Markham selecting their dinner from the selection of dehydrated backpacker meals they'd brought. Pork chops, mixed vegetables, and blueberry cobbler, which wasn't half bad, especially with a couple of shots of Evan Williams 12-year old bourbon.

"They keeping you busy, Pete?" Markham asked.

"Routine stuff, mostly. POTUS hasn't strayed too far from home base lately. Seems like the busier he is, the less work for the rest of us."

Markham nodded, half- reclining against a large rock, and extended his feet toward the fire. The evening was cooler than normal for this time of year, and there would be heavy dew by morning. He sipped the bourbon slowly.

The two men enjoyed each other's company and their solitude with a slow ease that allowed long, comfortable silences between short exchanges of shop talk.

As the moon and stars shone down on them through the rustling tree branches, their subject turned to world events. Trakis raised the subject of Russia, knowing it to be one of Markham's areas of expertise.

"Putin's moving in several directions at once, which makes him interesting. He's well on his way to making himself the next Tsar, as well as chief puppeteer in the Kremlin, but at the same time he's manipulating his natural resources surplus into a weapon that just might be more powerful than his tanks and missiles ever were. Take that pipeline he's building, for instance...."

A little bell went off in Trakis's head.

"Yeah, doesn't Uniglobe have a major stake in that pipeline?"

"They do. Why do you ask?"

"Oh, nothing."

"Really? Nothing?"

"Well, actually I'm not sure it's nothing. You remember that big traffic mishap on 270 a few days ago?"

"I do. It was a Uniglobe tanker that blew up, wasn't it?"

"Right, but that isn't what I was thinking about. It was the lunatic driver of the BMW who caused the accident. Toople was his name. I'd escorted him in to the White House just that afternoon, for a meeting with POTUS. He didn't look too happy on his way out..."

"And...?"

"...and he left a laptop with Claymore."

Markham sat up straight and looked hard at his old friend, then into the crackling flames in front of him.

"Hmmm. An unusual coincidence, don't you think?"
Trakis thought about it for a long moment.

"Maybe. To me the most unusual part of it came the next morning, after the news of the accident was broadcast the night of Toople's visit. POTUS was more jovial, happier than I've seen him in weeks. You'd think Toople was Farr's personal IRS Auditor, gone to his reward."

Chapter Eight
The Mall

August 30
1035 Hours.

Two men walked together along the Reflecting Pool, heading east from the Lincoln Memorial. Through a steady, windblown rain, their pace was slow, their heads down, seemingly lost in thought. Despite their solitude, their words were few, uttered barely above a whisper. Both men were aware of the latest NSA reconnaissance equipment operating in more than 200 public places throughout the Nation's Capital. Both were confident that the traffic sounds, wind, and rain were more than a match for that equipment today.

Their dark suits, hats, and raincoats gave them, at least from a distance, anonymity, no indication of their occupation – members of the Joint Chiefs of Staff. Gen. Jack Markham was Commandant of the US Marine Corps. He had called this quiet meeting.

The second man, US Army General Micah Sweisach, who'd last seen duty in Kosovo, was slightly taller, and much thinner. The others on the JCS had begun expressing concern about him, though it would be another six months before the doctors at Walter Reed could hold him still long enough to diagnose the cancer that would shorten his career.

They passed through the World War II Memorial and reached 17th Street, turning south and making their way across Independence Avenue and then east along the edge of the Tidal Basin, toward the Jefferson Memorial.

Halfway there, they were met by a third man similarly dressed in civilian suit and overcoat, walking under a large black umbrella, his own hat pulled low to further hinder a passerby from recognizing him. Admiral Phillip Peeler, stood nearly 6'4" and after 22 years captaining Trident Missile submarines, he joked that he'd been made a member of the Joint Chiefs before he could hit his head one more time on the low-hanging plumbing of the "tin cans" he'd been running. "It was either this or a nursing home."

The three men stood talking quietly near the ramp leading down to the little platform from which summer tourists would again rent pedal boats, still months away.

They seemed impervious to the rain and wind along the Potomac, and in fact were thankful for it, as it also minimized the number of passersby.

"This is too much. If it blows open, I'm not sure this Administration can survive it."

The others nodded slowly. Sweisach leaned against the iron railing, his back to the water, and looked hard at his two companions.

"To be honest, I'm less worried about the Administration than about the country. I'm not sure the people can stand it – if it's true. We've got to do something – but I'll be damned if I know just what…"

The third man removed his grey fedora and ran a hand through the short buzz of his silver hair.

"That's just the point, Micah. There is nothing for us to do until we find out. We need some hard evidence to know how far this thing goes. If Farr himself is in on it, there'll be hell to pay. If he had anything to do with this guy Toople's death, all hell is going to break loose. Dick Nixon's resignation and the cluster-fuck that led to it was a gut blow to everything we thought we stood for. Another of those and we'll like as not lose a lot more – maybe everything."

Their conversation was not their first on the subject. It had begun two weeks earlier, when Jack Markham had returned from his backpacking hike in the West Virginia mountains with Pete Trakis.

To Trakis it had at first seemed like nothing more than a weird coincidence. What made it more ominous, however, was the wall of total silence that rose up around the Tooples' visit and the laptop since then.

"We've had little enough success finding anything on this side of the Atlantic. I even asked the head of Farr's Secret Service Detail if he could "borrow" Toople's computer, but he wouldn't even admit to knowing of it. The only thing we can do is get someone over in Georgia and start picking up the trail from that end.

The three men had explored a variety of theories based on the few pieces of the puzzle before them. All of the theories involved Uniglobe, large, even huge amounts of money, and people in the White House. All of them also agreed that it likely involved the biggest thing Uniglobe was doing presently, which involved the construction of a major international pipeline through eastern Europe to bring Russian crude to the West.

"—when we have confirmation of that, heaven only knows what we do next. This could be the biggest can of worms any of us has ever seen."

The other two simply nodded, nobody replying.

Sweisach moved even closer to the other two. *"Is there anyone we can trust in Langley? Or the FBI?"*

Peeler shook his head. *"Not a soul. You know what a raging nutcase Farr is about leaks – he's barely even reading our dailies, let alone the CIA one-pagers. They're so far out in left field they probably aren't even getting their paychecks on time. And you guys know how holy they think they are – and how beneath contempt they think anyone in a uniform is."*

Finally, Markham got the message, and said simply, *"I'll put a man over there, one of our own"*

The other two raised their eyes and stared into his, their gaze full of question, even challenge.

"It'll take a damn special man, Jack."

General Markham was the junior man of the three, but the most widely recognized. Adm. Peeler and Gen. Sweisach had served on the JCS longer than he had and both had more experience in the shades-of-grey intersection of warfare and politics, having served through the large and small wars our patriotic civilian leaders are so fond of declaring – for too many years.

Markham returned their gaze.

The other two nodded slowly. Sweisach reached over to shake Markham's hand, then Peeler's. The three men left in separate directions.

Chapter Nine
The Pentagon

C Ring, C33203
September 12, 1023 Hours

Staff Sergeant Mickey Dopa stared into his computer screen, trying, and failing, to focus on the scrolling lines of text. His distraction? The four eyes of Lt. Col. John Tirada and Col. Peter Hackman, who sat behind him, waiting.

Normally, Dopa would be documenting duty assignments for each of the 825 Marines in his MOS, before passing them up the line. Normally he'd be fighting to keep his concentration sharp, because the work was repetitive, routine, and far remote from action Dopa thought he'd be seeing as a Marine. But today wasn't normal. In fact, the whole atmosphere of the office was different. Tirada and Hackman were men who cast a long shadow in the Corps, and today that shadow was just over his left shoulder.

He didn't know them, but though they hadn't explained why they were there, he knew not to ask. Both officers were senior leaders, among the elite of the elite in Marine Corps Special Forces. The two of them, and about twenty other senior officers were among the "Quiet Men" of the Corps, men about whom much was rumored, but little was known.

"*Sir, I have what I think you're looking for: Captain James Darden.*"

Tirada and Hackman shuffled through their stack of jackets. Tirada reached for his now-cold coffee. "*Run him down for me Sergeant.*"

"*Sir, Three years at Camp Pendleton as a Platoon Commander with 1st Recon Battalion. He was attached to Darkhorse 3/5 for the push to Baghdad in 2003 and the Battle of Fallujah in 2004. During Operation Phantom Fury he was awarded the Bronze Star for valor. He's in Quantico right now working a crash assignment, debriefing on Iraq Field Operations with the Special Ops Planning Group.*"

Dopa noticed both Tirada and Hackman raising their eyebrows. He stifled a smile and continued.

"*…300 PFT score, a Black Belt Instructor, and he has well above average relative value marks on his Fitness Reports. No injuries, Five years' service, two medals for valor in Baghdad operations. No injuries, single, no children, though – wait: here's a note here that he's engaged to the daughter of a Spanish diplomat and has requested 10 days leave for his wedding and honeymoon in two weeks.*"

Tirada stopped -- his coffee half-way to his lips. "*Darden…Darden. Colonel, is this the guy?*"

Hackman's eyebrows arched as he found and opened Darden's folder in his stack. "*It sure is, John.*" He snatched up the folder, stood up, and turned to leave.

"Hold his file, Sergeant. Make no assignment. We'll be back later. Keep up the good work."

"Sir, Yessir," Dopa replied, doing little to disguise the perplexed expression on his face, actually hoping the two officers would notice it and explain. They did. And they didn't.

Hackman and Tirada walked down the hall toward the E-ring and the Commandant's suite of offices, shoulder to shoulder, speaking in hushed tones.

"Something big, and strange, is up with this guy. Coded assignment expression translates to 'Embassy billet,' but it doesn't say what or where. That's crazy on its face. If it's 'Marine Security Guard Detail,' we'd have to bust him back to Staff NCO to fit the billet, even as Head of Detail."

Tirada nodded. "He's never been to MSG school. Even if he had, that kind of 'B' billet would be out of bounds for Special Ops personnel..."

"-- to say nothing of the Commandant's orders for theno ears lid on the whole thing. I've known this man since he was commissioned. He's one of the best. Imagination, new ideas, top drawer combat skills, and he's old, old school."

He spoke the last two sentences in an even softer half-whisper as they passed two officers heading the other way.

Hackman shook his head.

"We've never moved guys out from under General Toomey without his say-so, but this is a no-com/no paper move except to let the General know he's losing this guy. So I'd have to bet with you."

Once in the Commandant's suite, they went directly to an empty office and placed the call. As they expected, General Toomey was none too happy to lose a talented and seasoned combat veteran, hand-picked and trained to a razor's edge for special operations/desert and mountain warfare, especially with Baghdad still uncivilized and storm flags flying over Teheran and Damascus.

On the other hand, as they also expected, General Toomey was too high up the food chain not to suspect what they were already sure of. He knew that ignoring the wishes of the few men in the country higher than himself could endanger his fourth star, and a request this unusual and this quiet *must* be at least the Joint Chiefs, and possibly even 1600 at work. His three stars had been trios on his shoulders for long enough now, and he'd always preferred quartet harmonies, especially considering the bump in retirement pay.

"OK, Goddam it, snatch him out from under me. I don't want to know what his assignment is, but I damn well hope it's worth the price of losing a pro-bowl quarterback like Darden. Wherever he's headed, he'd better not have lost his fighting edge when he gets back to the real world, or we'll have destroyed a damn fine Marine."

Chapter Ten
Quantico Marine Base, Virginia

Captain James Darden, USMC

Jim Darden had lived the life of an arrow, flying hard and true toward goals he'd set unusually early in life.

At age five he had decided he would become a Marine. At twelve, that goal had remained strong, although he'd decided to become an officer in the Corps. At fifteen he had a momentary diversion, deciding that law was both honorable and important. He quickly regretted leaving behind his first goal and was relieved to find, a year later, that they were not mutually exclusive. The Marine Corps had a place for lawyers.

He graduated second in his high school class, with seven varsity letters, then in the top 3% of his class at the University of Michigan with two varsity letters in track and wrestling, and was the Editor of the Law Review his third year at Michigan Law. When he felt the need to relax, he read <u>War and Peace</u> in the original Russian, played chess, and exercised enough to know that Marine Officer Candidate Training would be a personal walk in the park..

He dated, but not often. The few women with whom he shared much of himself seemed disappointed by his single-minded rush toward his career goals.

After law school, Jim spent the summer studying for his bar exam in Michigan, which he passed with little difficulty. In the fall, he was accepted to attend the ten week Officer Candidate Course at Marine Officer Candidate School in Quantico Virginia. He spent another six months at The Basics School learning infantry tactics and developing the necessary leadership skills to lead young men into battle. He was selected as Honor Graduate for both of these demanding courses.

While his OSO at first assumed he would want to move directly into Marine JAG, he made it clear at Basics School that he wanted to lead Marines. Because he was Honor Graduate, he was given his first preference, Special Operations, and so was transferred. In 1st Recon Battalion he would spend his service life more in harm's way even than regular Marines, and so he learned many more ways to kill and maim with less noise and fuss than he would have believed possible.

He found that his physical limits were tied to his mental limits, and that both were far more elastic than he had realized.

His instructors grumbled that his near-fluent Russian was obsolete, wishing he'd studied Arabic or Farci instead.

In his second duty tour, he was stationed temporarily in the Pentagon, learning quickly why Marine Officers' morale in the Puzzle Palace was lower than a field latrine. His duties, like those of his fellow officers, centered around moving large masses of paper from one file cabinet to another, from one desk to another, and from one pile to another. Still, his own career docket grew to contain several verbal notations that this young man had a lot to offer the Corps and they had best use him wisely.

He had little immediate interest in the labyrinths of power and politics that is Washington, so rented a townhouse outside the sprawling Marine base at Quantico and drove the ugly commute each day up Route 95 and 395 through the traffic-choked arteries that make Washington a national gridlock. His days were long, but at 29, in peak mental and physical condition, he took it in stride.

Early in his tour of Pentagon duty, which began in February, he suddenly found himself surprised – to be unhappy, even discouraged. He wondered briefly what it was that ever made him think this was the life he'd wanted for so long.

(*"So, hotshot, here you are doing exactly what you've always wanted to do, but it sure doesn't feel much like 'hallelujah!*)

Chapter Eleven
The Embassy of Spain,
Washington, DC

The Ballroom
July 3, 8:05pm

For several months prior to his new assignment, an uncomfortable part of Jim Darden's Pentagon duties involved attendance at frequent Embassy Row receptions. Apparently, our State Department diplomacy experts felt incapable of making entertaining small talk with foreign military officers, and relied instead on our own officers who happened to be stationed in the Washington area.

At first he disliked the posturing and patent insincerity of these gatherings, but as he developed his ability to smile and murmur polite nothings, he found that about once an evening, he could find a conversation worth having.

Once he found a second secretary from the Polish Delegation who had seen all of John Huston's movies. Another time he got into an intriguing comparative law discussion with an Punjabi barrister serving with India's military mission.

Tonight, he had been introduced to the Spanish Consul, Don Alberto Something da Something, who seemed an agreeable man. The two fell into a comparison of the attack strategies of American football and European, or soccer to Jim. The Spaniard was using a pair of wine glasses to illustrate how Real Madrid executed the give and go when Jim felt another pair of eyes on him. He glanced up and instantly forgot all about Real Madrid.

The eyes were large, the darkest of browns…and calm… and perfect. They dominated a face that was stunning, oval, flawless…and perfect. The strong, but slightly turned up nose was likewise, perfect, the bud-shaped, perfect mouth below it somehow even more...perfect. Her skin was smooth and unblemished, a little creamy olive-rose tint…Perfect. Surrounded by dark, thick, shoulder length, shining, perfect hair.

The analytical/verbal cortex of Jim's brain began to count the little bell chimes that sounded each time the word 'perfect' had just popped up. The rest of his brain scrambled for an opening statement.

He smiled. The mouth did not move, but the eyes changed shape. They seemed to reflect his smile.

"It's perfectly delightful to meet you," he said.

She said, in an accent that softened her English, *"But you haven't."*

"True, I suppose…*but if I had, it would be."*

"Perhaps I am not delightful. Or perfect."

"I would never admit that to anyone."

"Then you think that I am not!" She sniffed.

"I think that you are certainly one of them. Quite probably both."

"Then if one, I choose delightful. Perfect is boring."

"I wouldn't know. I've never seen it."

"Scoundrel! You have not met me and already you insult me!"

"Scoundrel?"

"Is that not a good word? I discovered it in Thackeray."

"Thackeray is almost 200 years out of date. I suggest 'bounder.'"

"Bounder. Fine! You are a bounder, trying to pass off old fashioned words and insult me all in a mix."

She tapped him lightly on the nose with her fan and moved away.

The aging Consul moved to his shoulder and said softly, *"I have often wondered why she carries that fan. Now I understand."*

Jim could not take his eyes off the empty place in the crowd the lady had just occupied.

"Why?" he asked.

"To anoint one of whom she approves."

"That's approval?"

"Yes. That is my daughter, and that, I am quite sure, is approval."

Jim suddenly decided this gentleman had more to offer than comparative sports theories.

"Tell me Don Alberto, about your name. There seems to be a lot of it."

"Ahh," said the older man. *"That, sir, is much too long a story for this occasion, and I can only doubt you are truly interested, except to be polite, which I know is one of your duties."*

Looking back from the direction his daughter had taken to the man's face, Jim protested.

"No, sir, I am quite sincerely interested, if you don't mind, that is."

"Not at all, Captain Darden, but perhaps another time we might get together in more relaxed surroundings, and I promise I will bore you with all the family history you can tolerate. May I presume your curiosity extends to my beloved child as well as my revered ancestors?"

Darden actually blushed. *"Well, I surely wouldn't expect you to believe me if I said 'no,' so I might as well admit it, don't you think?"*

The older man smiled a gentle smile. *"If I am to consider you an honest man, indeed, you might as well."*

————————————

Nearly two incredibly hectic months later, Jim Darden and Maria Elena Contreras da Silva sat at his dining room table with plans for their wedding spread out around them. Jim had absorbed the Pentagon's need for contingencies and for every event, had planned three or four alternatives.

"What is that word you use for these 'backups to back ups'?" asked Maria.

"Redundancy."

"Re-dunnacy."

"Close."

"If your forward planning is so bad, how do you Americans win all the wars you fight?"

Jim thought about this. *"Our forward planning for our own actions is great. But we sometimes know too little about what the other side is going to do."*

"But in this case the 'other side' is our guests, and <u>we</u> know what they are going to do! There will be at least 250 of them to fill all my father's obligations. Many will come 12 to 34 minutes late. They are going to cry at the appropriate time. They are going to eat and drink more than my father can afford, though he will never admit it, and each couple will wish they are as handsome a couple as we are."

"What..." Jim asked, *"...will we do if the caterer does not come on time?"*

Maria's straight nose and large eyes wrinkled into indomitable hardness. *"I shall send my Marine Corps and they shall behave."*

"Me, you mean?"

"Precisely! You."

"I am only one Marine, not a Corps. Besides, I may have something else to do."

Maria frowned. *"What is more important than food and wine at a wedding?"*

"Suppose the priest forgets the key to the church?"

Her calm was not disturbed. *"Breaking the door down is only a matter of two well-placed kicks, and then you can go and capture the caterers."*

"And what will you be doing while I am riding around saving the day?"

Her smile grew wider as she considered this final question.

"Powdering my nose, so I am sufficiently beautiful for the best day of my life."

Jim looked at her and tried to imagine how she could be more beautiful, and how he could have fallen so hard in such a short time. He almost wished for years to pass in a moment, so that he could catch his breath. The thought of having been together for ten or twelve years, with children and routines having added comfort and serenity was almost delicious. The sudden arrival of feelings he'd only imagined before were overwhelming him, literally toasting his sense of himself.

She read his thought and a full smile slowly suffused her face. He stood and went round the table to her. She stood, and as she did so, swept a third of Jim's papers off the table. He looked alarmed at his careful contingencies cascading onto the floor, but refocused very quickly as her arms came around his neck.

She had a way of fitting her body to his so that all possible surfaces were touching with soft insistence. He pressed her close, wanting her so badly that he feared he could crack one of her ribs.

Soon enough he had kissed every possible place on her face and was working towards new territory below her collar line. She responded with little cat growls that vibrated against his solar plexus in wondrous ways. Each button on her blouse came undone and exposed new kissing zones, each with new and lower growls. They sank to the floor, rolling under the table, stopped by a table leg, entangled in a chair leg, pushing the damn thing away, her lower abdomen soft and beautiful. So beautiful that he didn't know how to hold it all or kiss it all but he tried and somehow they fell together into the zone in which each began straining for more and more, so utterly, totally together.

A long time later, ten minutes or maybe three hours, he still held her close but not too tight, for fear of cracking a rib. Her huge eyes looked into his, and she said, *"You are a brute."*

"I love you," he said softly.

"Of course you do. But you are still a brute."

"Tsk. You are supposed to whisper sweet nothings at a time like this."

She snuggled even closer and took the lobe of his ear in her mouth and whispered, *"I love you, brute."*

Then aloud. *"Now please untangle this chair from us. Or us from it."*

He pushed himself to recognition of his surroundings. There was indeed a chair involved in their goings on. He took hold of its leg and put it aside. He looked at her, and realized that her clothes, their clothes, were all around them, mixed up with his contingency plans. He decided that this style of planning had its advantages. He kissed her breasts, and she surrounded him with her arms and her love and they sank again from direct knowledge of their whereabouts.

Chapter Twelve
Quantico Marine Base

September 10, 0655 hours

Jim Darden arrived at Quantico's Special Ops Center, his uniform pressed and shoes prepped with extra care, though he wasn't sure what was about to happen. As he entered its Planning Group suite, General Toomey met him at the door, shook his hand, and informed him that he would be excused immediately from further SOPG meetings.

Surprised and puzzled, he was escorted to a small sound-proofed "safecom" meeting room on the fourth floor. Since 9/11, security on all US military bases had been the subject of extensive reviews and many improvements, though by some measures they were still far from invulnerable.

Once inside the room, the telephone on the conference table rang immediately. He picked it up. *"This is Captain James Darden."*

"Jim, this is John Tirada. Colonel Hackman is here with me. How the hell are you?"

Jim felt a small shiver of uneasiness. (*"What's going on here?)*

"Fine, sir. It's good to hear your voice. How long has it been?"

"Too long, Jim. Listen. You're there to meet someone. We're sure you'll recognize him. He'll join you at 0700 -- in a couple of minutes. He'll have some news about your next duty assignment. Normally, as you know, we'd deliver it without this little ceremony. In this case, however, it isn't what you're expecting, and some of the details may be a bit -- well, a bit unusual, and we're not in the loop. We <u>can</u> tell you there must be a very high priority on this assignment to yank you out of the Special Ops Planning Group."

Jim's face registered surprise, but only momentarily. *"What is the assignment, sir?"*

Silence. Jim waited, gripping the phone a little tighter.

"We don't know. You'll be briefed on it in just a minute."

"I don't understand, sir. Aside from General Corbet, is there a higher authority in Special Ops than Colonel Hackman?"

Tirada understood the question. Because Peter Hackman was Deputy Director of Special Operations, USMC, only General Mark Corbet was "higher authority" within Marine Special Forces. He knew for certain that the man who was about to enter the room was higher authority.

"No, son, there isn't. But you'll understand in short order."

Less than a minute later, Jim Darden was joined by the Commandant of the Marine Corps, and leaped from his chair to attention.

"At ease, son. Take your seat."

"Sir, yes sir."

"Captain Darden….Jim…we need you for a very special assignment, one in which you'll operate on two levels. On the outer level, the public level, you'll be assigned as Head of Station, Marine Security Detail at our embassy in Tbilisi, Georgia."

Despite his self-discipline, Jim lost all effort to disguise his surprise. *"A B-billet sir… Embassy Guard duty? I've never heard of sending an officer on that duty, sir. Even Heads of Station are staffed by SNCOs."*

"They certainly are. You will report as Gunnery Sergeant James Darden, replacing GySgt . Ordell Wickes. You'll retain your current pay grade during your tour in Tbilisi, but while you're over there you'll actually receive a Gunny's pay, with the remainder deposited in an account over here, actually in an off-shore bank. You'll have access to it when your tour is done."

Jim shifted his butt on the tan naugahide once more.

"What's more, we can't send you over there without training, so you'll be enrolled in a very special

one-student MSG School beginning this afternoon. I'm afraid your request for ten days leave will have to be reduced to three, and your wedding will...well, I'd suggest you may want to postpone it."

"Respectfully sir, is that something you can require me to do?"

General Markham had taken a seat opposite Jim at the small conference table. He smiled and looked past Jim for a moment.

"Well, yes and no. This assignment is top secret, and you'll be unaccompanied."

"-- But sir, if I may, my wife Maria is from a family of diplomats. She could be a real asset in an Embassy setting, and..."

*"She'll be no **kind** of asset, Captain. No <u>scintilla</u> of an asset, because not only will she not accompany you, she will know absolutely nothing of your mission. That is an iron-clad, non-negotiable aspect of this assignment. You'll agree to that immediately, and completely, or we scrub the mission."*

Jim stared at the Commandant, not moving a muscle of his own.

The hairs on the back of Jim's neck stood up so hard they practically pushed his shirt collar away. Still, one part of that statement was puzzling. Markham hadn't said *"you'll agree to that or we'll get someone who will."* He'd said they'd scrub the mission. It must be important, and he must be important to it.

"May I understand what this mission is, sir?"

"Jim, I'm sending you over there to find out what you can to separate facts from ugly rumors and half-cooked conspiracy stories. Or confirm them. It's important -- awfully important -- to the nation's security and its future. It's also got to be quiet. That's critical."

"How quiet?" Jim asked.

The General looked straight into his eyes for a long moment.

"How quiet? That's an interesting question, young man. I could just say 'totally.' But let me answer it this way. Once you know the mission, you're alone and you're on it. Period. Or you're dead."

Chapter Thirteen
US Embassy -- Tbilisi, Georgia

August 13, 10:08am

His Excellency, Peter Ambrose, Esq., second son of Archibald Ambrose and (second) heir to the Ambrose Enterprises import-export fortune, adjusted his worsted wool-covered bottom for the fourth time on the soft leather of his high-back desk chair, ran fingertips over his carefully arranged dark hair, and did his very best to stay straight-faced and focused.

As the military man seated before him prattled on, Ambrose fought his mind's tendency to wander into the bubbling cauldron of acid anguish and resentment in which his assessment of his life's injustice stewed.

("Ambassador to Georgia...what a joke! When the President's self-important boob of a third-level staff flunky first mentioned it, I thought I was being offered a position in Atlanta, not this God-forsaken pustule of a city in a fourth-rate ex-Soviet satrap. For all the fund-raising I've done for the President, milking every thoroughbred breeder in Kentucky and every country music hick in Nashville, even the smallest justice would have required more, so much more than this.")

Not that Ambrose was actually suffering, by any normal measure. The man was worth nearly $20 million.

Admittedly it was the much smaller portion of the old man's fortune. His older brother's share dwarfed Peter's.

(*"Worse, it's smaller even than my god damn baby sister's share. It says somewhere that middle children never get their due. It could be that..."*)

More likely, he decided, God and the world had been conspiring against him, withholding from him everything he most sought; a place on his prep school polo team, the Presidency of his college fraternity chapter, the hand of Stephania Pelatka, whose father's shipping fortune made his own family's look like chump change, even his own Daddy's approval, and finally, when the old tyrant died six years ago, a fair share of his money.

After running three of his uncle Fred's radio stations in Kentucky and Tennessee for four years and sucking up to every Derby breeder and hillbilly music impresario in the South, he'd decided to launch his career in public service, with a run for the U.S. House seat vacated by the retirement of one of Kentucky's white-haired throwbacks to Reconstruction Royalty, Henry Willingham.

Had he needed further proof that God himself was scheming against him, that run for office had provided it. He'd outspent his rival by nearly $10 to $1, including almost $3 million of his own inheritance. He used his own radio stations and every other media outlet to flood the airwaves, cooking the books with real skill to hide the fact that he wasn't paying but two cents on the dollar for the airtime.

He'd promised lower taxes, better roads, an end to
the failed Johnson era welfare programs, forced school
busing and affirmative action, and anything else the
"right people" clamored for...and he still lost.

After the humiliation of that defeat, he'd
wandered Europe for six months, (but nowhere near
Georgia,) licking his wounds, deciding what to do next.
Considering the outrages he'd endured, he felt certain
even the strongest of men could not match his resolve to
push on, and become something his stone-hearted father's
ghost would finally accept.

If not "upfront" public service (the elected kind,
with power and prestige that Daddy would have surely
respected) then he would work behind the scenes, by
becoming the campaign financier to the right candidates,
moving on to trusted advisor, counselor to Presidents, and
surely one day, in recognition of that service, a Cabinet
Secretary in his own right (Commerce, Treasury, State, it
didn't really matter.)

In the process he'd realized that a suitable wife,
and even the obligatory children were just that -- a
requirement. Beginning with Pelatka, he'd wined and
dined a succession of 'appropriate' candidates,
(qualifications: family financial statements of at least
$100 million and no siblings to steal any of it,) to no
avail. Four spurned him outright.

The fifth, Penny Hart (no relation to the sexy
Senator,) looked like the end of his losing streak. Pretty
face, great hair, filled a low-cut cocktail dress with the
best of them. Swarthmore grad, only daughter of Phillip
Hart, the mega-mega car dealer...she'd let him score on

their third date, though she'd seemed cooler after the event than before.

Still, things were definitely looking up, but when he popped the question, she blew him entirely away. Not by saying "no," but worse -- by demanding from him for a tightly-constructed pre-nup.

Defeated, embarrassed, but undeterred, he'd finally settled on the former Phyllis Smithwick of Louisville, third daughter of William Smithwick, a small-time local attorney who'd managed to accumulate two homes and a stock portfolio of $24 million.

William hadn't exactly gushed at his skinny, gawky daughter's good fortune, but he **had** forked over $80 grand for a decent spread at their wedding. Because Peter was actually worth more than Phyllis, there was no talk of pre-nuptial agreements.

(*"True,)* he thought, (*"with her face and figure she's more bow-wow than babe,")* but she'd let him into her bed on the *second* date and was actually grateful enough for his attention to give him an ongoing series of enthusiastic bj's, which had always been his favorite form of bedroom recreation, anyway.

Even after 20 years of marriage and two children safely installed in boarding schools in Connecticut and then college, he thought of her as a kind of cruel consolation prize, an ongoing part of God's conspiracy to deny him his destiny.

God must surely be enjoying his little Peter Ambrose game today. Here he was, nearly 58, sitting in his personally purchased $3895 heated/cooled and massaging leather and suede executive chair trying to keep concentrating on Major John Akers, US Army.

The Major was surely part of God's plot, assigned here to coordinate some kind of defense exchange program with the Georgians. (Twenty Georgian army officers were allegedly learning unit mobility theory at Fort Lee, Virginia while Major Akers drank Russian vodka in Tbilisi, "coordinated exchange operations," and looked for ways to get rich.

The ignorant fool probably thought a couple of million was all the money in the world, and had no clue whatever about the hundreds of things that one couldn't do even with Ambrose's money.

Today, the Major was fishing, as usual, searching for any means, legal or not, to turn his wet fart of a career assignment into a retirement bonanza. It didn't matter how he got the Ambassador's attention, as long as he had more of it than anyone else on the staff. He especially liked sitting like a mute stump, while Peter took calls from the State Department, some wealthy Georgian, or especially the White House, (which was not nearly as often as Peter deserved.)

"-- You may not consider it important, Sir, but I believe it's <u>critical</u> that we put a stop to this and any other form of criminal activity within the Embassy."

He was talking about the terrible possibility that one or more of the staff might be stealing office supplies from the embassy supply room. (*"God, you're playing with me again!")* Ambrose thought. *("…Wasn't Kafka a Georgian? He must be!")*

Peter kept his face blank as Akers worked himself into a long-winded exposition on why the missing supplies would have to be the first issue the new Marine Security Detail Chief tackled, else petty office thievery would threaten the stability of the free world.

Peter shook himself in wonder.   Akers had certainly not said those words…had he?

("Office supplies! Shit!"). Peter Ambrose, fundraiser and political kingmaker- extraordinaire, was being lectured about wiping the asses of his larcenous staff in this ass-wipe of a country. *("Paper clips, toilet paper, and ballpoints...Jesus!")*

Major Akers wound on and on, while Peter's thoughts slipped back to his own agenda.

———————————

One day, perhaps soon, there would be real money -- and real power in his hands. Despite the insult done to him in assigning him to this festering pimple on the global back lot, he might yet snatch victory from defeat.

How? Only recently had a clue dropped into his lap.

Soon after his arrival in Tbilisi, Peter had been introduced to General Alexei Viprotin, Chief of Staff of the Georgian Army, the Black Bear of Tbilisi.

He was a frightening man, a beast. son of a Russian father and Georgian mother, he was an anomaly in a country in which nationality seemed to mean everything. Georgia's 100% Georgian civilian President, Baladze Revaz, was, by comparison, a wimp, a hack, and a non-entity.

Viprotin was huge, a veritable mastodon. He stood at least 6'7", and carried almost 350 pounds on an iron-boned frame with no loose fat whatsoever. Ambrose literally shivered when the two men first met, especially when they stood face to face and he had to look sharply up to maintain eye contact.

He was not ugly, exactly, and obviously maintained his body, face, and hair with some care, but he was one of few people Ambrose had ever met whose physical aura was that of a large and very predatory animal.

The General had studied English in his Russian military school, and evidently had used it enough to maintain his modest vocabulary. He had an animal intelligence that added to his intimidation, an ability to literally smell fear, dishonesty, and double-dealing in anyone, even by phone.

Viprotin was no politician, though when he wanted to be, he could be charming, if one finds charm in a 350-pound jungle cat.

He had already climbed the ladder of his choosing, ascending to a military position from which he could pursue his ultimate ambitions: the power of every-day command over several thousand armed men, occasional absolute power over any one, two, or several women at a time, and the personal power to take what he wanted when he wanted it, be it money, a dacha or two, and any of a host of expensive toys that fascinated him for a day or a week.

He had no sense of his own nationality or ethnicity, cared little about local or global politics, and in fact harbored a long-nurtured cynicism about government and "public service."

Despite feeling personally intimidated, Peter Ambrose knew his challenge would be to create a relationship with the man -- in careful stages.

Familiarity first: He would walk the tightrope of respect and deference without tripping on suck-up or servility. Slowly he would work from familiarity to mutual respect and confidence. Trust might be unnecessary, and the two men didn't have to like each other much, but a degree of mutual confidence and confidentiality would be necessary.

Ambrose saw quickly that Viprotin carried a measure of respect for the power of the United States. That, of course was a good thing, and gave Peter a useful starting point. A second clue came quickly from his team, his "Listeners," who compiled a set of personal data about the General he could use to make a favorable impression.

The data they gathered made him aware of two of the General's personal appetites: Woodford bourbon and exotic women.

The bourbon was a key that unlocked a wealth of useful information, but it didn't come easily. The General never drank alone, and never trusted anyone who wasn't drinking out of a bottle he knew contained alcohol. One diplomat a few years previously had tried plying him with another Kentucky bourbon while swilling what he said was his favorite Russian vodka, but Alexei reached for the diplomat's bottle while the man was off peeing, and found it contained only water. That discovery ended in disaster for the diplomat.

Also, Viprotin could drink a fifth of the bourbon without losing much of his edge, while Ambrose began to feel its effects while sipping his third shot. Peter worked with painstaking care to develop a masculine version of chatty-Cathy verbosity, hopefully covering the fact that he was sipping while the General was out-swilling him by three to one.

Ultimately, he managed, and when the General was finally drunk enough to fall into his personal Slavic funk, he became a morose, but less-than-careful sharer of feelings, thoughts, and especially facts that Ambrose wanted desperately to learn.

What Peter had learned in his third one-on-one drinking session was of inestimable value.

Viprotin slouched on the Ambassador's couch, his boots carelessly plopped on Ambrose's favorite coffee table, and waved his nearly empty bourbon glass as he rattled on.

"Is fucking incredible, how these assholes lust after their rubles, dollars, and Euros, as if mere money is the only key to power...."

Peter nodded knowingly, his own heels carefully positioned on the opposite corner of the marble table.

"It is, indeed, but which assholes do you mean, Alexei?

"All of them, you simple shit! The Russians, the Saudis, the Americans, even the faggot Brits! All of them!"

Peter smiled. It was always a good sign when Viprotin started using locker room language with him. It was, he felt sure, the beginning of friendship, and though it was only a small part of a much larger and more cynical strategy, it touched a seldom-reached part of his heart.

"But Alexei, money has been the root of power for centuries. What's new about that?"

Viprotin leaned forward, grabbed the Woodford bottle and poured himself another glass.

"What's new about that, my criminally ignorant friend, is what's going on right here in Tbilisi, under your snot-filled nose!"

September 10, 1740 Hours

Jim Darden pointed his aging Mustang at the curb and eased forward until the front wheels tapped it, in front of his rented townhouse outside the Quantico base.

He smiled as he noticed Maria's yellow VW Golf parked three cars away. The smile widened as he opened the door to the smell of vegetables being sautéed and the sight of Maria in short shorts and faded tee shirt smiling back at him.

"Good evening, Mr. Man. Your timing is impeachable!"

"Impeccable, you mean, Ms. Woman!"

"OK, impeckable, if you say so, but how does one peck timing -- if it is somehow 'peckable'?"

He laughed as he hugged her tightly.

"This is quite a surprise, young woman! I was sure you were engaged in affairs of State in Washington. To what do I owe the gift of your presence in my humble abode?"

"A need of practice. I am afraid I am much more skilled at ordering from menus than at cooking, and as I will soon be living on American shoelaces, I cannot be sure I will see another menu for many years to come, alas."

Jim reached for her, spun her in his arms and whacked her behind.

"That, young lady, is for your impudence. And this...(he spun her to him and kissed her softly, then not so softly)*...is for your beauty as well as your skills. And by the way, it's singular, and a string, not a lace."*

She looked puzzled, then quickly understood.

"OK then, Mr. Expert. Shoestring. Shoelace. It's still poverty, and I must learn to adjust, mustn't I?"

"Indeed."

His one-word reply and serious expression changed the mood in a flash. Maria turned down the heat on the stove and followed him into the living room.

"You know there was no complaint there, I hope. Do I need to apologize?"

"No...not at all...it's just...I have some bad news."

"Don't tell me you're being sent to Iraq ?"

"N-no, but it might be just as bad."

"Afghanistan?"

"No."

"Where, then? For how long? Can I come with you?"

"I can't tell you, I don't know, and no, you can't."

Maria stood over him as Jim fell into his easy chair. Her hands on her hips, her expression suddenly serious, she looked ready for a fight.

"What do you mean, exactly, Mr. Man?"

"Just what I said, Maria. I have new orders, and I can't say anything about them – to anyone."

She sat on the edge of the sofa opposite his chair, looking smaller, as if someone had let the air out of her.

"What about our wedding? Our honeymoon? They are only a week away! Must we put them off until you are back? And when will that be?"

His silence made everything worse.

Finally, he said softly: *"The wedding can go on as scheduled. The honeymoon will have to wait."*

The sound of food softly sizzling on the stove captured her attention and she rose quickly and left the room. Jim heard her stirring something and moving about in the kitchen, and noticed that she was in no hurry to return.

Chapter Fourteen
Tbilisi

September 12
The Presidential Palace

Alexei Viprotin was hard at work on a project that would, if successful, increase his power ten-fold.

He knew that the pipeline discussions were reaching a critical stage. Not just any pipeline, but a major oil trunkline from the wellheads around the Caspian Sea and Azerbaijan west, across Georgia to its western port of Batumi, not more than 110 miles from his chair. The free enterprise capitalists running Russia today were in full stampede to make billions and spend them – wild dogs starved for a century, then let loose in a meat market with no one to say "enough!".

Selling Azerbaijani and Caspian crude to SUV-drivers in Columbus, Chicago and Ypsilanti was their Plan One. The fact that American air east of the Mississippi was barely breathable and that 2/3 of the rivers in Siberia and Azerbaijan were fouled with spilled crude and other drilling-related toxins was irrelevant to these quiet men. There were uncounted billions to be made, and no obstacle was big enough to deter them.

("At $50 or more per barrel, we are talking many, many billions. At $100 per barrel, it may be enough to control the world. So far the talking and planning are so

quiet there hasn't been a peep in the American press or ours, except for the industry journal no one reads.")

Still, he knew it was virtually impossible to keep something this big quiet forever. *("Even the slippery snake of an American Ambassador smells money in the air, and is obviously anxious to sniff up my drawers.")*

He was right. Ambrose was fascinated. Lately he had been sucking up to Viprotin with all subtlety of a five-day old mackerel.

For Viprotin, it had begun a week earlier, when he had been summoned to the Presidential Palace on the banks of the Kura River to meet with President Revaz himself. Once seated before the little man's huge and ornate desk under the Palace's glass dome, the President wasted no time.

"Alexei, I believe you may be able to be of some service...some unusual service on a matter of great importance."

"Indeed, Baladze? You have some rebels who need silencing?"

Revaz wrinkled his nose, furrowed his thin eyebrows and tried his best to look insulted.

"Not at all, Alexei. Georgia seeks not your military prowess, but your influence, your ability to negotiate and win the hearts and minds of your countrymen."

Viprotin smelled bullshit, and wanted to wrinkle his own nose at the odor, but merely raised one of his bushy black eyebrows in a look of passing curiosity.

"You see, Alexei, we find ourselves at a crossroads, so to speak, and a crucial one at that. We have an opportunity to influence great global events, and to create national wealth beyond our...beyond anything we might achieve by...normal means."

Viprotin leaned forward and casually reached across Revaz's desk, lifting the lid on an ornate lacquered humidor, and withdrawing a long, fat Bolivar Suntuoso.

Removing the Honduran hand-made from its glass tube, he bit the capped end, spat it onto the President's Persian rug, then rolled it on his tongue before lighting it. It was a show of deliberate intimidation which was not lost on the small man, despite his supposedly superior rank in Georgian politics.

"I am listening, Baladze."

Revaz shifted uncomfortably in his oversize chair, and cleared his throat three times, suddenly afflicted with an excess of phlegm. When he spoke, he made an effort to sound as Presidential as possible.

"Well, then...yes...I must...I am obliged to tell you...that what I am about to reveal to you is of utmost secrecy, and can be revealed to no one, even within our own councils. That is absolutely paramount!"

Viprotin merely puffed, and watched the curls of smoke rise in the air between them.

Twenty minutes later, Revaz had laid out the outline of the plan for the pipeline, and of his personal need for Viprotin's services.

"So you see, Alexei, the negotiations with our farmers and landowners must be swift, silent, and successful, with no controversy and no resistance, lest the Russians grow impatient and seek another routing."

Viprotin allowed a smile to slowly spread across his face. He took a long last puff on the cigar and ground its last inch and a half into the President's glass and leather ashtray.

"So, Baladze, you want me to personally convince six or eight hundred peasant farmers to accept a single payment of $500 for a 100-year lease on a right-of-way across their land to build this fucking pipeline so the Russians can get rich and the Americans can drive their Cadillacs.

"They cannot plant on this land, and in fact cannot even drive their tractors or plow teams across it except on roads your people will cut every kilometer or two, eh?

"Moreover, for $500 you want them to smile, accept, and be grateful for such generosity."

Revaz squirmed again, his trousers making a sound quite like a fart against the leather of his chair.

"That's $500 <u>American</u>, Alexei!"

Viprotin's smile grew wider.

"Indeed, Baladze, $500 <u>American</u>! Certainly more money than any of them has ever seen at one time, no? They should fall on their knees in gratitude!"

The President nodded enthusiastically.

"— and just in case one or two of them has the brains to count beyond twelve, you want me to 'convince' them, eh?"

The President swallowed another sudden wad of phlegm and nodded, a bit less enthusiastically.

Viprotin lunged forward in his chair and slammed both hands down on the desk top so hard every item on it literally bounced. The President actually uttered what could only be called a shocked, stifled squeak of fright.

"So, Mister President. Before I accept this dangerous mission for the greater good of the State of Georgia, precisely what -- did you say -- was in it for me?"

Less than two minutes later that negotiation was complete, and Viprotin stood to leave. Baladze Revaz offered his manicured, but thoroughly damp hand. The President remained seated, however -- not to insult the General, to be sure, but rather to conceal the dark stain of wetness on the front of his grey trousers.

Chapter Fifteen
Washington, DC

September 14
Dulles Airport

Peter Ambrose was glad to be back in Washington, even for only four days. This, after all, is where he knew he belonged. As his plane touched down on the Dulles tarmac, and the State Department driver met him at the baggage carrousel moments later, he actually smiled, looking forward to the two biggest Embassy receptions of the season and the way-too-rare White House dinner. Tired as he was from the flight, the first reception at the Russian Embassy was this evening. He even looked forward to seeing his wife for the first time in five months.

The latter anticipation, however, didn't survive more than thirty seconds after his driver dropped him at his Georgetown townhouse.

Phyllis met him at the door with an enthusiastic hug and kiss.

"Oh, Peter, it's been so damned long. It's so good to see you! Welcome home dear!"

"Thank you Phyllis, it's good to be out of that rat hole."

"Is it so bad? You poor thing! Oh, dear I couldn't wait to tell you the news! Amanda is in love! We feel sure by this time next month she'll be engaged! Isn't it wonderful?"

Peter took a step back from her embrace. As always, he could smell even the slightest whiff of her BS.

"Wonderful? Well, I imagine that depends, now doesn't it? Who is the fellow? Where's he from? Who are his people?"

Phyllis's smile faded rapidly.

"Now Peter, you know how hard it's been for Amanda. After all the money we've spent on her schooling, her therapist, her personal coach, and all, and after all the effort she's put in to slim down and get herself together…"

"—Of course, Phyllis. You can bet I haven't forgotten a bit of that. So who's the fellow?"

Her voice grew smaller, more timid, almost a whine. Even before she'd finished the next phrase, the stink of BS became overpowering.

"Well, his name is Ricky Stein, and he's from somewhere on Long Island. He's studying Sociology at Ithaca college and she says he's a perfect gentleman and…"

"—Ricky What?!"

"Ricky…Stein."

"Our daughter is in love with a Jew?! From precisely where on Long Fucking Island, Phyllis?"

True, any serious interest in his daughter was an unexpected gift, but why a Jew? A Jew was bad enough, but he said a quick prayer for the Hamptons as a consolation prize.

Phyllis melted into full whimper-and-whine.

"Peter, Peter please, for God's sake, this is your only daughter, who has been miserable for most of her life. She's 24 and hasn't had a single man pay more than one night's attention to her <u>ever</u>!"

He almost chuckled at that, but the thought of paying even one night's attention to his obese, homely daughter made his stomach churn. The Jew must be stupid.

"I asked a simple question, Phyllis. Where is 'Ricky Stein' from and who are his people?"

The response came in a tiny voice, barely above a whisper.

"He's from Queens. His parents own a business."

"What kind of business, Phyllis?"

"It's a...a resta-...a delicatessen."

Peter just stood there looking at her for a long moment, incredulity and disgust written across his face in bold.

"Shit!" was all he said, and turned away.

Pouring himself a drink at the bar trolley in the corner of their living room, he shook his head slowly.

("What a total fucked-up waste! What in the world have I done to deserve this unremitting river of crap? I hope you're having a huge fucking laugh up there, God!")

Phyllis came up behind him and squeezed a shoulder with each hand, laying the side of her face against his spine.

"You poor dear, working so hard in that God-forsaken place, then a long flight home and...and I knew I should have waited until tomorrow to share Amanda's news, I just knew it," she sniffed.

He spun out of her grasp.

"Phyllis, for God's sake, today, tomorrow, it makes no damned difference. We need to leave for the reception in an hour. Give me a few minutes alone and get yourself ready."

––––––––––––––

Jim Darden's head was spinning. Five days of double-shift, crash instruction at the Marine Corps MSG

School in Quantico had left him precious little time for anything except hitting the books and surviving on a half-ration of sleep…at best.

He awoke every morning at 0445, was in the base gym at 0500, back in his townhouse at 0640, showered, dressed, and wolfing down fruit and an egg burrito by 0710, and in his special class-of-one by 0730.

One ten-minute break in the morning, one in the afternoon, a 20-minute sandwich break at noon followed by a ten minute run, and then back at it until 1930. Home by 1940, a small meal, four hours of study, and maybe ten minutes of shared romance before he was out cold, intentionally or not. The "maybe factor" was Maria's attitude which she tried hard to keep positive, but found harder to maintain the longer this regimen continued.

She had plenty of time to consider her attitude, and what, if any objections she had to the situation. In moments of greatest honesty, she knew the thing she resented most was not his mission, nor even a postponement of their wedding. It was her fiancé's unquestioning obedience to orders that he keep secret his whereabouts, and the length of time he'd be away from her. That gnawed at her more and more as the days passed. He could also tell her nothing about what kinds of danger he would be facing – what risks of injury – or even death would confront him.

Chapter Sixteen
The Embassy of France

September 15, 6:48pm
A Ride in Silence

Diagonally across from Georgetown University Hospital, the French Embassy would have been a pleasant walk from Ambrose's house on P Street NW on a warmer evening, but as it was still chilly in early-April, and as she was always concerned about her husband's driving after drinking, Phyllis had called a cab.

They completed the short cab ride in mutual silence: his, still fuming; hers, painful almost to the point of tears. In fact, his reaction to what she felt was wonderful news about their long-suffering daughter caused her to begin thinking, what for her, were new thoughts.

"What, exactly, do I have here with this man? When he trashes Amanda's romance with this young man, it will just destroy her…and even if she still marries the Stein boy, it will be awful for her."

"And what about me? What am I getting from this relationship? He doesn't want me in Tbilisi, and after four months of absence gave me not an ounce of warmth or desire this evening. I've worked hard to give him everything I know how to give a man."

"For years I've convinced myself that without Peter I'd be alone and sorry, a typical, pitiful old maid. The fact is that in the last year I've spent less than two months with Peter and ten on my own. I've had several opportunities, even a couple of invitations to be with other men. And even if I'm alone, how much sorrier would I be than I am right now?"

Had Peter looked at his wife, he might have seen these thoughts in her suddenly cold eyes, but he didn't.

When they arrived at the Embassy, he completed only the bare minimum of protocol with Phyllis at his side. They walked receiving line and completed a few quick and perfunctory greetings. He got her a drink, and found a table a good distance from the dance floor of the Embassy ballroom.

Still thinking her new thoughts, she was not surprised when he promptly left her with two other Foreign Service wives and went off to find his own entertainment for the evening. Peter Ambrose was – above all – a master eavesdropper. He honed his skills to a high level and carried a passion for the task fully equal to any Red Sox fan's one-time adoration of Ramirez and Big Pappy. Tonight, he was on his usual hunt for useful news and opportunities for advancement.

He began trolling immediately, noticing that it was likely to be a good haul, given the fact that the majority of the A-list was in attendance tonight. He quickly counted nearly the entire White House staff, as well as the Secretary of State herself, and five…six…eight, no, ten of her Undersecretaries and Assistant Secretaries.

His first sortie through the Embassy's public rooms caught sight of at least a dozen Senators and Congressmen and at least twenty more expensive tuxedos worn by lobbyists from the K Street fraternity.

Peter had long understood the importance of memorizing faces and names, so the fact that he didn't actually know all of these luminaries personally didn't stop him from saying a casual "hello" to many. He also knew which ones to greet and which others to make himself visible to, hoping they might greet *him*.

As the evening wore on, he began looking for two things: first, a strategic spot to stand, sit, or lounge, from which he might overhear muted, but useful conversations, and more important, a "friend" who was drunk enough to carry on a quietly banal conversation in that strategic listening spot, so that he himself appeared occupied, rather than listening in on others.

Tonight Bud Skipwith would fill that role admirably. About to retire from the firm of Tillinghast, Skipwith, Ardsley and Herring after 30-odd years of questionable ethics and unquestionable profits, Skipwith was a dead ringer for Shatner's "Denny Crane" character on "Boston Legal."

Peter had known Skipwith for a dozen years, and worked with him to raise funds for several ungrateful politicians. They had enjoyed each other's company, and had shared a good number of nights on the town in restaurants with long tablecloths and young Skipwith interns who did wonderful things under them while the two men rolled their eyes and giggled into their drinks.

Having noticed groups of two, three, and even six "retiring" to the second floor Embassy library for quiet conversations, Peter tipped one of the bartenders $100 for an unopened bottle of Johnny Walker Blue and had it delivered to a darkened corner of the large room where he had staked out two chairs and deposited Phil in the larger one.

It wasn't long before he was able to filter out the soft buzz of conversations across the room and zero in on one particular trio standing several feet away near the fireplace.

What attracted his attention was the identity of two members of the trio. One was the Assistant Secretary of State for European Affairs, the second the President's Chief of Staff. The third man wore a naval uniform – in the flickering firelight he thought he saw Admiral's stars on the officer's shoulders, but didn't recognize him. They were speaking softly, obviously feeling the need of privacy.

He nodded toward Skipwith and leaned in to fill his glass, directing his ear toward the trio.

"...negotiations are nearly done...enough to buy a small country..."

"...ends in Batumi...less than two years..."

"Batumi" rang a bell in Peter's brain. He was onto something. The port city on Georgia's western coast was less than 150 miles from Tbilisi.

A few seconds later a louder bell rang.

"We've got that covered...some Army type...name of Vipo--Viprotsky or something like that...

"...taking care of the farm leases...no troubles."

"...keeping this quiet, even after we're out and collecting..."

Peter was fascinated, a sudden statue, almost forgetting to use his Skipwith prop to cover his interest. As the Admiral suddenly turned in his direction, however, he quickly covered himself by continuing, as if in mid-sentence, punching Skipwith gently in the shoulder in a show of old buddies being old buddies.

"You know, Skip, it's been a damn long time since I've tasted this stuff!" he said waving his single finger of expensive scotch and slurring his words. *"You remember that time..."*

The Admiral turned back and the three continued.

"...billions...start pumping in 13, maybe 14 months...need more tankers."

Ambrose reached across to refill Skipwith's glass – the next one should render him comatose. Peter chucked him on the shoulder again and giggled.

"Gotta go spring a leak, old buddy! Drink up!"

Every bell in his head was ringing. Five minutes later he had collected Phyllis and left the Embassy. He had work to do, and his first task was to book the next available flight back to Tbilisi.

Chapter Seventeen
Tbilisi

September 18
The Ambassador's Office

Four days later, Peter was back in Tbilisi, his mood instantly darkened. The more he thought about his post, and the nation he'd been sent to treat with, the more disgusted he'd become.

Georgia is in many respects a modern-day triumph – merely because it exists as a nation at all. One of several east-west crossroads on the ancient Silk Road trade route between the so-called civilized glories of Western Europe and the so-called mysterious treasure troves of the Orient, it had traced its history in spilled blood. Hundreds of battles of invaders, conquerors and would-be conquerors changed its name and redrew its borders as ancient tribes of Persians, Caucasians, Turks, Ottomans, and a score of other invaders lay this or that week's claim to it.

The country's service as a battlefield has continued from early Christian centuries all the way through last week's news, as Russian troops have continued to try to referee ongoing tribal animosities in Georgia's breakaway provinces of South Ossetia and Abkhazia. Even as multi-national oil firms have negotiated for choice positions in the coming contest for control of the huge petroleum fortunes to be made, they have had to learn complicated dance-steps with changing partners, often on a weekly basis, as ancient tribes and bloodlines skirmish for control of areas smaller than Rhode Island.

Ambrose saw no real hope for Georgia as long as these tribal "mini-wars" continued to rage. He had little understanding of this history of tribal warfare, and no respect for the cultures that have never yet found a way to live together in peace. In a sense, he'd built a grudging respect for the order and stability of the USSR, forced and brutal as it was. This chaos of small-town military struggles was, he felt, chaotic at best, ridiculous at worst.

Still, here he was, and there *were* opportunities for those who knew which buttons to press and when to press them. It didn't take much effort to assemble the jigsaw pieces he'd collected in Washington. Four days later, Peter Ambrose knew he'd found a new source of power – and if he played his cards right, a new source of income, beyond any he had imagined before. Quiet men on both sides of the Atlantic were hatching a major oil pipeline across Georgia to bring Caspian crude out of Russia to the West. The pipeline itself would be no secret, of course.

What few would learn, now or ever, if the quiet men succeeded, was their web of ownership shares and financial "commissions" shrouded in multiple layers of corporate structures and shadow entities.

Billions, alright. No doubt about that. It was a perfect "revenge" for unelected and underpaid public servants who never received the public adulation they felt they deserved. Peter Ambrose was definitely one of those -- and he would find a way in.

What he needed first was to make Viprotin open up. The question was "how?"

After considering several alternatives on the long flight across the Atlantic, France, and Germany, he settled on a direct power play.

He invited Viprotin to an immediate private meeting, promising him important news from Washington. The inevitable drinking took nearly an hour of desultory small talk. When the General had decimated another fifth of expensive bourbon, his casual conversation took a sudden turn.

"...So Alexei. How are you doing with the right-of-way negotiations with the farmers?"

"What? What did you say?"

"The farmers, Alexei. The pipeline right-of-way fees."

The General came out of his laid-back slouch and sat upright, suddenly almost sober. Though he tried his best to avoid it, there were tell-tale signs of surprise around his heavily lidded eyes.

"What the fuck are you talking about, Peter?"

Peter did his best to intensify his steady gaze into the General's eyes.

"Alexei. It's a simple question. I need a progress report on your negotiations with the farmers and landowners. Now."

Viprotin was suddenly, and visibly confused.

"I—I didn't know you were..."

"-- I was what, Alexei? -- In the loop? Of course I'm in the loop. You might say I'm the center of it."

Ambrose had to plan his next moves carefully. Knowing about the pipeline windfall and a couple of the insiders who would reap its proceeds was one thing. Actually inserting himself in its core group of beneficiaries was something else.

He had already decided to use a different hand with each of the principals. It was, he knew, a matter of leverage, and with each of those principals, his potential leverage was slightly different. Still, he had to feel his way along slowly, carefully, and ever so quietly. Moreover, he didn't yet know who all of the participants were.

Sitting alone in his office, he considered the possibilities, a yellow pad in his lap with a list of names, each a possibility, each presenting a different challenge.

Was the President himself on the take? He doubted it at first, and had started to cross Farr's name off the top of the list, but then decided to leave it there for the time being. With the President, his leverage was simply his ability to identify the man as a participant to the public. That revelation could be ruinous. That the President stood to gain perhaps $8-12 billion over the coming years was much more than an annuity. It was the key to a life of real power after the man's second and last term in the White House was over. At only 57, he undoubtedly considered himself too young to go into some kind of genteel retirement, and he'd never be caught dead hammering nails in Habitat for Humanity houses like Jimmy Carter.

This revelation might well destroy both the annuity and the mantle of honor and admiration that the man had assumed would be his.

With the Secretary of State, Samuela Breedmore, revelation would endanger her career just before it reached its pinnacle. She had carefully positioned herself as the right wing candidate for the top spot in the next administration. She would almost surely win if she kept her name clean between now and the next election. If she was a participant in the pipeline windfall, it was being held in utter secrecy, channeled, Peter guessed, through a mind-numbing maze of organizations who would pay her generous honoraria for her every speech and visit, who would contribute to her campaign, and employ her trusted aides at salaries well beyond their value, portions of which found their serpentine way into her own on-shore and off-shore accounts.

How about the President's National Security Advisor? Garland Hightower was the consummate power junky who must have at least 50% vampire blood, given his intense distaste for publicity and limelight.

With his corporate background and a large gang of corporate cronies, the revelation of his role would do relatively little damage, because the man had virtually no political ambition, and no particular interest in future history books' accounts of him. However, he and his corporate pals understood the higher and lower uses of wealth and they had utterly no moral doubts about their own plans for guiding the future of their country.

Ambrose knew he needed more leverage than just his knowledge of the pipeline's quiet owners, and aside from Claymore and the two others he'd overheard in Washington, he didn't even have that -- yet.

He also knew that becoming a member of this rarified circle was surely a matter of life and death -- his own. He had no doubt that if he made even the slightest mistake, he would find himself on some plane that developed tragic engine trouble, or on the wrong end of some Islamic terrorist abductor's sword.

Merely knowing the identity of the three players he'd overheard was enough to reduce his life expectancy. Using that knowledge to threaten even the most minor of them (and none were minor) would mark him for immediate 'disposition.'

("No. If I'm to get into their circle, it had better be entry by invitation. And I'd better buy some serious insurance.")

His last session with the General made him pretty sure Viprotin was either a member of the pipeline's inner circle or at least that he was "in the mix." Knowing the General as he did, that meant Viprotin also had established his own brand of leverage over at least some of the core movers and shakers.

Ambrose considered his position -- and his alternatives -- for days. The pipeline was going to bring a lot of money lapping up against the shores of this little country, and the silent circle in Washington, whoever was in it, would surely need a trusted man here in Tbilisi – a well-placed American, – *"and who better than me?"*

The rewards? Serious enough to assure one's own future within a more elite circle of movers and shakers, people who had so far rejected or eluded him.

The more he considered that higher circle and his membership in it, the more fascinated he became with its two most powerful characteristics: silence and secrecy. In the privacy of his office, his yellow pad still in his lap, Peter Ambrose actually had to reach up quickly to wipe a dribble of saliva from his chin.

———————————

Major Akers popped his head in the Ambassador's door, smashing Peter's reverie as if it were made of glass.

"We're all out here sir, ready for the meeting...?"

Ambrose waved him in, momentarily embarrassed that he'd let the minutes slip by in his private fantasy. His personal staff filed in and took up places around his conference table.

"Do we know exactly when the new Gunny -- the Security guy, what's-his-name, is coming?" asked the Chargé d'Affaires, Tyrone Roberts as he took his seat.

"Darden, James A." replied Major Akers. *"Four more days."*

"What do you know about him?" asked Roberts. As executive officer of the Embassy, he was point man on Ambrose's private team of Listeners, and he took his responsibilities seriously. They were as close as he would ever get to the career that he had been denied when the CIA had turned down his application some dozen years ago.

Akers' methodic delivery rose a bit. He, too, loved espionage lingo.

"My sources tell me Darden is nobody special...a typical jarhead on rotation through his assignments. No service record highlights to speak of. He's probably just another high school washout with a body by Bowflex and a big dick."

"Really?" Roberts arched an eyebrow. *"How ever did you discover that?"*

"Just a hunch, but a good one. The file on him says he's just married some big-tit Spanish hottie, daughter of one of Spain's top guys in their Embassy in Washington. Way out of his league. He's no son of a millionaire, so it must be she's hot after a uniform and his package. What else could it be...?"

Roberts merely frowned at Akers' crudeness. Ambrose didn't move, but his wheels began turning as he wondered why Akers didn't mention Darden's law degree. That was in his file too, though it should have been removed.

"-- and this is his first assignment in the field. He'll soon learn what life is like in the <u>real</u> Marine Corps," Akers continued.

Akers' venom impressed Roberts – and disgusted him. The two men were not close. Roberts despised the way Akers played tennis at the American Club, calling the lines liberally in his favor on his side, and arguing them narrowly and violently on the other. In addition, **Mrs.** Akers added nothing to any conversation, however much she talked. Roberts felt a flash of pity for whoever this Darden was.

Ambrose had heard enough. *"Well, Major, get the Gunny 'squared away' when he gets here – is that the Marine usage? Oh, and if his wife is accompanying him, be sure to get them both to our reception next month. She may be...useful to us...in a diplomatic sense."*

Akers grinned as if he understood, though he hadn't a clue. Roberts merely arched another eyebrow.

Chapter Eighteen
Quantico Marine Base, Virginia

September 19, 0505 Hours
Lake Lunga

Jim Darden slowed his pace to an easy jog.

"Come on Cade, let's get some breakfast."
"Cade" had been shortened from "Cadet," the name Jim gave the pale yellow Lab puppy when it bounded up to him a year ago during one of his runs on the many trails of the Quantico Base.

No collar, no tag, eight or nine weeks old, heart-break sweet, hungry, thirsty, and about 150 cockleburs tangled in his soft yellow fur. For nearly a year now, the two had been inseparable.

Jim had fallen in love with him in about twenty seconds, but worked hard to submerge it until he'd advertised the "found puppy" in the Base newspaper and especially until, after two months, no one had claimed it. It was only on the day he cancelled the ad that he felt he could really let himself feel the affection for the pup he'd been keeping since they'd met.

It was a storybook relationship. Some people love dogs, but all dogs love people, most without qualification and without hesitation.

Cade must have seen, or (more likely) smelled something in Darden that Sunday evening along the parkway. When Jim stopped and picked him up he licked his face like it was coated with nectar. Later that evening, after a bowl of cool water and a ball of raw hamburger, he stood perfectly still while Jim pulled and clipped the cockleburs out of his fur one at a time. That night he fell asleep against Jim's chest, cradled by one arm as Jim lay on his side. Jim awoke the next morning to a second tongue-bath of his face and neck.

"Aaaaaauuggggh! Dog germs," he cried, pushing the puppy away, but enjoying it nonetheless.

As was Jim's habit, his puppy became an instant mission. He scanned the internet and Borders Books for the best dog-training manuals. After studying three, he felt he was ready to begin, but quickly found he needed only two of their many rules for training Cadet. The first was to be clear and consistent with his commands. The second was to praise the dog enthusiastically every time a command was obeyed, with strokes, an occasional treat, and a warm tone of voice, and to ignore the dog when he failed or disobeyed. In fact those two practices made training this dog so quick and easy he wondered whether they wouldn't work just as well for training people as well as dogs.

When Maria arrived, he'd already enjoyed ten months of one-on-one bonding with Him. Now there was a new competitor for Jim's affection, Cade had taken the change in stride, deciding almost immediately that owning two caring humans was even better than one. Besides, Jim's very visible love for his puppy was one of the first things that attracted Maria to him. Cade seemed to understand instantly how the sequence goes. ("I do something cute. He smiles and pats me. She looks warm eyes at him. He hugs her. They kiss. She picks me up. I lick them both. Three way hug. Family. No problem!")

Right now his human was beginning to feel quite lost in a maze of sudden complication.

(*"Jim boy, your ass is grass. Just a year ago things were simple. No dog, no woman. Just a job and a simple-minded set of beliefs that made the job relevant. Now I have a wife who's already unhappy, a dog I love and who loves me big as all outdoors -- and responsibilities to both. Come to that, I never did give much of a thought to what I'd do with Cade when I go on a float or an overseas assignment.*

(*"Now I have Cade plus a job that matters to my country, and a woman who matters the world to me."*)

He let himself stop there, to consider the impact Maria had made on his life. He'd had a crush on a girl in his high school senior class, and his share of dates later, but nothing that even resembled this. He knew full well that he was stone in love, but at the same time he felt like anything but an expert in it.

He recognized that there was a whole new set of feelings that flooded his system, not only whenever he was with Maria, but even when he stood alone, thinking about her. There was a new happiness, a new excitement, a feeling of being "at home," of being "complete," whenever they were together. At the same time, the thought of being without her, even for a short time, was suddenly awful, a virtual Sahara trek with no water.

Finally, he had assumed a new personal mission that had nothing to do with national security: to provide for her, to make her happy, to protect her, to please her in every way possible. It was a mission that had taken up residence in the very heart of his heart.

("You have all this...and a dog to whom I mean the world. On top of that I've been selected for an overseas assignment that is obviously important, probably dangerous, and so secret I can't even tell my wife a thing about it.")

"What am I going to do with all of this?"

The questions were pretty clear, even if the answers weren't -- yet. In fact, he'd given no thought of leaving the Marine Corps until he'd met Maria Elena. True, he'd wasted no time falling in love with her. Now that he had, he recognized her life had been enough of a bouncing ball landing here or there around the world with her diplomat father and musician mother. Sure, she loved the whirl, learned the languages, and was proud of the skills and perspectives all the exposure to the world's cultures had given her. Still, she'd made it clear she wanted most of all to settle in one place, put down roots and make a real home for Jim and children.

("Leaving the Corps would be... for Maria,") he thought.

("In addition to travel and me being absent for long periods while she deals with our kids, there's the question of money. At my pay, I am no financial 'catch.' Supporting her on that pay won't be easy. We could get by, but it would probably mean her working instead of

staying home, which would make raising children really difficult. She's no snob and no Euro-royalty type, but PX groceries and Walmart aren't her style either. Right now she's so full of new love she swears it won't hurt, in but twenty years...?")

And if he <u>did</u> leave the Corps, what would he do? He supposed he could go to work for a defense contractor and do R&D work on the weapons systems he was using right now, but from what little exposure he'd had to those people, he knew there were about 16 reasons he'd choke on the job and bolt within weeks. Same for practicing law. He suspected that he'd be a staff toady for years, sucking up to senior partners and learning to lose at golf to clients with strong demands and fragile egos. If he hung out his own shingle, he'd be taking divorces and injury cases for 30-odd years.

He'd loved teaching Marines, and he'd probably love teaching kids -- at least older ones -- but he'd have to go back to school to get any kind of decent pay in teaching, and in all but the best paying counties, teachers' salaries are way behind the cost of living.

("Now I've got to depart for Tbilisi, for the love of God! I' never even learned anything about the place.")

Even that wasn't as painful as the prospect of saying "Good bye" to Maria.

Jim would not get a final briefing on his mission in Georgia until just before he boarded his flight across the Atlantic.

Chapter Nineteen
Over the Atlantic

September 22, 0640 Hours
En Route

The sun was barely peeking over the Atlantic as Jim settled himself in the seat of the C-130. Within seconds its engines roared to lift the plane off the Andrews Air Force Base tarmac and climb as it headed east at 31,000 feet toward Blenheim Air Base north of London, then on to Tbilisi. The seat itself wasn't all that bad, but for a variety of reasons, comfort wasn't possible.

First, there was Maria, now Mrs. Darden, and now alone in his rented townhouse in Quantico, with only their Labrador puppy for company. She'd taken the news of his assignment harder than he'd imagined, and not without a few hundred well-chosen words directed at the Corps.

"What do they think, these Generals and big heads? What runs through their veins? It must not be blood! They must have no soul, no human blood!"

His beautiful, self-possessed, incredibly talented, hugely intelligent, articulate wife was suddenly a fragile thing, momentarily vulnerable, angry, saddened, even a little afraid.

He closed his eyes and saw her again, her large brown eyes filled with sudden tears. He'd taken her in his arms, and held her, saying nothing. In that silence he realized there was nothing he *could* say to take away her anger or her sorrow.

She was full of questions for which he had no answers, and she was far too smart to satisfy with vague generalities.

"Listen, sweetheart," he had said, earlier. *"It is a serious assignment. It's important, and it's completely, totally, 100% quiet. I can't tell you anything more than that."*

"That's nonsense!" she nearly shouted. *"I am your wife! Are you telling me I can know nothing about where you are, what you are doing, what kind of danger you are in, when you are coming home? Nothing at all? That is inhuman! That is not America! It can't be true!"*

He tried to take her in his arms, but she pulled away.

"No! Your affection is not a pacifier! This is too important! I have had you in a legal marriage for what, five days? And now I am to lose you to some assignment that leaves me with what? Nothing! This is horrible! It's...how do you say...beastful!"

He'd laughed. *"Beastly."*

"OK, <u>beastly</u>, and don't laugh at me when I'm so angry! It makes me want to get a big stick and <u>whump</u> you!"

At this, he broke out laughing even harder, so hard she finally joined him. As their laughter subsided, he reached for her again, this time taking her face in both his hands, looking deeply into her dark eyes.

"It is that. Beastly. Terrible. I feel the same way. There is no way I would choose this. You must understand that."

She pulled away, suddenly angry again.

"Oh, please, Mr. Soldier – Okay, okay, I remember, you're not a soldier, you're a Marine! You HAVE chosen this! Don't think you can silence me with some stupid excuse like 'I am only following orders!' It didn't work for the Nazis and it won't work for you either. You volunteered for this. You must have! That is what hurts the most. It is insane!" she shouted.

Comparing him to a Nazi war criminal stung him – hard – and felt a momentary flash of anger at it. It wasn't fair. Still, he reached for her again, and gently guided her to a chair beside their kitchen table. He sat facing her, and again took her hand. When he spoke his voice was softer, but there was no mistaking his intensity.

"I did volunteer, and I expect you to understand. The job I've been given is an important one. Perhaps the most important of my career. But my career itself is not the point. It never has been. It is important to my country, Maria, so for me, it is also an order.

"When I joined the Corps I learned one thing immediately -- that Marines follow orders, without hesitation or question. Sometimes, once the orders have

been fully executed, there are opportunities to question them, to gain clarification, or even to re-think them. But first, a Marine follows orders. It has to be that way. Without it we would lose lives and battles. It is what I have done here...and I do expect you to understand that."

At that, her anger dissolved, the hot wall of Spanish temper collapsing in silent tears. This time when he reached for her, she came into his arms without protest, suddenly terribly present and terribly distant. She knew he was right, and that she respected him precisely for being right. As he held her, there was nothing he could say or do to bridge the distance between them. Then, that distance was miles – and two thicknesses of cloth. Now, as he flew eastward, the distance was just miles, and the number was rising.

"Gunny?

"Gunny?

"Uhh...Gunnery Sergeant Darden!?"

He practically jumped. His instructors in his special MSG course had called him "Gunny" for several days, but he was still having trouble connecting the rank with himself. Besides, he'd been daydreaming. Still, it was a mistake he couldn't afford to make again.

"Sorry. Lost in thought."

The crew chief smiled. *"Believe me, I understand. Would you like a meal?"*

"Sure. Not MREs, I hope." Jim's tolerance of Meals-Ready-to-Eat was on a par with most Marines. If you're near death, you eat them. They keep you alive. Period.

Jim's question had lit the veteran crew chief's fire.

"Wel-l-l son, it's your lucky day! You got yer choice of coo-senes today on account of this plane usually ferryin' three-stars and up. You got yer reg'lar standard MREs, to be sure...OR you got yer extra fancy box lunches...today we're featurin' a delicious black forest ham hand-carved and layered with pure Wisconsin cheddar, with handy foil-wrapped dollops of Hellman's Real and Gulden's brown. Accompanying the entrée is a bag of Utz's finest tater wafers, a highly responsible granola bar, a fresh-off-the-tree Granny Smith apple and a vintage juice box from nowhere near the Napa Valley. Which one most tempts yer palate?

Jim was laughing, both hands raised in surrender.

"Lunch box, please. You've sold me!"

Chapter Twenty
Tbilisi

Arrival

The ride from Tbilisi the airport to the Embassy complex was mercifully short, though the driver, a 20-something Corporal, was full of questions, obviously trying to capture the first low-down on the new Head of Detail.

"So, uh, Gunnery Sergeant, do you mind if I call you 'Gunny'?"

"Gunny is fine."

"Smooth flight over, sir?"

"Yup. Smooth enough…and long enough to be boring, I guess."

"Well, welcome to Georgia, sir. Is this your first MSG tour?

"It is."

"If you don't mind my asking, sir, how'd you come to land this billet? Piss off somebody important?"

A brief chuckle. *"Is that what could have caused this assignment? I don't know. Maybe I better retrace my sins since my last confession."*

"Might could help, sir. So, uhh, any ideas on how you want to run the detail over here?"

"Not many. Do the job, keep our noses clean, and our heads down. Go home with zero purple hearts and no Congressional medals. Make sense?"

It was the Corporal's turn to chuckle. *"Yeah, in a way, it sure does. Armpit of the universe that it is, I guess we can be grateful this isn't Kabul or Baghdad, right?"*

Jim had been careful in his answers, walking a line between friendly and vague. He was already surprised at the level of concentration he would need to maintain just to play the role he was assigned, let alone to complete the mission he'd been sent here to do. With its constant tension, he imagined such fatigue that he'd have no trouble falling asleep at night.

Once inside the complex, the driver had handed his bags to another Marine and then escorted Jim up the wide stairs in the ornate lobby to the second floor, through two sets of electronically locked double doors and down a long corridor to a second waiting area outside the Ambassador's corner office.

"The Ambassador asked to meet you immediately when you got here. He will be with you shortly. Nice to meet you, Gunny."

"Shortly" evolved into nearly 25 minutes. Finally, Peter Ambrose came out through his office's double doors, his face wreathed in a broad smile and each outstretched hand on the shoulder of a visitor.

He was in mid-sentence as the doors opened, but his voice was soft, just above a whisper. Jim watched him, taking inventory, a habit he'd acquired and developed since college and law school.

("The man must be 50, maybe 55. Either works out or doesn't eat much. Spends serious money on his hair and teeth. More on his suits. Appearances are important to him -- even the appearance of warmth and friendship. Knows how to toady up to people who have something he wants. Either that or he's just a great guy.")

As the Ambassador's visitors left, Ambrose turned back toward his office, and though he had clearly glanced at Jim on his way out, now pretended to 'notice' him for the first time, stopping and extending a hand and flashing a broad smile.

"Ahh, you must be Sergeant Darden, our new Head of Security! Welcome to Tbilisi! I've been looking forward to meeting you! Come in, come in!"

Turning to his secretary with a flourish, while still holding Jim's handshake, he continued: *"Suzanne, no interruptions at all, please, and Sergeant, how do you take your coffee?"*

"Black is fine, sir."

"Of course, of course. You Marines are all allergic to cream and sugar, or else there's a code of honor in the Corps. I suspect the latter." (Big smile here.)

("Interesting: the man calls me Sergeant instead of Gunny – a little slap or power play, and then does a suck-up when he thinks it'll earn him a point or two.")

As they entered the Ambassador's large and impressive office, Ambrose guided Jim to an upholstered easy chair near a small coffee table, taking one opposite it himself. Suzanne must have waved a magic wand, for she entered mere seconds later with two steaming mugs of coffee. She smiled what appeared to be a very friendly smile at Jim as she bent low to place his mug on the table in front of him, giving him an extraordinary view of her perfect breasts beneath her silk blouse. He smiled back, a flush rising quickly in his cheeks, followed by a second flush, already embarrassed by the first one.

"So, Sergeant Darden, how was your flight, and may I call you James?"

"Jim would be fine, sir, and the flights were smooth all the way, thank you."

"Great, great! Tell me about yourself, Jim. Where are you from? How long in the Corps? Family?"

"Pennsylvania, sir, near Pittsburgh. Five years, and just a wife."

"Ahh, yes, and if I recall correctly, a brand new one. A European and a foreign service brat, at that, isn't she?"

Jim heard a faint alarm bell. *("So, as I expected, all this glad hand chit-chat is just that. You've already done your homework on me. So what else do you know?")*

"That's right, sir."

Ambrose smiled a rather different smile this time, one that Jim had seen among locker room buddies in high school and college.

"A real pity to start a tour of duty in a place like this as a newly-wed, especially someone who's snared what I understand is a real beauty! Georgia isn't exactly honeymoon central! Do you have a photograph with you?"

Small hairs began rising on the back of Jim's neck, little flags of discomfort on its way into distaste.

"Yes..sir...I believe I do...(though I wouldn't be surprised if you already have a few.)"

He reached for his wallet, extracting from it a fresh photo he'd snapped during their short honeymoon. He was proud of it, possibly the best photo he'd ever taken. A close up, across a candle-lit restaurant table. The lighting had been perfect, and indeed, Maria had been perfect too. He handed it across to Ambrose.

"Ohh, myyy, yessssindeedindeed! She's quite spectacular! A truly great catch, young man! Congratulations!"

As Jim retrieved the photograph, his little neck hairs were whispering to him. There was something...just below the surface of the man's enthusiasm...that felt like the slime on a three-day old fish left out of the fridge. Maybe it was the word 'catch.' Maybe it was something about the expression that flitted across the Ambassador's face as he gazed at the photo. Maybe it was nothing. *("You're getting weird here. Don't get ahead of yourself, Jim boy!")*

The Ambassador was certainly curious. The next half hour was a rather intensive game of twenty questions, asked in a pleasant, mild, even fatherly tone, but all adding up to "what the hell are you doing here, son?"

Jim's answers were equally pleasant, mild, and by-the-book, and thus increasingly frustrating to Ambrose, who probably considered himself a skillful interrogator.

Finally, Jim decided it was time to change hats, and so started his own line of questions.

"Sir, I'd really appreciate an intel-report on the Embassy situation here. I'm afraid I didn't know a thing about Georgia prior to my assignment, and I'm not all that well prepared on the country's situation."

Ambrose suddenly shifted position in his chair, pushing himself up straighter, leaning forward, then, as if he thought better of that posture, resuming a more relaxed slouch, and waving one hand as if to dismiss the request.

"Sergeant Darden -- Jim, let me assure you, there's precious little to tell you about this hole -- and I use that word quite advisedly. It is just that, a hole. A third-rate backwater of the once proud Soviet 'Evil Empire' that today signifies damned little. The locals are so proud of their history they worship the stones of church towers that fell down 500 years ago. Ever since they climbed out from under Moscow's Soviet blanket, they've been reverting to their ancient tribal animosities. Even now, they can't make up their minds to be one country. The Ossetians and Abhkasians want out, and have pretty much gotten out… and they all talk as if they're the ghost of St. George the Dragonslayer. It's laughable.

"The so-called leaders of this little backwater twist themselves into pretzels in a vain effort to pretend Georgia has any strategic importance on the world stage whatsoever. It doesn't."

The man's tone was an odd mix of bitter sincerity and too-fast cadences that suggested he was performing an act.

"Surely that is at least a bit of an exaggeration, isn't it sir? I have done <u>some</u> *homework, and clearly, a man of your stature and influence would not be assigned to a third-rate backwater." (My, my, I can do suck-up myself, can't I?)*

The Ambassador fixed him with a suddenly intense gaze, as if trying to peer beneath the surface of this Marine's handsome face -- to see which way the man's wheels were turning. He wanted very much to believe they weren't turning at all, to satisfy himself that the last words out of the man's mouth were just *honest.*

"Well, thank you for the compliment, Sergeant Darden. I would like to believe you're right, but there really isn't much I can tell you about Georgia that would impress a young wife such as yours with the importance of your assignment here. We'll just have to work something up for you!"

(Shit! Back to my wife again! What's up with his fixation on Maria?) The smile that accompanied that statement was both warm and condescending. Jim decided he'd earned a point or two with the man, and also that he would have to be very careful.

"Getting back to more pleasant subjects, Jim, is your wife with you?"

"No sir, I'm afraid not. My orders are that this is an unaccompanied tour, which is partly why I asked for the briefing on our situation here. You can understand that being separated from Maria Elena so soon after our wedding..."

"-- I certainly can! I certainly, certainly can!" Ambrose said, with yet another smile that lacked warmth and tiptoed toward a leer. Jim's little hairs jumped to attention and his skin did a short crawl. Fish slime.

Chapter Twenty-One
The Arc

October 19
A Game of Tennis

The American Recreation Club occupies the grounds of what was once the rather opulent home of one of Georgia's pre-1917 oligarchs, a Greek emigrant who had made a tidy income from a shipping line he'd inherited and expanded in Batumi and other ports serving eastern Europe before Marx, Lenin, and Trotsky changed the landscape.

It's 12 bedrooms were for overnight guests of the Embassy, while its dining room, billiards room, bar, and library were for the off-duty enjoyment of the Embassy staff and guests. What was once an estate of more than 600 hectares has long since been reduced to 62, but it still boasts a large a rear veranda overlooking a rectangular swimming pool, three tennis courts, and six holes of rather decent golf. Surrounding woods and the mountains that ring Tbilisi on three sides serve the staff well during hunting season, including a target range for archers and shooters.

After five days of hectic activity becoming acclimated to security detail procedures and chasing phantom office thieves on the impassioned advice of Major Akers, Jim felt a couple of Saturday hours at the ARC would be a welcome relief.

He drove his Embassy-issue Jeep Wrangler out of the Security Detail's quarters near the Embassy compound and across the city to the ARC's hilltop location nearly 4 miles out of town. Arriving a little after mid-morning, he showed his ID to the Corporal on duty at the gate, received a hearty *"Welcome to the Country Club, Gunnery Sergeant!"* and headed for an open parking space near the main entrance.

The usually brisk fall weather was warmer than anyone could remember at this time of year, almost enough to break a sweat just by standing in one place, but the Club's air conditioning was more than up to the task, and felt immediately refreshing. Nevertheless, Jim felt good to be out of uniform, relaxing in shorts, a sleeveless t-shirt, and Nikes, and so headed toward a wicker chair on the warm back veranda.

The bartender had just placed a tall iced tea by his side when he felt a punch on his shoulder. It surprised him, not hard enough to hurt, but quite clearly harder than just friendly -- especially as he'd made no 'friends' here yet.

"Well, well, we were wondering when our newest guard dog would deign to socialize with us! Welcome, Sergeant!"

He looked up quickly at John Akers grinning face, and found himself a tad slow in returning the smile. *("Guard dog?")*

It was impossible for Akers not to have known that calling a Gunnery Sergeant "Sergeant" was an insult that within the Corps would have gotten him on every shit detail to come down the pike. He had tactfully asked the Major to call him "Gunny" several times. Now it was clear that the insult was no mistake.

"Good morning, sir. Nice to see you."

"How's your investigation coming, Sergeant? I haven't heard any messages about your progress."

The edge in the Major's tone suggested care in Jim's response, but his neck hairs and gut were sending their own warnings: *("Asshole Alert! Asshole Alert!")*

"Progress, Major? I can't say there is much to report, sir. There is nothing we've found to suggest that someone is into wholesale thievery. Mostly it seems that we may be losing a pen or two or a stapler at a time. I'm sure you know how office stuff migrates to home stuff when folks work overtime by taking office work home?"

The Major's grin disappeared. *"Is that so? Well, I certainly expected a bit more professionalism than that, Saaargeant. When we're losing thousands of dollars in less than a year, one might hope you'd be able to find <u>something</u>! Perhaps we expect too much of rookies, even in your business."*

Two voices vied for Jim's attention. *"Asshole Alert Confirmed! Asshole Alert Confirmed,"* vied with *"Watch your ass, buck-o. Don't make this guy your sworn enemy!"*

"No sir, I don't believe you do. Our work isn't finished, and if, as you suggest, this goes beyond petty thievery of the negligent, rather than pre-meditated sort,

we'll find out what's going on and take appropriate action, sir."

The Major prided himself on recognizing suck-up when he heard it, though like many, he suffered a hearing loss of 30-50% when it was directed at himself.

"Well, that's more like it! You keep at it until you catch the thieves and string'em up good. We need to send a message here, know what I mean?"

Jim nodded as earnestly as he could. *"Sir, I certainly do, sir."*

"Great! Well that's bygones. How about a little tennis action for the price of a superb ARC lunch. What do you say?"

"Oh, well, thank you sir, but it's been a very long time since I've played, and I'm sure I would..."

"--Nonsense! You're not gonna let a mere Army man challenge you and refuse to respond, are you? It'll be the disgrace of the entire security detail, and you'll have an open insurrection on your hands for failing to uphold the dignity of the Corps."

Jim rose from his chair, a bit hesitantly (*"This guy makes my skin crawl. I don't know what it is about him, and he probably isn't a bad guy at all. Maybe you've got a case of the crabs, Jim boy. Gotta watch these foreign toilet seats."*)

Once on the court, with a borrowed racket, Jim found himself almost enjoying the warm-up rallies, especially because even after a long, long lay-off, his strokes seemed to come back to him quickly.

Akers, on the other hand, was enjoying himself less and less as their warm-up continued.

"OK, Sergeant, what do you say, $50 for the match?"

"What?! You want to play for money? A little one-sided, especially on a Sergeant's salary, don't you think, Major, sir?"

"Come on, come on, Darden! You jarheads are supposed to be the hotshot warriors of the western world. Did they suddenly change the TV ads? The few, the frightened, the phony, right?"

Jim stopped, stood still for a moment, and another, just looking across the net at Akers.

("No, Jimbo, you don't have the crabs. It's the guy in your gunsight. Wonder what his problem is? Did some off-duty Marine bouncer do whup-ass on him in a bar somewhere?")

Jim took another moment, just staring across the net, before nodding slowly.

"Fifty dollars, sir, two out of three sets."

Akers grinned. *"That's more like it. I'll go easy on you, just to level the court a bit, OK?"*

("You do that, asshole.") *"Thank you, sir. I'll appreciate any kindness!"*

Major Akers spun his racquet for serve. *"Up or down, Saaaargeant?"*

"Down, sir."

Akers aimed the briefest glance at his racquet strings, then smiled. *"Not your day. I serve."*

("Why am I not surprised?") Jim asked himself.

Akers' first serve was an ace. Flat, straight, angled to the outside of the court, but very, very fast.

The two moved to the deuce court. The second serve was a carbon copy of the first. Jim moved a little faster and got his racquet on this one, but only the top of the frame, so his swing resulted only in a weak lob that landed in the next court. The Major smiled again.

Jim's third return was a little better. Still weak, and into the net, but the net of his own court. He was beginning to adjust to the speed of the Major's cannonballs.

"Forty-love, Saaargeant!"

Akers' next serve was a carbon copy of the second. Jim's anger and adrenalin were no longer fighting each other, one to increase his violence, the other to rein it in.

This time he got his racquet's sweet spot on the ball, his return was every bit as fast as the serve. It cleared the net by an inch, landing not more than six inches inside the Major's baseline, sneaking under the Major's surprised and late backhand swing. Jim stifled his urge to yell "*Yes!!*"

"*Out! What a shame! Your serve, Saargeant.*"

"*What?!*"

"*I said 'out! -- Sergeant. The shot was long. Congratulations, though, it was a <u>real</u> nice try. I mean, you got it over the net and everything!*"

The next 45 minutes were a test of nearly every one of Jim Darden's abilities, but most especially his ability to endure a continuous stream of cheating and humiliation. The Major actually allowed him to win a few points, but his own service wasn't strong enough to hold a service game, and though he quickly adjusted to Akers' cannons, his returns had to be at least a foot inside the lines to be "allowed" and returned.

The final score was 6-1and 6-2.

Akers grinned as he leaped over the net. "*That'll be $50, buck-o. Welcome to Tbilisi.*"

"*Thank you, sir. Here. You certainly are a powerful player.*"

(Sneer.) "*Nonsense. Didn't have my "A" game at all today. If I did, you'd never have stolen those two games from me in the second set. I played bullshit the whole match. But hey, who's complaining? An Army of One just whupped a whole United States Mariiiine! Will wonders never cease?!"*

"Well, I guess it's a good thing tennis isn't my mission over here, sir. We'll do a good bit better job at protecting our Army of One… <u>sir</u>."

Akers sneered again, his sun-reddened face flushed darker with an anger whose source was a mystery to Jim.

Akers glared at him. *"What the hell is that, Saaargeant? You trying to give a superior officer some shit?"*

Jim smiled back, his eyes locked on Akers'.

"Absolutely not, sir. I'll leave that for when we're both out of our respective services. If our paths should cross then, I'd be delighted to feed you a whole mess of shit, sir, turd by turd, but right now, no way, Maaajor. I recognize a superior officer…when I see one."

It was the slight pause in the last sentence that gave Akers the shot that nearly made him erupt, but Jim had turned and begun walking away. Over his shoulder he smiled again. *"Thanks for the tennis lesson…<u>Sir</u>!!"* (

("You son-of-a-bitch. I'll have your ass for breakfast one day soon, Sergeant, one way or another.")

Chapter Twenty-Two
Embassy Patrol

October 21
Night Walk

At 0212 hours , the Embassy compound was mostly dark and silent. The Communications Officer was at his work station, but for little purpose, other than studying the latest Corvette road test in *Car and Driver.*

Jim had walked the inside patrol route three times with the Corporal whose watch ran from midnight to 0600. The route took 22 minutes, give or take, and the intervals between walks ranged from five to forty minutes to minimize the ability of intruders to use the walk schedule to get in and out undetected.

The previous three interior tours had been routine, punctuated only by casual small-talk between the two men. When it ended, both settled down at the security desk in the Embassy lobby to enter their notes on the watch log and wait for the next tour. Outside, two Marines stood at each of three entrances to the building, and four more patrolled the perimeter. It was quiet outside as well.

"I'll take the next tour myself, Warrior. And I'm gonna take it at half speed, so don't expect me back for about 45 minutes, OK?"

"Yessir, Gunnery Sergeant. But why the slow pace? Was I going too fast?"

"Not at all. I just want to spend a little extra time memorizing the details of the place, look for chinks in the armor, think through any ways we can improve what we do. Capisce?"

"Sure...no problem, sir."

Part of Jim's crash course in Security Detail duty was a trio of lessons in crime scene investigations. He would need to remember everything he'd learned, because he'd just arranged for about 40 minutes alone in the Ambassador's office suite to conduct the first of what would probably be a number of quiet searches.

The Ambassador's desk was locked, of course, but his preference for French provincial furniture had resulted in a lowest-bidder purchase from a North Carolina company that provided only the silliest of locking mechanisms. A letter opener with a flexible blade opened the center drawer and top right hand drawer in seconds.

Jim's concentration was total, his adrenalin rush giving him both intense focus and a rapid heart rate. Even the softest rustle of the Ambassador's papers seemed terribly loud in the deafening silence.

The documents in the right-hand drawers were routine administrivia. Staff credentials, invitations to social functions, weekly briefs to Washington on the 'state of the state,' nothing out of the ordinary.

The desk's center drawer was the messiest, a jumble of pens, paper clips, pinch clips, half-used packs of breath mints, message slips, and perhaps a hundred or so slips of miscellaneous paper. Jim wondered whether the Ambassador himself was the imaginary supplies thief.

Ambrose was evidently a doodler, a rather advanced one, suggesting too much time on his hands and not enough to do. The scattering of pages from small note pads with random words and phrases might as well have been code.

Jim had donned latex gloves in the Ambassador's private bathroom prior to beginning his search, then washed the glove fingers in a vinegar solution and rinsed them with clear water. No finger prints, or even partials would remain after he'd dried them. He even found them helpful in leafing through the piles of pages.

("Damn! This is going to take time -- a long time -- to find anything useful among all this scattershot.")

He glanced at his watch and swore again. He'd already been in the Ambassador's office for nearly 15 minutes. He hurried his pace, leafing through another 20 or 30 of the small squares of note paper.

"Akers...office supplies...asshole."

"Vilishnava -- wants more Broadway tkts. Screw him. Get him 6, but introduce him to idea of quid pro quo."

"$100 mil...$150 mil....$450 mil...and a place at the table."

"Phyllis B-day. Flowers. Bracelet. B-day fuck."

"Martin needs push. Not listening hard enough."

"Akers: new Head of Marine Security Detail is an AH."

"Staff picnic. Hold Bailey to ~~$500~~. $800."

"Reception for asshole VPN. Pussy gift."

"Mega Millions lottery, $286 mil. 500 tkts."

"New File Clerk -- <u>Tirana</u>. Akers: No tits, but great BJs, likes back-door. Check WebMD. HIV from BJs?"

Jim leafed through a few more. He was beginning to feel half bored, half disgusted. He was about to close the drawer when he decided to scan four more.

"Ag Min. threatens farm revolt on lease fees. Call SS with 'early warning' -- reward?"

"Angushets making noise up north. Useful?"

"SS memo on p-9/11 global threat assessment. ~~Akers? Darden?~~ Ears."

("Who are 'ears?'") he wondered, as he turned up the last of the little squares.

"Sudden need for New Ag Min. More reward?"

("What lease fees? Is SS?...it has to be the Secretary of State. Why would there be a 'reward' for warning him about something as minor as a farmer revolt on some kind of 'lease fees' in this backwater? Is somebody leasing farm land? For what?")

It was something. He decided he'd have to come back to finish this search later. For now, he'd do some homework from his own office. He replaced the sheets, as close to their random scatter as he'd found them. Closing the drawer, he used the letter opener to gently reset the lock without leaving marks on the keyhole face, and dusted the edge of the desk above the drawer to be sure there was nothing of his search left behind.

His heart didn't slow down until he was in the stairwell, heading down to his own office.

Chapter Twenty-Three
2315 Pennsylvania Avenue

October 29
The Embassy of Spain

The Chargé d'Affaires, Raimondo de la Cruz Bottegas was enjoying what had become a nearly three-month "window of opportunity" to run Spain's Embassy in Washington during an unanticipated vacancy in the Ambassador's post.

As the person-in-charge, he had decided, a little uncomfortably, to use the Ambassador's office for full staff meetings and high-level diplomatic hostings, as it was the only one large enough, save for the main conference room and the grand hall, both of which he deemed inappropriate for business, albeit for opposite reasons.

"I find the conference room far too corporate, in the worst American sense of the word, and the grand hall is a wretched excess, fairly reeking of a desperate attempt to impress our guests. No, indeed, the only proper place for hosting international guests is His Excellency's Office."

Today's staff meeting had gone well. He had wielded the baton with grace and dignity, and had been rewarded with attention and immediate, if not authentic consensus on his every suggestion.

He had, of course, been careful to tread lightly on any issue on which he knew his Consul held strong views. Don Alberto Contreras da Silva was nearing 70, an age by which most diplomats had long been put to pasture. Indeed, it had been rumored that now that his daughter had married, Don Alberto would soon be taking his last eastbound flight across the Atlantic.

Still, it was unwise to contend with the man. In conflicts large and small, his victories were both final, and very quiet. Moreover, he never lost. Neither did he ever play overt power games. He never name-dropped, never appealed openly to any higher authority when his own appeared insufficient to the task. Yet he seemed to know everyone he needed to know, from God to the King to the Prime Minister to the military and the quiet people who did things unofficially and without accountability. Not only knew them, but could arrange for them to support his position, no matter the issue, no matter the opponent.

This power had become the stuff of legend, a legend spoken only in whispers, for fear of becoming his next opponent. Yet Don Alberto was nothing if not the epitome of old world charm and courtesy. He spoke with a deference that made him seem little more than a humble servant. In fact, he spoke much less than most of the others, yet he reminded Bottegas of the thirty-year old American television commercial for the investment firm.

"When Don Alberto speaks, people listen."

He was an enigma to most of the Spanish diplomatic corps, for throughout his career, he had seemed surprised at each promotion, and ambitious for none. He had served under four Prime Ministers and one King, and it was well known that when he was regularly called home to Madrid, it was his private and personal briefings that were more sought after by both than the official journals and bulletins sent back by the political hacks who had "earned" Ambassadorships through their campaign largesse.

The meeting was breaking up, and several staffers were already filing out when Bottegas' personal secretary poked her head in the door.

"Signor Bottegas, excuse me, but Senora Darden is here to see her father. May I show her to his office?"

"Of course, of course, we are finished here anyway, but bring her to us here so I can greet her!"

The secretary nodded and turned, but Maria Elena was standing right behind her, so needed no relay of that message.

"Buenos Dias, Signor Bottegas, and Papa. How are the affairs of State today?"

Bottegas rose and held his arms wide. She came to him and folded herself into his embrace, as always a little too tight, his arms reaching a not nearly far enough around her, instead copping the edge of a feel of the sides of her breasts. Her response was a quicker escape from the hug and a dazzling smile -- of steel.

"Superb!" Bottegas replied, noting the steel and wishing, momentarily, that he had controlled himself more thoroughly. *"And how is the young bride today.*

Surely a bit lonely, and, shall we say, somewhat disconsolate after such a short honeymoon?"

("If I was ruled by my vagina as much as you are by your penis, I suppose I would be, and if so, I am sure you would be glad to help relieve me of my tensions, you drooling idiot!")

"How prescient of you, Signor. In fact, that is precisely why I am here -- to see Papa about a job!"

"How wonderful! I am certain we could find a place for you. As a matter of fact, I would be delighted to have your services as a personal assistant!" Bottegas cried.

("You couldn't pay nearly enough for the kind of assistance you want, you rutting boar,") she thought.

"I need something a bit different, Signor Bottegas. Not here. As a matter of fact, I'm not sure where, but not here."

The Ambassador's face dropped, his blush of excitement suddenly drained.

"Ahh, well then, I shall leave you in your father's care, but should you change your mind..."

"-- Of course, Excellency. You would be the third to know."

"The third?? Oh, I see. Well, thank you for your advice during the meeting, Don Alberto."

The Consul escorted his daughter to his office down the hall. When they were behind closed doors, he sat at one end of his sofa, one knee drawn up, turned toward her as she took the other end. He studied his daughter's face, waiting for her to speak. She seemed uncomfortable, hesitant. Still, he waited for her.

"Papa, I need your help."

His gaze held her eyes, and he continued to wait for her to be specific. In the face of that gaze, she felt suddenly smaller, younger. It was not that he was intimidating with her, he had never been that, but his expression reminded her that try as she might, she had never been able to manipulate him, or coax a thing out of him that he didn't want to say or do, no matter what feminine tactics she might employ.

"I need to find my husband. When I do, I want to go to him. I know I can't do that directly. His 'assignment' as he calls it, is secret, and there is no room for me in it."

Don Alberto lifted one eyebrow. *"So? How then do you 'go to him' as you say?"*

Again she hesitated, searching for the right words. She knew her request was extraordinary, probably insane in his mind. Nevertheless...

"I want you to find him. When you do, I want you to pull one of your many strings and get me a job nearby, perhaps in our embassy if he is in some country's capital. It doesn't have to be a big job, only a small one, and..."

He sat very still, fingers still steeple under his chin, saying nothing, but only closing his eyes, which told her what would come next.

"Impossible," he said softly.

"It's not!" she said instantly. *"You could do this with your left hand, in a matter of minutes, Papa. You have done more than this hundreds of times with only a snap of your fingers!"*

He shook his head, slowly, and spoke softly, equally slowly, as if choosing each word with great care.

"You are a grown woman, smart, independent. What is so special about being next to this man now, when you have a whole life together when he returns?"

It didn't work. Maria's temperature began to rise.

"Everything is special about his man, Papa. He is special because he is my husband."

"Really?" he asked, relishing every shade and detail of his precious daughter. He knew he was baiting her, but he continued anyway.

"What in particular do you find so wonderful about this man. He is, after all, just a man, and as you know, there are millions of those walking around."

("Oh Papa, why must we play these games? You picked arguments with me ever since I could talk, just to make me furious enough to debate with you. I never knew what you found so entertaining about it, but I

always honored you, so I suppose I will still another time...")

"Well, let me see. First of all, there is his huge...what do you men call your things these days?"

He shut his eyes and covered his ears with both hands, a man in sudden shock and horror. One round to Maria.

"I cannot hear such tramp talk from a woman I have raised to be a..."

"-- a woman?"

"Precisely," he replied too quickly, then caught her meaning, and swallowed the rest of his argument.

" Seriously, I haven't spent enough time with this man to know him well. As usual, you young people want everything in light speed. He should have courted you for three or four years at least."

She grimaced, but decided on a different tack. Sincerity.

"Papa, you may think of me as a grown woman, and with your help and Mama's, I suppose I have had enough education and experience to have become one. But in some ways I am still your little girl, because I still cling to many of the dreams I had when I was six and seven and read Cinderella and Snow White.

"James Darden is my prince. He fulfills every dream I have ever had."

Don Alberto started to shake his head again, raising his hands toward his ears.

"--No, no, not just those dreams. I am thoroughly, thoroughly respected by this man. He seeks my thoughts, my ideas, my preferences. He puts me ahead of himself. He is as tender as he is tough, as patient as he is demanding. He also has a purpose in life far beyond dinner and a ball game.

"He will make a father to fine children of whom you will be proud."

When her father spoke again, his tone had changed. It was no longer a game.

"Does he have a God?"

"Yes, he does. But he is no cookie-cutter Catholic or rubber-stamp Christian. Once when I had the TV remote and stopped at a televangelist who was spouting about being 'washed in the blood of the lamb,' Jim said he has been washed in blood several times, but felt clean only when the blood was washed away.

"His beliefs are strong and he has the humility of a child of our Creator. But he has many, many unanswered questions, and what you would probably value most, Papa. He has a patient and teachable spirit."

It was enough. He held out both arms and reached for her. Her words gave him great comfort, even if her request did not.

He sighed, as if suddenly exhausted.

"You are right, Maria, in what you said earlier. As a matter of fact, I have already learned where he is, though it took me considerably more than minutes and a few phone calls."

"Well then, that's wonderful!" she said, suddenly excited.

"No, my darling daughter, it's quite far from wonderful. It took a good deal of work and calling in favors from people who have long forgotten that they owe me any, plus a piece of sheer luck. Your husband's mission is very secret, so deeply covered that I doubt more than five, maybe six people in this country's entire government even know of it."

"That may be, father, but what is most important is that <u>you</u> know of it -- of his location. How hard can it be to find me a small job nearby? I'll do anything!"

Again he closed his eyes, as if her face had become painful in his sight. It was his turn to struggle for words.

"Maria, listen to me. A mission as quiet as his must come with more than a little danger. To him. To others. To anyone around him. It can be no other way. To send you into that country, that city, would be to subject you to that danger. I would sooner cut off this hand than do that."

Her excitement began to ebb. She knew this would be difficult, at best.

"Papa, you listen to <u>me</u>. I am no longer your little girl, weak, innocent, and foolish. You have given me an education few women on this earth ever get. You have seen to it that I got the best of instruction in several arts of self-defense, and the arts of handling all kinds of difficult people. I understand danger, but where Jim is, that is where I want to be. I need your help now, not your protection."

A long silence was excruciating. She knew he was watching a movie on the screen of his eyelids, and not a comedy. When he opened his eyes and gazed at her, he still said nothing, but quickly closed them again.

"No."

"What do you mean, 'no'?"

"Just that. I cannot do this thing. You are all that I have in the world. You know that. Sending you into harm's way is the last thing I could do. You may say I am a selfish old man, but you mean too much to me, and to your husband. You must understand me. You would not only endanger yourself. You would very likely endanger him, and even his mission."

Maria felt crushed. It was her turn to gaze at her father, her eyes a fiery mixture of hurt and anger. It was a look that cut him deeply. She held it through a long silence. Suddenly, she stood, and moved toward the office door. Halfway there, she turned.

"This is the first time you have ever rejected me when I needed you, needed your help. It hurts. And it insults me."

With that, she turned and left. But not before he saw the tears beginning to fall from her eyes. He sat very still, remembering no time when he had ever made her cry before.

He softly opened his desk drawer and removed his small appointment calendar. Flipping to the blank note pages at the back, he found the page on which he had written notes from the conversation he'd had the previous morning with an old friend along the Potomac on the Virginia shore.

Juan Gonsalvo had been a trusted friend for many years, a good, and very useful confidant. Now a Division Director at the National Intelligence Centre in Madrid, Gonsalvo had long since retired as a full Colonel in the Spanish Army. Intelligence had been his life. Recently, he had overseen the work of the Fresdnedillas-Navalagamella Satellite Monitoring Station in the Sierra Mountains north of Madrid. The Station's ten parabolic dishes were aimed at geo-stationary satellites 16,000 miles up, and they intercepted satellite communications for nearly 1,000 miles around Spain.

However, it was not the dishes which had enabled Gonsalvo to locate the American Marine. It was old fashioned on-the-ground footwork and networking. At first it had been a cold trail, as he had been searching for a Marine Captain. An exhaustive search of personnel lists in Afghanistan and Iraq turned up no Dardens.

South Korea had taken longer...then America's far-flung global military bases. Nothing. Finally, there were the 164 American Embassies around the world. The ranks of recently rotated Marine Embassy Security personnel was the last place he looked. Having found him, newly minted as a Gunnery Sergeant, the next chore was to learn what he could about the man's mission, for it was inconceivable that he would be demoted several grades from commissioned officer to enlisted ranks just to serve guard detail.

The product of his work was no certainty, just the best-educated guess he could make. The State of Georgia held no present strategic or tactical importance to the US except for the rumors of a new pipeline. Though it would clearly become a major strategic delivery route for millions of barrels of Caspian crude, there was little about the pipeline itself that would have necessitated a secret mission. As Gonsalvo surmised, however, there could well be urgent curiosity in high places about who would benefit most from the pipeline's completion and operation. He had learned quickly that the 'public' face of the pipeline's ownership was a consortium of British and American oil companies. The private face of that ownership, and the source of their funds, was another story – a very quiet story that his sources knew nothing about.

Now, Don Alberto studied the cryptic notes of his short, softly spoken conversation with Gonsalvo.

Darden in Tbilisi. Embassy Security cover. Seeking data on oil pipeline silent investors -- Ambrose connection? Must be higher than that – who sent him? Washington connections? High level?

Softly he tore the page from the notebook, and three pages following it as well, though they were blank.

He folded them carefully and tucked them into the inside breast pocket of his suit jacket. He would destroy the pages, but not here in the office.

He had done the right thing. He was sure he had. It must have been right, because it hurt almost more than he could bear.

Chapter Twenty-Four
R Street, NW

November 1 6:15pm
The Contreras Residence

Don Alberto's afternoon was suddenly chaotic, distracting him rather thoroughly from his problem with Maria and her young husband.

Instead, it was taken up with urgent news of sudden arrests in the case of jihadist bombings in Madrid. The entire embassy staff was deluged with requests for information and updates on the situation in Spain, and queries about heightened security alerts in light of the arrests of four men who appeared to have been behind the deadly explosions that had taken place nearly a year ago.

When he finally left the embassy a little after eight, he headed straight home to his townhouse on R Street. The Washington weather was unusually cold, a stiff wind out of the northwest stinging exposed flesh. Once there he poured himself a large scotch and filled the tub in the master bath to beat back the chill . His body was stiff with the tensions of the day, and when the tub was full enough he turned on the Jacuzzi jets, disrobed, and climbed in. There was nothing like a good long soak in the steaming, thrashing currents, a medicinal single malt as accompaniment.

Many is the time he would enjoy this particular relaxation, often falling asleep for short "power naps" in the tub. The jets would cycle off in 15 minutes, but when Don Alberto lay back in the tub and rested his head on the plastic air pillow, he was asleep in less than five.

Less than a minute later Maria opened the front door. She had come to apologize, to make amends, if possible, and to try one more time to make her father see things as she saw them.

Stopping in the foyer, she listened to the silence, then picked up the hum of the tub's jets upstairs, and knew where her father was. Across the living room his small bar was open, the scotch bottle and ice bucket still out. She decided to pour herself a short one and wait for him upstairs.

"Papa!" she called as she climbed the stairs, glass in hand. No answer. He almost surely hadn't heard her over the roar of the jets, so she peeked in through the crack in the open bathroom door.

Seeing him lying in the tub, head back, mouth slightly open, probably snoring, she smiled. It wouldn't do to wake him just now.

Glancing around the master bedroom, she saw his suit, dropped in a casual heap at the foot of the big bed.

"Oh, Papa. You work too hard, and too long. It is time for you to retire and go back home," she said softly.

Moving to the bed, she picked up his trousers and folded them neatly along the creases. Then she picked up the jacket and shook it out a bit. As she laid it atop the trousers, she noticed two lumps in the pockets. She shook her head, almost sadly. It was so unlike her fastidious father to carry anything large or lumpy in his suit pockets. He had always been proud of his appearance, careful in his choice of clothing, immaculate in his grooming.

There was his tray atop his dresser. She reached into the jacket pockets and removed car keys, a lump of loose change, and his cell phone, carrying them over to the dresser tray. As she turned back toward the bed, she checked the inside pockets. Nothing there but small folded slips of paper folded inside one another.

Quickly she placed them both on the tray and returned to place a neatly folded jacket on the bed. It happened as she laid the jacket down. A silent shiver ran up her back, tensing the small hairs at the back of her neck, making her stop.

Without knowing anything about why, she quickly returned to the slips of paper and unfolded them.

It took her less than five seconds to read the cryptic note on the second slip. The shock of it ran blood to her heart and just as quickly to her face. Stunned, she fought back a curious panic, a rush of excitement combined with a strong sense of dread. She knew where her husband was…but she didn't know what to do next.

("*I can't let him know that I know. I can't. Think, woman!*")

She wanted to slap herself, to get moving, to do something, ___***anything***___.

Suddenly, it came to her. In a sudden rush she picked up the car keys, change, cell phone, and papers and ran back to the bed, replacing them in the same pockets of his suit. Then she dropped the slacks and jacket back onto the floor, in her best effort to duplicate the abused state in which she'd found them.

She sprinted silently on the soft carpeting along the hall and down the stairs. The Jacuzzi jets were still roaring. Perhaps he hadn't heard her at all.

When she got to her car, and had turned the corner, moving out of sight of her father's house, she began to breathe more normally.

("What to do? Tbilisi. Isn't that in Eastern Europe? Where? The Russian, Schevardnadze had been President, at least once if not twice. Georgia, isn't it? Yes! Of course it is! Georgia!")

Having answered that for herself, she faced the next question , though it didn't take long. She knew what she had to do, distasteful as it was.

She stopped at the next intersection and made a left onto Connecticut Avenue, heading north. The Chargé's residence, unlike that of many other Euro diplomats, was in a lovely old home off Connecticut Avenue near the National Zoo. Perhaps not as posh as the Massachusetts Avenue diplomatic neighborhoods, but quite pleasant, quiet, and luxurious in its own right. She was not planning to visit his home, however.

Finding Bottegas would not be a problem, though she would have to wait for almost three hours. His wife generally kept him on a short leash after work hours, though that only meant that his affairs and dalliances were restricted to office hours or during trips around America or home to Spain.

It was Thursday, which meant he would be at his gym between 9:00 and 10:00 pm. For many months he had exercised in the early mornings, but then found that more young women, especially the ones who were already in great shape, exercised in the evenings, so he changed his schedule, explaining to his suspicious young second wife that he wanted more time with the children before work and school. Maria was sure she would find him there.

Her performance would be a challenge. It would not be easy, but in fact she had little doubt she could get what she wanted from him if she played her cards skillfully. The key was to play it up large without overdoing it. The fool was a slobbering idiot over her, but if she could do this right, she could use that annoying fact.

Happily, she was already dressed appropriately for the occasion. Her skin-tight black leggings and V-neck tee shirt under her jacket left little mystery about her own wonderful figure.

She stopped at the desk of the Gold's Gym on Connecticut Avenue, purchased a guest pass, and asked if, by any chance, Signor Bottegas was there. The young woman on desk duty smiled broadly.

"He sure is. By now I'll bet he's pumping -- iron or some babe.... Oh, sorry! He's not your dad, is he?"

Maria smiled back. *"Not a chance! Just an acquaintance -- and a horse's ass."*

A minute later she found him working the free weights, putting on quite a show, grunting and sweating profusely. She had to admit, the man had taken good care of himself, his slim body taut and considerably more youthful than most 60-year olds.

"Ahh, Signor Bottegas! I am so glad to find you here!"

"Maria! How delightful! What brings you to Gold's?"

She lowered her eyes and turned away slightly, her best imitation of a virginal 13-year old, as she shrugged off her jacket.

"It is difficult to say this, Excellency, but in truth, I have come to see you. Now that I am here, I feel -- embarrassed. I have never seen you -- without your suit and tie, and I was not prepared for this -- this sight of you."

He smiled broadly and flexed, watching his own biceps glisten in the lights, accepting her statement as a compliment -- and as sincere.

"A man must do what he can to maintain himself -- for the rigors of duty, my dear."

He finished a set of repetitions and dropped the hand bells to the floor, again flexing his muscles, this time in the mirrored wall.

It was hard not to blurt out her thoughts. *("You hopeless ass. The 'rigors of duty,' eh? So now diplomacy is defined by sticking yourself into as many young American girls as possible? Last time I looked, that thing between your legs is not one of Spain's recognized export items.")*

"Well, my dear, what exactly brings this surprising visit to my 'torture chamber'?" he asked, patiently.

She nearly choked. *"I came to...to beg for your help."*

"Indeed?" (The picture of her begging before him was enough to ignite his shorts.)

"Let me guess. Your papa was not able to provide what you requested this afternoon, eh?"

That was her cue to lose the virginal coquette and become the frustrated, enraged victim.

"That was too easy for a man like you to see," she fairly spat out the words. *"Much too easy. My father is an old man, a man of another time, another century! He does not understand my needs. He sees me as some sniveling teenager, not as a grown woman like..."*

"-- Like what my dear?"

"...Like...like you see me."

She looked away as she said this, which was fortunate, for he was taking a rather obvious inventory of her body's charms, noting that likewise, he had never seen *her* before in such an outfit.

("Oh, my God, yes, child...") he thought. *("I certainly do see you as a woman, and what a woman! Such a waste to dedicate all that to some half-wit Yankee Marine!")*

"Of course, my dear. After all, we are both adults, both wise in the ways of the modern world. We men are not the only ones who have needs. Those of us who are mature understand that women have their own needs, and it is up to us to satisfy them, is it not?"

Though Maria nearly gagged, she dropped the rage and resumed the shy, demure pose.

"I knew you would understand, Signor," she half-whispered.

"Oh, I do, I do so understand! Tell me, child...how may I help?"

"First, Excellency, I must ask that you never reveal even a word of this conversation, or of my meeting you here, to my father. Can I ask this, that you keep this strictly between the two of us?"

He reached for her, pulled her to him in a sweaty embrace.

"My dear, dear child, it is my delight to maintain our little confidences strictly entre nous, as they say in Paris. Have no fears."

"Thank you, thank you, from the bottom of my heart!" she said as she leaned into his embrace, already sensing the bulge below his waistband.

He continued to hold her close, so close that she could not see that he was looking down her V-neck, to see if he could find her heart at the bottom of her wonderful cleavage.

"Then, Excellency, here is my request, my hope, my prayer." The intimacy of her half-whisper was positively inflaming him as she described what she wanted.

A long moment later, he released her and sat down on a padded bench, pulling her down next to him.

"This is no small thing you ask, Maria. I doubt whether my 'influence,' as you refer to it, is adequate to arrange such things, especially immediately."

"Oh, Excellency, I <u>know</u> you can arrange such things. I have heard from many others how respected you are in Madrid -- even my father says so, and he never compliments a -- a superior."

She watched him smile again, virtually basking in the glow of her words. She wanted to laugh in his face. *("This is so easy it's obnoxious!")*

"Well, only out of respect for the loyal service of Don Alberto, and my admiration for you, dear child, I will do what I can. Still, it is not a small thing. Exactly how grateful might you be for such a favor?"

("You drooling dog!) Maria lowered her head, and spoke in her small voice. It was difficult to say the words, but she got them out.

"Grateful beyond measure, Excellency. I have no way to pay you what this is worth in money, signor, but anything I have is yours. Anything!"

He smiled even more broadly, and opened both arms in a gesture of power and, he believed, mercy.

"Then consider it done. I shall make the necessary calls tomorrow morning. And when you return from your little adventure, perhaps I shall have some ideas about ways in which you might share your, uhh, gratitude. N'est-ce pas?"

Chapter Twenty-Five
Tbilisi

November 8
The Ambassador's Office

Throughout the US, and now even in Japan, Britain, and parts of South America, more business decisions and political actions occur on the golf course and in the club bar than in boardrooms and corner offices.

In the world of diplomacy, relationships are forged and "arrangements" defined as often in embassy receptions, dinners, balls, and soirees as in offices and conference rooms. They are the indispensable lubricant of international relations, not only because premium alcohol lubricates minds and tongues, but because the very phenomenon of eating, drinking, dancing, gossiping, and laughing together seems to encourage diplomats in their hopes and beliefs that advantageous relationships can be forged across human tribes without resort to fissionable material or napalm.

Peter Ambrose had just such expectations in mind as he went over the details one final time before his annual embassy gala.

Tyrone Roberts, his Chargé d'Affaires was seated to his right, with four staff members arrayed around his conference table. Major Akers had asked to sit in as well, and though Peter had rather resented the man's naked

ambition to insert himself in affairs in which he had little
or nothing to contribute, he had shrugged and allowed it.

"Guest list?" Ambrose asked.

Virginia Kieffer, his personal secretary reached
into one of three manila folders in front of her.

"Complete, sir, as well as the PR." The PR was
the protocol rank file, assigning a social rank to every
individual on the list.

"Anyone new?"

*"Uhh, I don't think so...oh, yes. One. A new
arrival is due at the Spanish Embassy. Actually, she's
arriving the day before the reception, sir."*

"Anyone we know... or need to know?"

*"Again, I don't think so. Cultural Affairs
Assistant, if you can imagine. I mean, do you know of
any cultural affairs in Georgia, or any culture, for that
matter?"*

A ripple of laughter around the table, and a
nodding of heads in agreement. Ambrose himself even
chuckled.

"Name?"

*"Uhh...where is she?...Oh, here it is. Senora
Maria Elena Contreras da Silva-Darden."*

A little bell tinkled. Akers raised his eyes from his own notepad, and caught Ambrose's expression of sudden curiosity.

"Did you say "Darden?"

"Yes sir."

Akers and Roberts shared a look with Ambrose, but said nothing. Ambrose was not so circumspect.

"This is too coincidental for words. It must be our dear young Marine's wife. Has he said anything to either of you about her arrival?

Both men shook their heads. Everyone around the table remained silent. Roberts offered a guess.

"Could be he doesn't know about her arrival yet, sir. I checked our comm. logs and Darden hasn't received any calls from stateside or from another embassy here in Tbilisi. Possibly it's a surprise on her part, sir."

"Hmmm...How's our newest Head of Security Detail doing, by the way?

Akers responded immediately, and a little loudly.

"He's a typical jarhead, sir. A dipstick who you might say looks good in a uniform, but he's all hat and no cattle. I whipped his behind two Saturdays ago on the tennis court, and he took it like a twelve-year old. A true dipstick, sir."

"Mr. Roberts? You agree?"

"Not precisely, sir, but if you don't mind I'll share some thoughts with you later."

Akers bristled, suddenly erect in his chair, as if trying to sit taller than the Chargé, glaring across the table at him.

"Fine," said the Ambassador. *"Back to our new guest from Madrid. Thank you for bringing her to my attention. Any other developments -- or problems in your preparations, people?"*

Ambrose's gaze went around the table, stopping at each face. All shook their heads, indicating no problems.

"Thank you, people. We're adjourned."

All arose, except for Roberts and Akers.

"Thank you, Major. We won't be needing you."

"Well, sir, I thought you just might. After all, I, uh..."

Roberts interrupted. *"Actually, sir, it might be appropriate for Major Akers to hear what I have to report,"* he said.

Tyrone Roberts held an informal position of trust and confidence with Peter Ambrose that thoroughly outweighed his formal position. His informal position was Chief Listener. He was very, very good at it.

His responsibility was to watch his boss's back. Actually it was to protect his back, his flanks, and even his face from direct and indirect threats of any kind. To do his job, he inevitably needed to recruit others, often several people in a variety of positions surrounding his boss. He had to be careful to assign 'quiet responsibilities' to each member of his team, but never to allow the existence of those responsibilities to become public. In fact he never revealed to any member of his team the identity of the other members. He wanted each one to operate independently, and believed that all worked better if they believed their assignment was unique.

Furthermore, each one had only one real task: to identify any pieces of information, no matter how slight, that might represent a threat when combined with other actions, events, or words uttered by anyone in the Ambassador's larger circle of colleagues.

Roberts brought to this task an intense curiosity, a well-oiled imagination, and an enormous capacity for storing and managing seemingly unrelated data. The latter was particularly important, because he never knew when two or three seemingly innocent and unrelated bits of data might add up to an unanticipated and immediate threat to his boss's plans, his strategies, even his very position.

He was also hugely skilled at an unusual mental gymnastic. Whenever any of his "listeners" brought him a new piece of data, he received it, asked any questions he needed to understand it completely, then assured the listener that it was of little or no consequence. That half of the gymnastic was relatively easy, but the other half was just as critical. He also took steps to convince each listener that no matter how inconsequential their discovery had been, their service was deeply appreciated and would be promptly rewarded. His rewards were usually small, but often thoughtful and personal, and therefore highly motivating to each listener.

Add to this a near-phobia about potential conspiracies in every corner of his boss's work and life-space, and Ambrose had what he knew was an invaluable aide. Unlike the simpering and self-seeking Akers, Roberts was a very special resource, but one the Ambassador protected by never revealing to anyone else just how special and trusted he was.

Ambrose had been especially careful to keep the depth and closeness of his personal relationship with Roberts a matter between the two of them here at the Embassy. For one thing, the grasping and jealous Major Akers would be a problem if he thought that anyone else was closer to Ambrose than he was.

"Especially now," he realized, *"when I am so close to my own justice, my own payback for all the crap I've had to endure."*

He allowed himself to dream the dream for perhaps the hundredth time. Four hundred million dollars. Perhaps eight hundred, or even a billion, and a

place at the table with the real movers and shakers --
including the hack he'd worked so hard to put into the
White House -- the hack who'd paid him off with this shit
hole of a job.

There was no way he'd ever be invited to the
table, no way the oil men or the White House players
would voluntarily give him a share of the profits. He
would have to make his own power play, and there was
real risk in that. He'd have to have people watching his
back, and he'd have to create some fail-safe leverage, but
he was closer than he'd ever been. So close he could
taste it.

_____

"*Sir,*" Roberts began, when the others had left
him alone with Ambrose and Akers, "*our new security
chief seems to have taken his job quite seriously, perhaps
even beyond the call of duty.*"

"*Oh?*" said Ambrose. "*Go on.*"

"*It seems he's been more than a little ambitious.
Demanding of his staff. I'm told by one of his Marine
subordinates that he has even taken to walking interior
night tours. An unusual bit of ambition by a new chief of
station.*"

"*Really? Is that all?*"

"*Of course not, sir. That in itself would be
merely an act of commendable devotion to his job, I
would think.*"

"I'd agree. So where's the rub?"

"His tours take significantly longer than the other members of his squad, sir."

Ambrose began to grow impatient. One of Roberts' annoying habits was to lay out information bit by bit, rather than coming straight to the point.

"So he's being careful. He's new. So what?"

"Yessir. He's being careful. I thought so too, so I had my source shadow him during one of his 'longer' patrols. What took him longer was the time he spent searching your office."

That brought Ambrose to attention. In fact, he visibly jumped, a move Roberts catalogued in his data base.

"Searching <u>my</u> office?! What the hell was he doing? What was he looking for?"

"I don't know, sir. Neither does my source. He had to remain outside your door and keep perfectly still. But he heard faint sounds of drawers opening and closing, and of papers being moved. On two successive tours the Sergeant spent twelve and sixteen minutes in your room. It seems he's also been spending significant amounts of time reviewing e-mail communications and checking secure line channels. Your own, sir.

"When the Corporal walked by his desk the day before yesterday and asked if he could help in whatever

*Gunny Darden was doing, he immediately flipped his
screen off and replied in an angry tone, 'whenever I need
any help from you, Corporal, I'll ask for it.
Understood?"*

Ambrose concentrated all his effort to remain still,
to think clearly, and carefully. What came to him,
ironically, was the tactic Roberts himself had used so
consistently.

He sat still for another long moment, then
dismissed the issue with a casual wave of his hand.

*"Well shit, maybe he's counting paperclips like
you ordered him to do, Major. I guess we should be
grateful he's paying attention. Anything else, Tyrone?"*

Roberts frowned. This was not the response he'd
anticipated, and it certainly didn't fit with the little jump
he'd just seen. It was a totally unfamiliar experience
being on the outside, and he didn't like it a bit.

*"No sir. Not at the moment. Shall I continue to
have Darden's 'patrols' monitored?"*

Another wave of dismissal. *"No need, Tyrone.
I'm sure our young jarhead is just being zealous in his
new duties. No problem there."*

Roberts searched his face for a moment, then
nodded.

"Yes sir," he said, and got up to leave.

He didn't believe a word of the Ambassador's nonchalant dismissal. He would have to watch closely. Something was up, and he was suddenly **_not_** on the inside.

Chapter Twenty-Six
The Embassy

After Roberts' Departure...

...John Akers didn't waste any time.

"Sir, I'm sure you want something done about Darden. Am I right?"

Ambrose hesitated. He was running through a hundred sudden scenarios, and none of them were good for him. Had he been willing to share the truth with his military attaché, he'd have admitted he was both confused and frightened.

Fortunately, Akers was alert enough to grasp that truth without the Ambassador having to admit it.

"Ye-ess, John, I do...but exactly what I'm not quite sure."

"Let me take care of him, sir. I'd be delighted."

Ambrose held up a hand, as much to slow his own thoughts as Akers'.

"Hold on, Major. This is no time for carelessness. There's...too much at stake. I want something done alright, and quickly, but whatever we do

has to achieve certain objectives, or it'll come back to bite us in the behind."

"Objectives, sir?"

"Yes. I want Sergeant Darden out of my hair...right away...and permanently. But it can't happen because of anything I did. Something else has to cause his exit."

"Uhh, an accident, sir?"

It was suddenly clear to Peter Ambrose that he was going to have to be even more careful than he'd already realized. Subtlety and indirection were absolutely required here, and John Akers clearly didn't know how to spell either word.

"If you mean a tragic event that looks accidental, John, I'm not confident you or I can arrange that. In fact it would probably better if we could just get him recalled to the States and a new assignment of some kind. Something that doesn't stimulate anyone's imagination that we wanted him out. You get my drift?"

It was Akers' turn to hesitate.

"Certainly, sir."

Ambrose studied Akers' face, watching wheels turn beneath the military buzz cut that on Akers resembled a monkey. (*"The man actually earned an engineering degree at West Point. Sweet mystery of life, how that could have happened."*)

"I may just have an idea."

Ambrose was not exactly reassured.

"That's fine, John, but no way I want anything **done** *until I take some steps of my own. Is that clear?"*

No hesitation this time, though Akers burned a little burn at the evident lack of trust. *"Certainly, sir. But..."* (a cat-eating-the-canary smile) *"...I believe you'll like it."*

Peter Ambrose smiled, but it disappeared almost immediately. *("Am I getting ahead of myself here? I probably am. Damn!")*

He sat very still, his fingertips steepled under his chin. *("It is time...")* he decided. *("...time to make the call.")*

Chapter Twenty-Seven
The White House

November 9, 8:44am
The West Wing

Barry Wicker had taken the call on his secure line, listened carefully, and grown more and more puzzled as the caller's cryptic phrases were delivered. It had been a short conversation, and quite one-sided. Now that it was over, he was still unsure what to do.

As Deputy Chief of Staff, he'd taken the call because Lawrence Claymore, his boss, was en route to the Caribbean to run errands for the President, who was beginning a weekend golf and business meeting with one of his Leadership Circles.

Ambassador Ambrose had told Claymore's secretary his message was "urgent," but when Wicker had taken the call, Ambrose was suddenly hesitant, fumbling for phrases that he guessed Claymore would understand even if he, Wicker did not.

It was something, he remembered, about a recent series of "eavesdropping" and "surveillances" that might relate to Claymore's "personal interests" -- not "*in* Georgia," but "*across* Georgia."

Wicker had declined the Ambassador's request to patch him into the Chief of Staff's GPS phone, hoping to win a few points by handling whatever the man wanted himself. Now he wasn't so sure he'd done the prudent thing.

It could be a crock, nothing of significance except in the fevered mind of the hack who'd been "rewarded" with an Ambassadorship to a third-rate ex-Communist backwater. Still, what could the man have been referring to? *"Claymore's <u>personal interests across Georgia</u>??"*

What interests? Wicker had heard nothing about any political machinations in -- where was it? -- Tbilisi? Of course with Claymore, it could be anything. Though he'd served the President for nearly three years, he was still fresh from well-cushioned seats on a dozen Boards of Directors in nuclear, chemical, pharmaceutical, and energy industries. Was it a business deal? If so, it had to be a problem. National interests were fine, but "personal interests?"

Wicker decided he'd have to be careful...and quick. He dialed Claymore's private phone and engaged the scrambler.

"Claymore."

"Sir, it's Barry."

"Yes, Barry."

"Sir, you just got a call from a Foreign Service guy, a Peter Ambrose... our Ambassador in Tbilisi...that's Georgia, sir."

"I know where Tbilisi is, Barry. What the fuck did he want?"

"Sir, I'm not sure. Alice took the call, which Ambrose said was urgent, but when she put me on the line, he got kind of weird and, well, nervous, I guess. A bunch of short phrases that sounded like code you'd understand and I wouldn't."

"I'm waiting, Barry."

"Yessir. He said there'd been some kind of problem at the embassy with 'surveillances' that might jeopardize... and I really didn't understand this, sir...'your personal interests – <u>across</u> Georgia. Does that mean anything sir, or am I just imagining things?"

There was the slightest pause, and then Claymore's response, which came at a suddenly rapid pace, almost as if his boss had been jolted.

"It means nothing whatsoever, but I'll get back to him. He's a small-time dipstick who sniffed up my ass for months during the campaign, hoping for a place at the table. I'll deal with it. I'm damned if I'll let him succeed, so have his call removed from the call log, will you?"

"Removed, sir?"

"Removed, Barry. Erased. Eliminated. Wiped out. What do you not understand about these words?"

(Ouch.) *"Yessir. Right away."*

*"That's right, Barry. Right away. As in, **<u>Now</u>**."*

Barry Wicker hung up the phone and sat very still. A moment later he actually shivered so hard his shoulders shook. His mind raced, a string of fevered fears that pushed out little droplets of sweat beneath his carefully trimmed hairline.

He could just feel it...like the subtlest hints of electricity in the air before a spring storm. It was "Oh, shit!" time.

He was going to have to make a few urgent calls, right after he executed his boss's order. Even though he'd carefully feathered his nest with a half-dozen law firms and high-tech outfits back home in Seattle, the scent in his nostrils was the need to flee right now, not 16 months from now.

What made the sweat droplets grow, however, was a greater fear. He could resign today, for health reasons, or to spend more time with his two toddlers. But once he'd removed Ambrose's call from the call log, and even though he had no idea why he'd been ordered to do that, he sensed it was already too late.

Chapter Twenty-Eight
Tbilisi

November 9, 12 minutes later
Ambrose's Office

Peter Ambrose smiled in satisfaction at the ring of his secure line. It would have to be Lawrence Claymore.

"Ambrose."

"It's Claymore, Peter."

"Lar-ry! So good to hear your voice! How are things in the Big House?"

Claymore fought the urge to hock up a wad of phlegm and spit it through the phone. He didn't suffer fools gladly, but most of all, he detested ambitious fools with an inflated sense of their own importance. Above all, no one called him "Larry," except, of course, the President. To everyone else, it was "...Lawrence...sir."

"It was your call, Peter. What do you want?"

This was it. Peter Ambrose was literally tingling with anticipation. He was finally getting his one chance to sit at the table when the big hand was dealt. He was ready to bet hard – in fact, to go all in, because the pot was huge, and even a share of it would be life-changing. He'd even thought through the downside risks, and taken prudent precautions.

"Nothing you can't handle, Larry. Just a slice. A nice slice, mind you, but just a slice."

"A slice? Are we talking improving your golf swing, or your appetite for pecan pie, Peter?"

Ambrose smiled. He was going to enjoy this.

"Don't be dense, Laa-arry. We're talking a nice slice of your secret little petroleum pie. Say a nice, plump half-billion. Golf?! Sheesh! You are one shamefully arrogant motherfucker, you know that?"

"What the hell are you smoking, Ambrose? You suddenly high on testosterone pills or what? Remember who you're talking to, you two-bit ass-wipe!"

Ambassador Ambrose was no physical specimen. Nor was he particularly brilliant in any serious area of academics. At moments like this, however, he surprised even himself with his ability to get really...really furious. Had he been within reach of Claymore, he might have just risen up and hit him with something hard and heavy.

Peter changed his tone. His next words were slow, hard-edged, angry, but with no mocking tone.

"Mister Claymore. It's time, right this second, for you to learn a whole lot of new respect for this public servant. I know about the pipeline.. .and its ownership. I want in, right now, this very minute. Slice the god damn pie...Mister Claymore."

There was silence at the other end of the line. Ambrose waited in patient confidence.

"Even if there __was__ such a pie, what in God's name do you imagine would make anyone include the likes of a sni – of someone like you?"

Peter lost his smile, and much of his enjoyment.

"OK, let me sort it out for you in small words. I know the game. Pipeline ownership kept quiet behind the expected multinationals and a dozen shell layers. You're in it, along with at least a few others there in the Big House, maybe including POTUS himself. How you got in, what kinds of promises you made to the corporate types, what kinds of arm-twisting you did, I don't know – yet, but it doesn't matter. The key to your black gold parachute is silence. You let me in, you have one more mouth to feed. Big deal. You don't let me in, silence goes out the window. Without silence, instead of a stream of billions, you get a minimum security cell and bologna sandwiches for a whole lot of years.

"Oh, and I've taken out a little insurance. I've got five personal services firms on two continents under contract to mail letters to __The New York Times__ and __Washington Post__ Managing Editors if anything happens to me or mine. The letters grant the editors access to a safety deposit box where I've deposited documents that lay it all out and name your sorry ass, among others. I've paid their fee for 35 years. After that, you can have me drawn and quartered, but not until."

"Now… Mister Claymore… what part of that do __you__ not understand?"

A different tone came back.

"My goodness, Peter! Aren't you thorough! I'll have to talk to some people, and get back to you. Won't take me more than a day, two at the outside. That OK with you?"

Peter Ambrose smiled again, but his smile would have been a disguise of serenity, had anyone been watching. Inside, he felt a surge of excitement so violent it caused a momentary urge to throw up. He was finally where he had wanted to be for so long, on the very edge of real money, and the real power that would come with it. He could dump his consolation prize of a wife and begin a life of importance...

...until he remembered the message he had left the White House Chief of Staff that had brought him to this edge of greatness. The excitement in his gut departed just as suddenly as it had come.

"Oh, that's just fine, but I had another message for you when I called earlier."

Claymore grimaced. What he had already heard was enough, plenty in fact.

"What was the other message, Peter?"

"Well, It's just that you have a problem...here in Tbilisi."

Claymore gripped his phone tightly, wishing mightily that the two-bit hack at the other end of the line was in front of him right now. He'd kill him with his bare hands.

"What would that be, Peter?"

"It would be a Marine. Head of Security Detail, newly arrived. A Sergeant James Darden. Seems he's been taking his duties a good bit more seriously than he ought to. He's been searching my office during his night patrols. Don't know what he's searching for, but it smells to me like an ugly coincidence. What do you think we should..."

Claymore wasn't listening. Hadn't been since the name 'Darden.'

One of the most critical skills of a White House Chief of Staff is a memory function that exceeds most mortals. The sound of that name engaged a synapse, caused a small bell to tinkle softly.

("Darden...Darden. Where the hell have I...? Yes, Darden. Jim Darden, but not Sergeant Darden. One of the White House Dinners, or was it an Embassy reception. Whatever, there'd been a Captain Darden, not a Sergeant. Can there be two James Dardens in the Corps at the same time?")

Lawrence forced his attention back to Ambrose.

"Excuse me, Peter. I have to make another call. I'll get back to you on this right away. Keep you secure line clear, will you?"

The call came to the Commandant's office in the Pentagon, taken by Megan O'Reilly, a civilian Administrative Assistant. Megan explained to the caller that the Commandant was out of the office and the city.

When the caller identified himself, she snapped to a good imitation of military attention.

"Sir, let me give you to Colonel Al Wheatley, the Commandant's Staff Director. Yessir, right away."

When she identified the caller, Colonel Wheatley took the phone immediately.

"Al Wheatley, Mr. Claymore. What can I do for you?"

"You can locate a Marine for me, Colonel Wheatley, and patch him in on this line, right now."

"Is there some kind of emergency, sir?"

"There will be, if he's not on this line in a very few seconds."

"Yessir. His name, sir?"

"James Darden. Sergeant James Darden."

The name rang no bells in Wheatley's memory. He plugged a headset into the phone to free up both hands to attack his computer keyboard.

It didn't take more than 25 seconds. The entire Marine Corps was at his disposal within a mere 24 keystrokes.

"Sir, did you say <u>Sergeant</u> James Darden?"

"I did, Colonel Wheatley. Why do you ask?"

"Well, I have a Captain James Darden and a Sergeant James Darden. The Sergeant is on duty in our Embassy in Tbilisi, Georgia, sir. The Captain is..."

"--I want the Captain, Al. Get him on the line, will you?"

"Certainly, sir. I'll have to ask you to hold. The roster says he's at Quantico, so it shouldn't take long..."

But it did. Four minutes and forty seconds later, an embarrassed voice apologized.

"I'm really sorry for keeping you so long, sir, but nobody at Quantico could help me find Captain Darden for the longest time. Finally I reached General Toomey himself. The General said Captain Darden is on 30 days leave – 'an extended, and well-earned honeymoon' he said."

Claymore's wheels were turning rapidly.

"So just where is Captain Darden honeymooning, Al?"

"No luck on that, sir. The General laughed when I asked him that, and said 'State Secret, Colonel! He calls in every third or fourth day, and when his next call comes in, I'll put him onto you.' Best I can do, sir. May I ask what this is about?"

"It's about national security, Al. What the hell do you think?" The connection was broken.

No bells were tinkling in Claymore's brain. Instead it was his olfactory sense that was in high gear, and right now he smelled a whiff of bullshit, and behind that, like layers in a fine wine, a darker scent of trouble. Real trouble.

He reached for his secure line and dialed Ambassador Ambrose.

"Yes Larry?"

("So we're back to the familiar, eh? Well fuck it.")

"Peter. You were half right. There <u>is</u> a problem, alright, but it isn't mine. It's definitely <u>ours</u>, now that you're a member of the team."

Ambrose smiled again. This was delicious. Money, power, and being a "member of the team." Still...

"So Peter, I'm going to ask you to take care of Sergeant Darden. Right away. You might think of it as a way to earn your way in, rather than worm your way in. Get my drift?"

"(Ouch...!) Absolutely, Larry. Any suggestions as to how?"

Lawrence Claymore felt as if he'd been dropped into the Pacific. The water was cold, and it was suddenly very, very deep. All the work he'd done, all the i's dotted and t's crossed, seemed suddenly fragile, wobbly. He said a short prayer for the effectiveness of secure phone lines and private conversations.

"Peter, I don't particularly care whether he's dead or alive. I don't know how he got assigned over there, but somebody pretty tall in the saddle has to be involved. He probably isn't even a Sergeant, but an officer masquerading as one.

"He has to be taken out of the loop in your Embassy before he learns anything or does any damage. We've done an enormous amount of work to maintain total silence on this project, and as you stated so eloquently, any breaks in that silence could destroy it..."

Claymore's influencing skills were second to none. A significant facet of those skills was an uncanny sense of timing in his use of flattery. That he was parsimonious with it made it all the more effective.

"...It's frightening enough that you discovered it, Peter, but a man with your intelligence and networking skills probably should have been with us from the beginning..."

It did the trick. Suddenly Peter Ambrose wanted to reach through the phone and wrap his arms around the President's Chief of Staff, a hug of sincere warmth and gratitude.

"Why, thank you, Larry," he said, his voice suddenly soft.

"Well, facts is facts, Peter. But listen. Whatever you do, there can be no trail of evidence, no questions for

anyone to ask, no details left hanging, no accidents that seem 'un-accidental.' He has to be taken out, but it has to be totally, antiseptically clean. You understand?"

"I do, Larry. Leave it to me. I'll take very good care of Mister Darden."

Chapter Twenty-Nine
The Marine House
Tbilisi

November 8, 2155 Hours
A Late Supper

Jim bit into a ham and Swiss sandwich and chewed slowly. The sharp mustard he'd spread on the dark bread, usually his favorite condiment, now tasted both bitter and sour at the same time. He wasn't enjoying it -- or anything for that matter.

It had been a challenge to fit in with the other Marines at the embassy

He took a long pull on the pilsner. It didn't cleanse his palate. He felt like crap. The silence of his room was more than silence. It was a fog that separated him from everything and everyone. He felt more alone than at any time in his life, and the weight of it felt like an anvil.

He thought of Maria and how much he missed her. The distance between Tbilisi and Quantico seemed light years more than miles. He found his memories of her both painful and frustrating. They were so sweet they made his longing for her almost unbearable, but at the same time they were nothing more than diaphanous shadows, thin and wispy things so damned inferior to having her here, in his arms. He knew he loved her with all his heart, but right now, it was an ache, pure and simple.

What made him sigh, and almost sob with a rolling wave of heart pain, however, wasn't Maria. It was Cade, his Labrador. The bond between them was incredibly special, incredibly close. He didn't just miss him, either. He felt suddenly terribly guilty for leaving him alone for weeks now? What must Cade be feeling? Abandoned? Afraid?

"Jesus Christ!" he said aloud.

("What are you doing to yourself, asshole? Turning into some kind of mushball? The dog has Maria, and she has him. You have your mission and a strong right hand for when you get horny. Get over yourself.")

It didn't work worth a damn. He felt every bit like a wet turd and there was no getting around it. Still he couldn't give in to it, so he did what he always did when he needed to relax.

Tossing the sandwich and his loneliness aside, he put on his running shoes, strapped a compact Kohner automatic into a tight cloth shoulder holster under his sweats and headed outside.

The night was cold and damp, so a jog wouldn't be enough. He started slowly, but then ramped up his pace to a dead run. Fifty-one minutes and eight miles later he was back in the Marine House. After twelve more minutes he was showered and asleep. It was a good four hours later that the dreams started. Sure enough, they woke him up.

Lying awake, flat on his back, eyes probing the darkness of the ceiling overhead, he retraced his steps for perhaps the tenth or eleventh time.

"So what exactly have you discovered, Mr. Undercover Man?" he asked himself.

The answer was frustrating, and the frustration was growing. The more he searched, the stronger the odor of corruption, but what exactly was causing the stink?

Peter Ambrose was a political hack, a cynical, ambitious, devious slimeball who despised his own job and wanted more, much more…one of those political placekickers who gets rewarded for licking stamps on campaign envelopes with a job like this and hates every minute of it. But where in that was any crime? Truth be told, he'd probably hate being Ambassador here himself.

So far, he had uncovered no smoking gun, and time was of the essence. What background he'd received back in Quantico suggested that something very large was suspected to be going on here, something that involved people much bigger than Peter Ambrose, though no one had been much more specific than that. He'd been ordered to trace and track any and all communications between the Ambassador and Washington, and to identify any off-mission business dealings that the Ambassador might be conducting, as well as any of his staff.

The only big business in all of Georgia, as far as he'd been able to learn, was the giant oil pipeline that was being built to take Caspian and Azerbaijani crude across the country to Batumi and out the Black Sea to the West. Three of the global oil giants were purportedly behind it, and the Russians were furious at their own failure to retain a controlling interest. In fact, they were shut out. Again, so what? No crime in that, as far as he could see.

He scanned his memory of the slip-notes he'd read in Ambrose's desk two nights ago.

("There were references to money – big money…fairly obviously falling into his own hands…from the pipeline? Is that what the 'lease fees' were about? If a pipeline were to be built across privately owned farmland, would the oil companies have to pay the farmers? Could he be dreaming about syphoning off some of that revenue? No…no way that would amount to hundreds of millions…what about the oil itself?" Is there some way for him to be…?

Jim had reported his fragmentary findings in coded emails back to Washington, but was almost certain they were of little help – so far.

He closed his eyes, as if staring into the dark actually hurt. He turned onto his left side and pulled the covers tight around his neck. The room was cold, as he preferred it, and he should have been sound asleep. Even a fetal position on his favored left side brought no comfort.

He remembered the short conversation he'd had with the Commandant just before he'd accepted his mission.

"Son, I have to ask you one question. I know you've sworn to defend your country against its enemies. But in this case I'm sending you to find what could be evidence against your own countrymen – up to and including our Commander-in-Chief. I need to hear that you're OK with that."

He'd had to think about that – he remembered feeling uncomfortable with his own delay in answering.

"Sir, I've sworn to protect and defend the Constitution of the United States – against all its enemies. It's been awhile since I've read any 'Pogo' comic strips, but I sure as hell remember the phrase that made it so famous – 'we have met the enemy – and it is us.' I have to admit, there's a special kind of ache in going after bad actors in our own city—our own government, but if we can't keep our own house clean and straight, there's little we can expect from enemies outside, except greater desire to destroy us and the freedoms we cherish – and greater confidence that they can. Does that make sense?"

The Commandant had said nothing for a moment. But he offered his hand in a firm handshake that quickly became a tight hug and a softly whispered "Godspeed, son."

Sometime later, much later, it seemed, Jim finally fell asleep, though when he finally awoke just before dawn, he felt as if he'd gone two out of three falls with a big-time WWF tag team...and lost.

Chapter Thirty
Tbilisi

November 11, 8:52pm local time
The Embassy Reception Hall

The room was ablaze with light, its decorations elaborate and festive, attendees dressed and coifed to a standard seen nowhere else in this city. A twelve-piece orchestra had been dredged up from somewhere, and played spirited facsimiles of standard 1940s dance tunes, though its string instruments seemed perpetually on a different page from its two horn players, who were old enough to have played the originals.

The invited guests were nearly all there, sitting, standing, dancing. From a great height, they would have resembled nothing so much as a hive, though in this hive there was no queen...yet. The gowns and tuxedos were festooned with gaudy jewelry and silk sashes in what purported to be national colors. The clutch of military men wore enough chest salad to shame Eisenhower, Patton, Schwarzkopf and Alexander the Great, leading even a casual observer to wonder if Georgia's surplus stores had been laid bare of their entire supply of used battle ribbons.

The social and political hierarchy was manifest in the physical arrangement of the guests throughout the Embassy reception hall. Not only were social friendships to be found in the small conversation circles here and there across the hall, but power levels were also visible in the arrangement of various wannabes around the two epicenters of power in the room: Peter Ambrose near the entrance to the hall, and General Viprotin perhaps forty feet away, near one of the two bars busily dispensing champagne, vodka, and Woodford for the most unabashed of the General's suck-ups.

Standing with his back to one wall near the orchestra, Jim Darden looked immaculate, but more than a bit stiff and wooden in his dress blues. His own set of ribbons and medals was certainly modest in this company, though he'd exchanged the ones he'd actually earned for a set appropriate for an average Gunny when he suffered his "demotion" for this assignment.

Wooden and stiff wasn't just his uniform and posture. He felt out of place, unsure of himself, to say nothing of lonely. He'd even gotten off poorly with a couple of the marines he was supposed to supervise, which was also a first.

Glancing around the hall, he caught sight of himself in the square mirrored column nearby, and saw that he wasn't keeping his mood a secret from anybody.

("Shake it off, bucko. The world isn't about your little feelings. You've got a job to do, and nobody guarantees straight A's in this life, so get over your poor self!")

He shivered once, straightening his shoulders and inhaling deeply. As he did so, a pair of women came up, obviously curious. The first, reaching out her hand in greeting was older by a few years, but certainly under 40, blonde and dressed to leave little to one's imagination, therefore probably single.

The younger one, a step behind, was a lighter shade of blond, equally endowed with feminine equipment, but an even sweeter face.

"Good evening, is it Lieutenant? You're new here, are you not?"

"No, ma'am, it's Sergeant. Gunnery Sergeant Jim Darden, and yes, I am. Been here only a few weeks."

Even though the look on her face dimmed for a moment, in obvious recognition that "Sergeant" is not nearly as interesting as "Lieutenant," the older blonde placed a hand on each of his shoulders and leaned forward to touch each of his cheeks with her own.

"Good evening, Sergeant. I am Helga Kronenbourg, and this is Mariska, my sister. We are here with the legation from Denmark. So, how do you find life in Georgia?"

"I would have to say rather quiet, so far. I would imagine you miss Copenhagen yourselves."

Helga smiled and Mariska giggled. *"You cannot imagine how much!"* Helga said. *"If it were summer here we could entertain ourselves by watching the grass grow, but in winter there is so very little growth!"*

Jim chuckled. It felt good to crack a smile.

"I understand. Still, there must be some life in the round of these parties and receptions?"

It was Mariska's turn to respond.

"Parties are only fun if there are fun men to play with. Here there is only married boobs, frustrated second-raters, and General Viprotin, the beast of Tbilisi. Altogether not much better than watching grass grow, which is what we're doing here. Are you married, Sergeant Darden?"

Jim glanced quickly at his hands, as the two women already had, finding no wedding ring, and allowed himself to consider, in a flash, how he should answer the question. Even the two or three seconds of consideration made him blush with sudden guilt.

"Well, ah..."

Just then there was a sudden motion among the people gathered near the entrance to the hall, a rise in the murmur of conversation. Someone had just arrived and was being greeted by Peter Ambrose. For a second he couldn't see who it was, and then, just as suddenly, he could.

Helga and Mariska had become rather intimate witnesses to a moment of intense shock, now coursing across every inch of Sergeant James Darden.

His eyes widened, his face grew a deeper crimson, and he had suddenly stopped breathing altogether. All body motions stopped entirely, and he had become a marble pillar – very nearly a pillar of salt.

While both women watched in utter fascination, Mariska in particular felt a twinge of sadness that whatever was causing this trauma, it wasn't her.

The sight that was causing it was a vision in red. The sleek black coat that had just been shed revealed a woman in a fiery red gown that set the room ablaze. She had so captivated Peter Ambrose that the man was falling all over himself in greeting, bowing to kiss both her hands in what he imagined was a charming way here in Eastern Europe. The woman smiled gracefully, giving the Ambassador a moment of her full attention, uttering some pleasantry that Jim couldn't hear, which was understandable because he'd suddenly gone deaf.

It might have been ten seconds, or fifteen minutes, that he'd stood there, transfixed, not breathing, not hearing a sound, not even blinking, his wide eyes fixed on the entrance to the hall.

"Err...ahh...yes, ladies, I am. Quite," he said, finally completing a sentence he'd begun an eternity ago.

He forgot entirely to take polite leave of the two ladies from Denmark and moved as quickly as possible toward the entrance.

"Well, well, Sergeant Darden, from the look on your face I see that we have a surprise for you!" said Ambrose as he came up the three steps to the edge of the grand foyer.

"And quite a surprise for us as well! I must say your description of this young lady did not do her nearly enough justice. She is stunning!"

Jim said nothing, but wrapped her in his arms with an embrace that might have cracked several of her ribs, had it been any tighter. His eyes closed tightly, he inhaled her, instantly frustrated by the wool of his uniform jacket and her clothing that separated his skin from hers. At the same time, he felt waves of emotion washing over him – waves of fear, even anger.

After what began to seem an embarrassingly long moment, Maria broke his embrace and smiled at the Ambassador.

"So, my dear husband, you are describing me as a wizened old hag, and this after less than a week of marriage, eh?"

Jim's face was still red as a beet, the look of shock on his face almost humorous. He smiled once, briefly, at Ambrose, and muttered an *"Excuse us, if you would, sir,"* then steered her toward a momentarily quiet corner of the hall opposite the orchestra and dancing.

"My God, Maria! What are you doing here?"

She smiled one of her most imperious smiles.

"Checking up on you, of course, and just in time, apparently! Not only are you describing me as a hag, but you are surrounding yourself with blonde babies with huge bosoms. I think I have arrived not a moment too soon!"

"Nonsense. And they're babes, not babies. You've still got work to do on your American slang.

Seriously, what are you doing here? How did you find out where I --?"

"Seriously, my darling, I am here to be married in life as well as in legal documents. I missed you too much and finally decided to take matters into my own hands."

"That was wrong. Damn it! You have to leave, right away. You can't be here!"

She pulled back from him and glared, her dark eyes blazing.

"I have two questions: you will do well to have the right answers. Do you love me?"

"Of course I love you! I love you with all my heart, with every fiber of my being!"

"Right answer," she said, her tone still icy. *"...do you own me?"*

He was shocked by this question, and so hesitated.

"I see you need help with that one. The answer is 'no' you do not. Kindly keep that in mind. Now, dance with me!"

He gritted his teeth, tried unsuccessfully to think of a useful reply, and then finally took her into his arms. They moved into the flow of dancers, her flare of temper fading with the music and the feeling of being close to the man she loved so much.

What did you do? How did you...?" he asked.

"I asked for my father's help, but he refused me -- for the first time in my life. But his boss has unending dreams of being in my pants, so I simply encouraged his dreams a bit, and here I am."

"--You <u>what</u>!?"

"Listen carefully, my husband. I <u>encouraged</u> his dreams. I did not fulfill them. You understand the difference, you pig?"

"Oh, well..."

"-- So, with his help, I have a job here in my country's embassy. But fear not. I will stay out of your business as long as I can stay in your bed. It is a nothing job, but at least I will not cost you money. So after all this explanation, may I please have one kiss and one dance before I start my job as Assistant Cultural Affairs Attaché?"

Jim's mouth opened to say something else, but she stopped him by covering his lips with hers, biting his lower lip softly, choking off any thoughts of mere words.

The dance was, he decided, the most blissful four and a half minutes he had ever known. The band the embassy had hired was on a break, replaced by a recording of Phil Collins' "Give me One More Night." It was perfect. He even enjoyed the sight of Helga and Mariska watching him, sad looks on both their faces. That, however, was the limit of his enjoyment, for the rest of his consciousness was suddenly boiling with a stew of fear, confusion, and even anger.

_____

Peter Ambrose sat in his expensive chair behind his carved mahogany desk. Major Akers was seated across from him, a frown of concentration on his narrow face, a pad in one hand, his lips sucked into a tight "o" around the eraser end of a pencil.

(*"Nobody's going to steal <u>that</u> piece of our office supplies!"*) Ambrose thought.

They had been brainstorming for almost 20 minutes, and the pieces had not yet come together. Ambrose was getting nervous. He really should be downstairs, seeing to his guests, especially Viprotin.

"I think I have it, sir. It's a bit convoluted, but if we can get the pieces to come together just so, I believe you'll get exactly what you want."

"Oh?" Ambrose cocked an eyebrow. *"Why don't you lay it out for me?"*

"Well, sir, it starts with Mrs. Darden, as you suggested. That part is simple enough. We introduce her to Viprotin…"

"Yes. And…?"

Ten minutes later, after several revisions to Akers' plan, Ambrose fell silent, going over it step by step, asking himself every "what if?" he could think of. Finally, he looked up at Akers with a truly strange expression, as if he was seeing him for the first time.

"OK, let's do it. Now."

"Yes sir," Akers said. His grin of obvious pride resembled a leer. He was going to enjoy this.

("Maybe John has half a brain after all...!") Ambrose thought, trying to keep the surprise from showing. (*"Who knew?"*)

Jim felt a tap on his shoulder as he moved slowly across the dance floor, still inhaling his wife's scent as if he'd come upon a fragrant oasis in the desert. It was his fifth dance, but he'd long since decided that if the world were to end suddenly, this was not a bad way to go out.

He turned quickly, surprised to face the smiling Peter Ambrose.

"I hope you'll pardon the unwanted interruption, Sergeant Darden, but protocol requires me to steal your lovely wife for a few moments. May I?"

"Well, I, uh..."

"Of course you may, Signor Ambrose. I am at your service!" Maria said brightly.

"How very kind of you! I must introduce you to our guest of honor, General Alexei Viprotin, Commander of the Georgian Security Apparatus and a valuable friend of the United States. He likes to know as many of the

international diplomats in Tbilisi as possible, and he would consider me both rude and negligent if I did not introduce you personally."

Jim looked around quickly. *"I believe I saw him over by the bar less than half an hour ago."*

The Ambassador cleared his throat importantly. *"Harrumph! Well, I guess you haven't been thoroughly briefed on all of our social customs hereabouts, Sergeant. You see, General Viprotin is something of an introvert, dislikes crowds. Does much better, more comfortably in small gatherings, so during these receptions he usually retires to a VIP suite upstairs for quieter conversations. I'll have your bride back in ten, fifteen minutes at the outside. You continue your mingling, Sergeant, it's part of the job, I regret to say."*

The expression on Jim's face suggested quite clearly how he felt about that duty. Maria stuck a polished nail in his chest, a wicked smile on her lovely face.

"Yes, my darling, let me suggest several targets for your mingling while I'm gone. Let's see, there's the fat bald man by the bar right now, the decrepit crone seated behind the potted palm, and oh, yes, there are the two big-bosomed blond <u>babies</u> from Denmark, but you've mingled quite enough with <u>them</u> already!"

Jim blushed again, while the Ambassador enjoyed a hearty chuckle at his expense. A second later, they were gone, and he was left to his own devices, feeling an enormous sense of dislocation and shock. *("What the hell are you going to do now, bucko? This is a fine kettle of fish!")*

In fact, it was a fine kettle. Much finer than the one he'd been pouting and feeling so sorry about just thirty minutes earlier. Still, along with the blazing sunshine of Maria's arrival, there were clouds sailing along the edges of his mission, fat dark ones.

"Yes, General, her name is Maria Elena Contreras da Silva-Darden. I guarantee you, sir, she's the best looking bimbo to show up in Tbilisi in many a moon!"

The General took a long puff on his Macanudo and studied the silver ash at its lit end as he rolled it gently between fingers and thumb. Akers watched, fascinated. The man might as well have been fondling one of the woman's nipples.

"And she's being brought to me now?"

"Yes sir. Right away.   A uhh, a gift from Ambassador Ambrose."

"A gift you say? What a generous thought! This woman is from where?"

"Spain, sir. Daughter of a Spanish Consul in Washington."

*"Ahh, yes. I am familiar with the Spaniards.
There is hot blood in them. Quite a spicy treat, unlike the
cows here and in Russia."*

The conversation was interrupted by a knock at
the door.

"Come!" the General shouted.

Ambrose entered, arm in arm with Maria. As he
introduced her with heavy flourish, she felt the General's
eyes taking a thoroughly rude inventory, and obviously
liking everything he saw. The tip of the long cigar
clenched between his teeth had suddenly become wetter.
*("My God, the beast is actually salivating! What an
animal!")*

Maria was shocked when the Ambassador
suddenly halted his flowery introduction and signaled his
aide, whereupon both men left her suddenly and
completely alone with Viprotin.

The General had been seated in a huge leather
wing chair set before a fireplace, a side table at his right
hand with an ashtray and a large snifter of brown liquor.

The General stood and walked toward her,
reaching for her right hand.

"Good evening, and welcome to Tbilisi!" he said,
as he grasped her hand and raised it to his moist lips.

The man was huge. A great bear was a good
description. He towered over her, made her feel small
and vulnerable. It was the first time she'd actually been

frightened by a man in memory. A subtle odor assaulted her nostrils. Was it this man's tobacco and liquor? No. It was more bitter, sourer. Could be his obvious failure to bathe, but she shuddered at the thought that it was the smell of her own fear.

"So, little Maria Elena, you are a Spaniard, yes?"

"Si, -- Yes, General. From Madrid."

"Ahh. I understand the Mardrillenas are quite hot blooded. Is this true or mere bragging in women's gatherings?"

Fear increased, but with it a wave of anger. Who was this brute that he thought he could talk this way to a complete stranger, a woman at that? .

"I would have to say, General, that it is most often the skills and charm of the man which heats the blood in women the world over. I doubt that we are more passionate than your own Georgian women or those of -- Denmark, for example."

The General flicked the lengthening ash of his cigar toward his ashtray and missed, dropping a half-inch onto the Persian rug. He hocked up a huge brown wad from deep in his throat and spat it toward the fire. Maria was shocked as it hissed and bubbled on the hot hearth stone beneath the blazing logs.

"The women of Georgia are cows. Ignorant, fat, boring cows. Even the young ones. They know nothing about serving a man. They are pieces of meat. You, on

the other hand, would bring some flavor, some spice. I believe I would actually enjoy fucking you!"

It was a race now to see which emotion eclipsed the other, fear or anger. It didn't really matter, she decided. Both were ugly, and so unanticipated. *("Where is Jim? What am I doing up here alone?")*

"General, I will do my best to ignore the insult and accept the compliment, however sick and ugly your delivery of it. As to fucking me, you will not get that opportunity in this lifetime, so enjoy your belief."

With that she turned to leave. But before she was able to complete three steps toward the double doors to the suite, he was on her, moving more like a great cat than a great bear. With one arm circled around her waist from behind he simply lifted her off her feet and carried her quickly into the bedroom portion of the suite, tossing her onto the bed as if she was nothing more than a rag doll.

Anger won the race.

As he lunged forward to press himself atop her body, she raised a knee and caught him squarely in the groin, so that his own weight crushed one of his testicles on her kneecap.

He howled in pain that was stunning, but not debilitating, as he rolled to the left, reaching out with his right arm and swinging a blow that caught her full on the left side of her face. Though it was a heavy blow, her anger would not allow her to lose consciousness. She felt him yanking at the top of her strapless gown, pawing her bared breasts.

She moved with the speed of another great cat, rolling away, then reaching back and stabbing four newly polished nails at his eyes, lacerating one and raking his face, drawing four streams of blood.

He roared again, his own rage supplying a ferocity that was way, way beyond reason. He literally leaped from the bed and reached under his coat for the polished pistol he always wore beneath his left shoulder. As he drew it out, Maria kicked both feet as hard as she could. Sharp pointed dancing pumps were luckier in their placement than she had any right to hope. One popped the pistol from his right hand, sending it spinning into the air, while the other caught him squarely beneath his chin, snapping his jaw shut with a sickening crunch and causing another spurt of blood.

Because his eyes were already lacerated, he didn't track the spinning fall of the gun accurately enough to catch it, allowing it to fall onto Maria's chest. Without thinking at all she picked it up, pointed it at the center of the beast and fired twice.

The first bullet hit him in the chest, a little high, and to the right of his heart. The second was higher still, striking him in the neck, but missing his carotid artery.

Still, the impact of not one, but two bullets shocked him more profoundly than he could ever remember. There was pain, immediately, and the sick smell of his own blood along with the metallic odor of smoke from the gun, but what was most stunning was the extremely vivid sense of losing his life, actually feeling it ebb out of him in a kind of slow-motion rush that he could experience quite thoroughly and exquisitely.

Maria leaped from the bed and stood over the man, who had slumped, first to a sitting position, now almost fully supine, his head propped up against the side of a teak night stand. He breathed raggedly, a look of shock and bewilderment in his bleeding eyes. The huge beast of a man was neither dead nor dying, but he was suddenly no further danger.

Maria felt a sense of composure returning, and so remembered to breathe. In front of her was a long dresser with a large rectangular mirror above. She glanced at her own reflection and started to pull her gown back into place. Aside from the redness and swelling on one side of her face, and the damage to her hair, she was little the worse for wear.

The glance in the mirror couldn't have taken more than two or three seconds, before the sound of footsteps on the stairs outside the suite, and the double doors being thrown open in the outer room. In a few more seconds she was surrounded by chaos.

The chaos sorted itself out quite rapidly into two concurrent streams of action: the first to save the life of the General, the second to separate her from the smoking gun that was still in her hand and to prevent her from shooting anyone else.

There was a torrent of questions from what sounded like a dozen traumatized throats at once, a torrent that was overwhelming. Maria found herself suddenly mute, unable to gather herself to answer in anything like an orderly way.

It would have made no difference, she would understand later. Ambassador Ambrose and a certain Major John Akers were particularly unhinged, frantic. Both were shouting for the Marines to take Mrs. Darden into custody immediately. Jim was trying to calm them down, to find out in a more rational way what had happened, but he was being shouted down.

After what seemed like an eternity, another voice arose and the chaos suddenly went mute.

"There will be no Marines! Colonel Balnavia! You will take the woman to the City jail where she will await a judge to try her for attempted murder. That is an order, and it is final!"

Ambrose and Akers looked at each other, both men frantic to regain some semblance of control over a situation that had come thoroughly unraveled.

"I'm afraid, General Viprotin, that you are in no condition to –"

"--Ambrose. Shut your mouth. This woman tried to kill me. Me! This is my city, my country!" She will have my justice.

It was Akers' turn to speak up, though as the world's communication analysts are fond of saying tone is 93% of any communication. Given the Major's weak tone, he was not about winning friends and influencing people.

"General, excuse me, but this act took place on the sovereign soil of the United States of America, and because it did, we retain jurisdiction here. You can be sure that…"

Viprotin was now sitting up, holding a bloody towel to his neck. With one great paw he reached up and pulled Akers down by the lapels of his uniform jacket, so that the Major was suddenly kneeling, his face was inches from Viprotin's own.

"I am totally sure, Major, that neither you nor Ambrose will deny me my justice in this matter, and live to tell about it for even a single day. Of that, I am most particularly sure. Now get out of my way."

He turned to his aide, Colonel Georgi Balnavia, who while considerably smaller in stature than Viprotin, was still a formidable specimen, his gray hair cropped in typical buzz-cut 1/8 inch length and his jaw square and hard.

Balnavia shouted an order to four Georgian soldiers in tuxedos, and Maria was escorted, rather urgently, from the room, and then from the premises.

As for Viprotin, a specially equipped embassy van was at the front door, engine running, waiting to drive him to the city's hospital, less than two miles to the east.

As soon as the General was helped out, a different kind of chaos arose. The reception was at an end, and protocol required a reasonably mannered explanation and farewell from the Ambassador and senior members of his staff. That in itself was complicated by the need to control Sergeant Darden and to figure out how to move from here to Plan B for his departure. What made it difficult was the fact that there was, at present, no Plan B whatsoever.

Ambrose marshalled enough of his staff to see the guests out in reasonably good order, apologies made all around, and assurances of a resumption of the evening's festivities as soon as practicable.

Then there was Darden. Jim was as shocked and furious, as unprepared for this turn of events as anyone. In fact he was still shocked by Maria's arrival, and now this.

"This can't be happening! You two know damn well that Maria would never have done anything except in total self-defense. You have to know that! You've got to get her back, and I mean now. Right now!"

Ambrose raised both hands in a gesture meant to say either "calm down" or "I surrender." Jim wasn't sure which.

"Sergeant Darden....Jim...please. Give me a few short minutes with Major Akers. We've got to get control back before we can do anything constructive. Give us a few minutes alone to make some phone calls and take some action. We're with you on this. Entirely!"

Ambrose grabbed Akers and headed upstairs to his office. *"We'll call you up to my office as soon as possible. Just give us a little time to determine how best to proceed."*

Jim just stood there in the foyer. In the silence that followed, he admitted to himself that he had no idea what to do. He was suddenly over his head -- way over.

Chapter Thirty-One
The Ambassador's Office

Ten-Thirty-Seven PM

The Ambassador sat behind his great desk, elbows on his blotter, head in hands. He was suddenly submerged in a shark pool, and the sharks were hungry. Ironically, he felt himself in precisely the same position as the object of his little plan. Both men were frantic, yet both had no idea what to do next.

"God damn it, John, it didn't happen the way you planned at all! What the fuck do we do now?"

"Jesus, Peter, give me a goddamn minute, will you? I had no idea that Viprotin would jump her in what, 20 seconds? And she must be some kind of martial arts freak. How the hell could we have known? There was no damn time to get Darden up there!"

Peter was growing frantic. He didn't even notice Major Aker's sudden use of his first name, as if somehow he'd just been promoted two or three grades.

"We've got to get her out of there. If she starts squawking about him trying to rape her, we'll have a goddamn world class international incident going on here and no way to get him out of here. I mean the guy's done nothing, not a single goddamn thing!"

Akers hung his head for a long moment, making Ambrose feel even worse as he watched helplessly. He closed his eyes, but on his brain's private movie screen millions, no billions of dollars flew off in all directions, leaving him in this hell hole with his consolation prize of a wife and no prospects -- in fact the more he thought about it the more he realized even this fourth-rate job would soon be gone. He'd be out of the loop entirely. What the hell would he do *then*?

Finally, Akers looked up, as if a light bulb had suddenly lit.

"Wait a minute! I think I have it! It's even more convoluted than our first plan, but I'll bet we can pull it off!"

"Jesus fucking Christ, John, this better be good, or so help me, I'll have your ass, so help me!"

"Listen, Peter, enough with the tough guy threats, OK? You just aren't nearly the guy and the threats don't tweak my nuts even a little bit. I'm on your team and I'm doing my best here, OK?"

Ambrose felt the bile rising in his throat. He hated the bitter taste of it, and sensed that if there had been a gun in his hand at that moment, he'd have been sorely tempted to use it on his Military Attaché.

"OK, OK, John, what's your brilliant fucking convoluted idea? We've got a loose cannon Marine downstairs and we damn well have to get the genie back in the bottle for Christ sake!"

"Yeah, well, we still gotta get him out of here, right, and now we've got to make sure <u>she</u> makes no noise, either, right?"

"Right on both counts, so what?"

"So we help Mr. Sergeant Jarhead spring his wife from jail and get her out of the country."

"So she can run back to Washington and raise holy hell? You're fucking brilliant, John! What good does <u>that</u> do us?"

"None at all. But...we succeed by failing."

"We what?! Goddamn it John, a little simple English here, will you?"

"We help him get her out of the jail, right now, tonight, but we <u>fail</u> to help him get her out of the country."

A candle was lit in the back of Ambrose's fevered brain. Not a lightbulb, but a distant candle, and in the darkness of his scattered mind he ran to the flickering light.

"You mean <u>he</u> fails. What happens to <u>her</u>?"

"She dies. And he gets caught trying to get her out. Makes him an obstructor of justice, an accessory after the fact, whatever, all that sort of thing."

The candle flared, became a whole candelabra. *"OK, sounds great. I'm with you, but how?"*

"Give me a couple of minutes."

Akers had his yellow note pad in his lap, and Ambrose finally noticed that he'd been doodling for some time now. He wondered whether there was actually some engineering formula for getting rid of Darden -- and his wife. A couple of minutes passed, and then a couple more. Ambrose was ready to tear his heart out when Akers finally looked up, an expression of something that looked like optimism on his face.

"Well?"

The optimism turned into one of those smiles that Sylvester the Cat always wanted to smile in the Loony Tunes cartoons, but he never could because Tweetie Bird always got away.

"OK, now follow me. Step One. We help Darden spring his wife from the town jail. Can't be too hard, right? Especially if we let Viprotin in on the plan...if he's still breathing. Given our objective, he's likely to love it and cooperate fully."

"Fine...then what?"

"Step Two. He's got to get her out of the country, fast. We tell him we have no immediate access to planes, so no air escape. Best way, in fact the only way is to driver her west to Batumi and sneak her on board one of the tankers or freighters headed out. You with me?"

Ambrose felt seeds of doubt sprouting under his hair follicles, but nodded, nonetheless.

"Now there's tight security at the port, especially after Viprotin's Colonel puts out an emergency APB on his missing female prisoner. We convince our jarhead that there's only one way to get her down to the wharf and on board without going through security."

Seconds passed in silence. Akers was enjoying himself, and Ambrose found himself imagining his own revolver again, and several new holes in the man's face.

"John, for Christ sake! Don't fucking play with me here. What's the one goddamn way through the security?"

Akers smiled his Sylvester smile one more time.

"You're gonna love this, Peter."

Seven minutes later, an amazed Peter Ambrose did love it. It was so far out of bounds it was almost delicious. His face, tightened and twisted by fear now relaxed into a lecherous grin. He was amazed that the doofus he'd come to disrespect so thoroughly actually knew a bunch of techno-details that he could summon up at a moment's notice. But then, he'd forgotten again that Akers had actually earned a degree in mechanical engineering from West Point before paying his tuition debt to the Army.

"You are some kind of a weird son of a bitch, Major. I've obviously not been paying enough attention."

Akers returned the smile. This was his moment, one he'd been struggling for -- and missing -- for years.

Ambrose closed his eyes…and smiled. Sure enough, there at the other end of the long tunnel of darkness was a light, and it wasn't an oncoming train. It pained him to admit it, but he was probably going to have to revise his opinion of John Akers. He was still a dipstick, of course, but it was clear that at certain moments, the man could be actually useful.

Ambrose picked up his phone and punched his secretary's button. He knew she was still on duty after the evening's emergency.

"Sarah, get me Colonel Balnavia, Viprotin's man, right away."

When the man was reached at the City Hospital, Sarah rang her boss back.

"Colonel, how is the General doing? Oh? That's wonderful… My God the man is invincible, a true man of steel! Is he, by any chance, alert enough for a short conversation?...He is?...Please!"

Minutes later, Ambrose replaced the phone, and smiled one of his own Sylvester smiles, but this was a Sylvester-who'd-actually-munched-Tweetie-Bird-smile.

"Sonofabitch! The man is out of surgery. They took out two bullets with only local anesthetic, and the doctors say the only way they're keeping him in bed is to claim he has to have antibiotics by IV to prevent infection.

"As to our plan, he's thrilled. He could care less about Darden, but wants the woman to suffer as much as possible."

Akers smiled his best imitation of the Ambassador's Sylvester-burping-up-Tweetie-Bird smile.

"Ohh, she'll suffer alright. So will our Marine. Just leave it to me."

"OK, you've got it. Everything will be in place in Batumi. John, you're goddamn right. This is convoluted beyond measure, but it sounds like it's going to work."

Then, in a softer voice: " It's got to."

Ambrose finally shook his head to clear his momentary fog of anxiety.

"Let's get our poor Marine in here and help him save his darling wife."

Chapter Thirty-Two
The White House

November 8, 4:40pm
The Chief of Staff's Office

Lawrence Claymore was one of the country's true over-achievers. Born in Eufaula, Alabama, on the Chattahoochee River, the son of a small-time shoe store owner, he had come a great distance to be sitting today in a spacious office in the planet's most famous building, directing most of the political machinations of the free world.

It had been a long road, a hard one, and a truly expensive one, though not in the ways he'd expected. His father's shoe store in Eufaula should have closed long before it did. Finally, Wilmer Claymore gave up and moved the family to Kansas to work in his father-in-law's grain wholesaling business. Lawrence survived his one youthful brush with crime and graduated from the University of Kansas, then worked his way through full load of PhD studies at Columbia.

Kansas couldn't take the deep South out of his Dad, but by his own reckoning, he'd done everything a man can do in one lifetime to escape the odor of the Chattahoochee. He'd cleansed himself of every linguistic nuance of the south, every culinary preference. He hadn't eaten fried chicken in 30 years, and the last time he'd tied into collard greens or a poke salad was when he was 12. Catfish gave him indigestion.

If someone asked him today what the Crimson Tide was, he'd have said it's a microorganism that poisons shell and finfish in the warmer waters of the Atlantic and Gulf of Mexico, brought on by random weather shifts and possibly indiscriminate dumping of toxic materials in ocean trash yards.

What made his climb so expensive was, more than anything, fate...or dumb luck...or the comic/tragic coincidence that aligned his climb with that of another man, a New Englander who had fought, charmed, and clawed his way south, reversing Claymore's odyssey, ending up first in Tallahassee, then in Washington, as President of the United States.

The New Englander should have been in Hollywood. He'd have been better than Tom Hanks, better than Ben Kingsley, better than Harrison Ford or any of them, because he could play any of a dozen roles convincingly and almost simultaneously.

One role the President kept hidden from all but his most senior staff and a few members of his Cabinet was the role that was probably closer to his heart than any other: the blue-blood Bostonian who carried a pathological disdain for anything created south of the Mason-Dixon Line.

His own time served in Tallahassee was perhaps his most triumphant piece of acting, because while there he'd actually captured the hearts and votes of 53% of native Floridians (while holding 78% of the New York/New Jersey union members and Wall Street wonders, a true feat of modern politics!)

One of the President's cruelest habits was his incessant use of a nickname for Claymore, especially in the presence of other staff members and Cabinet Officers. "Lawrence" was never used, and "Larry" rarely, if ever, unless it was with half-dozen "r"s, to turn it into a caricature. Despite the fact that he'd explained gently, and then more seriously, how much insult he took from the nickname, the President never ceased to use it.

Today, Lawrence Claymore had a full load of stress and anxiety working, and an appointment with President Farr in 12 minutes, during which he'd have to deliver news that would get him his hated nickname again, and a serious ration of Farr abuse that would give him that near-asphyxiating urge to assassinate the man; an urge that he'd felt perhaps 500 times before.

Nonetheless, he popped an antacid, his third of the afternoon, and headed out of his office and down the hall. As he rounded the corner and entered the maze of smaller West Wing cubicles nearer the President's Office, he thought for maybe the 60th time how faithfully the producers had captured the rhythms and ambiance of the White House on the TV program "West Wing," even if the show's politics was the stuff of liberal fantasy.

The President's secretary was her boss's polar opposite. She had an enormous grace, the ability to project dignity and full respect for every man, woman, and child who passed by. Many times he had wanted to just lift the woman out of her chair, hug her, and tell her how wonderful she was.

"He's waiting, Lawrence. Go right in. I hope you have something wonderful for him, because he's in

one of his moods. Personally, I think we ought to investigate the first lady. She's probably putting arsenic in his hot chocolate again."

Claymore let his shoulders sag just half an inch, but she caught it, as she always did.

"I know, you poor dear…listen. Just hit him with whatever you have and scram. It'll minimize the loss of body parts."

As he opened the door and entered the Oval Office, his first glance at the President confirmed every nuance of Marion Applegate's characterization. The President was angry: probably frustrated and surely loaded for bear. Larry knew he was about to skate on some very thin ice. He had to bring the President in on his urgent need to get Darden out of Tbilisi, even get him to make it his own personal order, without revealing why.

Even as he stepped across the thick wool of the President's famous Great Seal rug, he could hear the ice cracking beneath his wing tips.

"It's been a shitpile of a day, Bubba. Shut the damn door and give me some honest-to-God good news, or I'll tear you a new one, so help me!"

Claymore gritted his teeth. There was nothing to do about the man, except ignore, smile, and stick to your knitting.

"Mr. President. I'm fresh out of good news. In fact, I have what may be very <u>bad</u> news, sir."

"Jesus H. Christ! Can you save it for another day?"

"I don't think so, sir. In fact, if I'd saved it for another ten minutes I'd expect you to have my ass, sir."

*"Shit on a stick, **Bubba!** What is it now**?!"***

"*Mr. President, sir, we uhh, we have a uhh, a problem in our Embassy in Georgia...in Tbilisi, sir."*

"I know what the fucking capital of Georgia is, Bubba! What the hell is the problem?"

"Sir, it seems the Marines have just sent a new Security Chief over there, and he's...well, he's..."

"Jesus Christ, Larrrry, spit it out!"

"He's creating havoc with the Ambassador and his staff, sir, going beyond his authority, snooping into areas that are, uhh, sensitive, sir. The Ambassador has called a half dozen times. He's worried about – you know...the pipeline thing. We've got to get him out of there."

"Why the hell am I not hearing this from Breedmore at State? This is his god-damned sandbox. He can clean up his own messes!"

"Yessir, he can. But I thought it best to take care of it myself before it becomes any kind of embarrassment for you, sir."

Farr glared at him, but one raised eyebrow hinted at recognition -- finally. Then he shook his head.

"That's just wonderful, Bubba. So what the hell are you doing in my face with this crap? You angling for some kind of medal or what?"

Larry lowered his eyes, his heart on fire with rage, but beneath that, the heart of his heart breathing a sigh of relief.

"No sir. Not at all. Just reporting, sir. I didn't want you to be caught off guard if the situation over there gets any worse before we can get this Marine out of there."

"Fine! Take him out. Is that it or do you have more crap to darken my day with?"

No, sir. That's all. Thank you, Mr. Presi...

Larry closed the door softly on his way out.

Chapter Thirty-Three
Crisis

November 8, 11:09pm Local Time
The Ambassador's Office

As Jim Darden was ushered into the Ambassador's office, Ambrose and Akers wore expressions of care and concern, both obviously having been hard at work.

"Jim, the situation is awful, just awful," Ambrose began.

"Maria is in the city jail, and even though we've learned that General Viprotin is out of danger and practically back on his feet, he has ordered her held for immediate trial on a charge of attempted murder with a number of lesser charges thrown in. If she's convicted by a judge she can serve 50 years at hard labor, and from what we know of this country's prison system, she won't last five of the 50.

Jim was still in shock, though he'd had time to sort out his thoughts while the other two were closeted.

"This cannot happen. If you can't get her out, if we can't work through channels, I will myself. I won't let her be railroaded when we all know damn well that anything she did was entirely in self- defense."

Akers piped up, using a tone that Jim had never heard from him, a tone of warmth and almost friendliness.

"We're with you Jim, 100%, all the way. We've been calling in chits and exploring alternatives through our contacts here and across the country. There is a way out, Jim. One way, but it's way too dangerous, way too risky. I'm afraid you'll never make it."

Ambrose watched Jim's face, and found himself shocked to discover Akers as a sudden master of manipulation.

"I'll take the risk. What is it?"

Akers was about to explain, but Ambrose raised both hands to cut him off.

"Jim, before we get into that, let me assure you we've turned over every rock, explored every alternative, and there weren't very many to begin with. What we've discovered is a desperate course of action, one that's way, way outside the law here in Georgia, and it requires some bold, determined steps on your part, and I'm sorry to say, on poor Maria's, as well."

"Fine. I'm ready. For God's sake, what is the plan?"

Ambrose raised his hands a second time.

"Jim, we're about to get to that, but there's one more thing. We cannot be a part of this plan. We can share it with you, and set you on it, and give you all the

silent prayers and support we can, but there's no way this can be traced back to us or to the United States Government or we'll have an incident here that could cause real problems for the President and for our country."

"Understood."

"Good, but let me be perfectly clear. If you are apprehended at any point in the process of getting Maria out of the country or even afterward, you're entirely on your own. We cannot protect you, we cannot give you asylum, we cannot admit to having any part in it. This is terribly difficult for me to say, but I must say it and we must have your word on it. Do you still want to go forward?"

"Of course! Sir, all due respect, get on with it!"

Akers smiled at Ambrose as the Ambassador offered his hand. When Jim reached to shake it, Akers put his hand atop the other two in a three-way shake. Ambrose returned the smile. Jim wanted to join them, but couldn't.

Several minutes later, Akers had taken him to his own office to describe the plan's details.

As Ambrose sat alone in the glow of his new respect for Akers' usefulness, his secure phone rang. He picked it up immediately. The voice on the other end was cold, hard, angry, and quite obviously frightened.

"Peter, have you got the situation with Darden cleaned up?"

"Almost, Larry."

"What the hell do you mean,' almost'?"

"We'll be sending him out in a very few minutes. The plan is in place, and we have every reason to expect a successful conclusion. If all goes well, we'll have... complete success... in just a few hours."

Claymore picked up the hesitations and careful wording.

"Is Darden in front of you right now?"

"No sir."

"Will he be dead in those few hours?"

"No, sir. That's not the plan. But he'll do his duty, and protect our national security at all costs. We have his assurance on that, and we've been very clear that if he's caught we can't protect him in any way."

Claymore wasn't sure he understood, much as he wanted to.

"I want all the details of this 'plan' of yours."

"Absolutely. I'll have Major Akers, our military attaché call you with those in just a few minutes. It's his plan, actually, and I must say, it's damn good."

"I don't give a shit if it's totally awesome, Peter. If it doesn't work, it's crap. Tell me it's got no chance of failure. None!"

Ambrose hesitated for half a beat.

"It will all be over in just a few hours, sir. You'll have to pull a few strings from your side, but it'll all be cleaned up, nice and tidy."

"What strings are those, Peter?"

"Nothing major. A quick court-martial for our Sergeant Darden and perhaps a long sentence at hard labor somewhere outside the country…if you can arrange it, Larry."

Claymore thought through the calls he'd have to make, the chits he'd have to use up.

"OK, I can handle that. Just take care of your end – now, Peter, not later. Got it?"

"Absolutely…<u>Larry</u>."

Peter hung up the phone. This was getting positively delicious.

———————————

Akers was maintaining a tone that to Darden sounded both urgent and reasonable, tones he'd never heard from the man before.

As he described the plan in detail, Jim's mind reeled with its difficulties. It was truly desperate.

"You've got to be kidding. This would be insane even if it was me going down inside the port's water pipe. With Maria, she'll never be able to…"

"—Jim. Listen, man. No argument, it's likely more than most women could do. If we had a day or two to prepare, maybe we could rig up a small compartment behind the back seat of one of the embassy cars and you could stow her in it and drive her down to the dock. Even if we could, if the fucking security guys brought out their dogs, no way they wouldn't sniff her out, especially if we left even a small air hole for her to breathe. But we don't have the luxury of that time. We've considered other routes across the border, but just getting across it doesn't make you safe. We don't have access to a plane on this short notice either. Believe me, Jim, we've thought this through. There's no other way. You're going to have to 'Marine up' here, Sargent, and get your woman to tough it out."

Jim listened carefully, and Akers earnest tone overwhelmed the ugly details. Still, what tore at him was the realization that he was almost totally dependent on two men whom he wouldn't have trusted with a dime an hour ago.

"I have to ask one question: How is it that you know all these details about the port and this water pipe?"

Akers smiled one of his best cynical smiles.

"Bureaucratic bullshit by the ton, brother! Two years ago when this oil pipeline was first proposed, our wimp liberals at the EPA ordered an entire fucking

Environmental Impact Statement before they were going to let any American oil company participate. I'm the only one on the staff here with an engineering degree, so I had to spend two fucking weeks in Batumi with a contractor team from Dallas, going over everything with tweezers and nitpicks."

Jim's mind was racing. OK, so Akers might know what he's talking about. Still, Ambrose had been right. The plan was insane, the risks huge. Had it been Jim escaping alone, it would be different, but while he felt sure he could carry out his part, he wasn't sure about Maria.

"...there's a problem, John."

Akers raised an eyebrow.

"What's that, Jim?"

"When Maria and I were hiking together in the mountains a couple of months ago, before we were married, we came to a cave that I wanted to explore. She refused to come in, told me she has claustrophobia. I don't think she'll be able to make it down the water pipe without totally panicking. If she doesn't get all the way down...she's dead."

Akers' face fell. *"Oh, that's terrible."*

But then he brightened up quickly.

"Wait a minute. I think there's a drug that she can take to conquer her fear. I forget the name of it, but I took it once when I was a rookie in paratrooper training.

If the doctor has some, we can get him to fill a syringe of it for you and you can give it to her just before you get to Batumi. It worked like a charm for me when I made my first jumps!"

Akers dialed his phone.

The doctor wasn't answering. After several rings the Major hung up, and left to go find him.

"Sit tight, Jim. I won't be a minute."

The doctor was still in the reception hall with the two blond Danes and one of the bartenders. Happily, he was drunk, but still alert enough to function. On the way to his office, Akers told him what he needed. The doctor was about to identify the drug, when the Major had a better idea.

"Hey, doc, what I really need here is a syringe of water, maybe 40 cc's."

"What happened to the need for valium, Major? And why would you want water when you need valium? Is this a practical joke of some kind?"

"What it is, doc, is my business. Right now your business is to take care of my business and keep your questions and comments to yourself. You think you can do that -- and then go back to your little love triangle?"

"I have a bad feeling about this, Major."

"Just get back to your two babes, doc. They'll give you a real nice feeling in short order, and you can just forget all about your bad feeling, OK?"

The doctor knew better than to protest further. Five minutes later Akers had a syringe of distilled water, 40cc's, in a plastic container. He handed it to Darden as if it was the world's first cancer cure.

Jim took the syringe and grabbed Akers' hand. The sudden lump in this throat made it difficult to speak.

"John, I-- I appreciate what you and Peter are doing for me here. It means...more than you know. Thank you...both."

Akers smiled back. *("Asta la vista you dumb shit. Your ass is grass, Mr. Marine Corps hero. -- Grass!")*

Through his smile, which Jim found strange in some undefined way, Akers actually said *"Think nothing of it, Jim, boy, we're just doing our job. Semper fi, guy..oh, and wait, I have a couple of things for you."*

Jim would remember, weeks and months later, feeling a brief shiver at those words coming from a non-Marine who obviously had a chip on his shoulder about the Corps.

Chapter Thirty-Four
City Jail

November 9
0015 Hours

Jim had removed his dress uniform and pulled on cammies, his shirt and pants matching, with large thigh flap pockets. Over his shirt, he threw on a black sweater, his winter jacket and cap.

Peter had given him the use of one of the Embassy's better cars for his purpose, a black Subaru Impreza WRX wagon with all-wheel drive, a 2-litre turbo and Georgian license plates.

The drive to the City jail would take only a few minutes. If all went well, getting Maria out would be quick work, but from there he had a 262 kilometer drive through the mountains ringing the city and then west to the port city of Batumi. He could still be there well before dawn, which he thought fortunate, for the security details would be at the end of their graveyard shift, a time when things are usually quietest, and soldiers are sleepiest. He worried, however, that Maria's jailers would see Batumi as his obvious destination and cut off his trip long before he could get there.

Akers had shown him the Georgian words he'd be looking for on signs within the jail building, which also housed many of the city government offices. He'd also told him to leave the car a block or so away and search the building on foot from outside, to see if there was an unguarded entrance on a side or rear of the building.

As he drove the short distance to the 250-odd year-old stone fortress, he felt himself alive in a way he hadn't in some time, the old adrenalin rush giving him an alertness that seemed as though it even sharpened his eyesight, though he knew that was foolish.

His thoughts ran again to Akers and Ambrose, and to gratitude for their concern, and help. He'd felt a twinge of resentment at Akers' use of the phrase "Semper Fi" as if the man had no right to use it, not being a Marine, but he knew that was silly as well. With their help, he had a chance to save Maria's life. That was all that mattered.

He drove slowly around the building once, noting an unguarded entrance on the building's west side, at ground level. He stopped the car briefly to peer in through the half-glass doors on that side entrance. A guard sat at a desk perhaps 50 feet down a hall from this entrance. Turning left, he noted the two guards at the top of the flight of stairs leading to the main double-door entrance on the building's south side. After completing his circle, he chose the rear entrance in an alley on the north side of the building and found a quiet spot to park the car two blocks away.

He pulled out a small leather bag containing a woman's outfit of stretch denim pants, cotton turtleneck pullover and heavy wool sweater, socks and running shoes, size, six, which he hoped would fit her. The suddenly thoughtful Ambrose had obtained them from an embassy staffer.

Unless she was already in some prison outfit, he was pretty sure she was still in her ball gown, which was impossible for what lay ahead.

He also picked up the heavy steel wrench and the four-foot length of steel pipe that was wide enough to swallow the wrench's handle, to give Jim greater leverage if he needed it in opening the water pipe's lower end. He left these in the car.

("He's thought of everything. God bless him, God bless them both.")

Climbing the tall iron gates with the bag straps in his teeth was not much of a problem for him, but he wasn't sure Maria could do it on the way out, so decided they may have to exit via the west doors, past the guard at the desk.

He was over the gate in a few seconds, treading softly down the dark alley. One large dumpster and a row of eight heavy duty trash cans lined the wall of the alley opposite the building and gave off a stench. The alley itself was littered with the detritus of city administration and some kind of food service operation.

Sure enough, there was an opening, a loading platform and overhead door about 40 feet down the building wall. Next to the overhead door was a flight of stairs leading down to a narrower iron door, a single light bulb glowing above it. He padded silently down the stairs and stopped at the door, listening. Nothing.

He tried the knob, and felt a surge of shock when it turned freely. Could the jailers be this stupid?

As he pulled the door open, however, it screeched, rusted steel against dented, rusted steel. He stood perfectly still in the silence, holding the door a couple of inches open, hoping he hadn't attracted anyone's attention.

The narrow corridor inside led directly into a large kitchen, which gave onto a cafeteria with perhaps a dozen steel tables and benches, each capable of feeding a half dozen prisoners or city workers, he wasn't sure which. He hoped it was prisoners, for that would mean he was already in the portion of the building used for the jail.

The rest of his mission could not have gone better had it been scripted for him. In fact he began to wonder half way through it whether security was always this light, or perhaps it was some Georgian holiday.

Down a corridor from the cafeteria, around a corner, up two flights of stairs, and he was in a wide corridor leading to a cell block. At the entrance to his right, was an iron barrier with double gates, and behind it, was a desk with a row of six small video screens. The guard sat with his back to the stairway which Jim had climbed, grateful for his gum-soled boots.

Silently, he drew his gun, then thought better of it, and watched the guard for a minute, then another. Five of the video screens were silent, showing views of several rows of cells, most apparently occupied, but quiet at this hour. The sixth screen ran a commercial TV program, the volume turned low. It was obviously a comedy, from the canned laugh track, but the guard wasn't laughing with the studio audience. In fact he was slouched in his chair, the back of his head resting on its top, and his shoulder rose and fell with a slow rhythm that had to be sleep. Still, Jim wasn't sure until he heard a rumbling snore.

He moved swiftly but silently. When he was within reach of the slumbering guard, he reached down and applied a sleep hug he'd learned in his special forces training, applying pressure to a nerve synapse in the back of the man's neck that quickly deepened his slumber.

From the desk in front of the guard he retrieved an electronic remote hand switch that opened locked doors leading to the cell block, and a ring of keys that would hopefully open individual cell doors. Glancing quickly at the video bank, he found the off-switch and shut it down. Then he took from one pants pocket a small flash light and headed down the corridor.

Pressing the button on his electronic remote, he opened the sliding door to the cell block and entered. Immediately ahead was a double row of eight cells, and half-way down it was a flight of stairs leading up to another level and another double row of cells.

Once inside the cell block, he stopped, stood still, barely breathing. He had to avoid waking the prisoners and starting a torrent of noise, so he held his hand over the lens of the flashlight, allowing only a small crack of light as he moved forward as silently as he could.

Five men slept in the first three double cells. One empty cell followed, then eight more men in the final four. Damn!

He climbed the stair and walked back to the first cell on this level. Maria was lying on a narrow bed, a single blanket wrapped tightly around her. Another lucky break. She was alone, and the next two cells were empty.

He had to arouse her, but gently, so as not to frighten her. He aimed the flashlight up into his own face, and made a soft "pssst."

Nothing. He did it a second time. "Pssssst." She moved slightly, and must have opened her eyes a bit, for she recognized light where there had been only darkness on her way to sleep. She raised her head, peered intently at the light, taking a little forever to recognize the face bathed in the narrow beam. In the first moment of recognition it looked like a disembodied head of her husband and she nearly screamed, but quickly covered her own mouth when the head whispered,

> *"Maria! It's me. Jim! I've come to get you out!"*
>
> *"My God! Jim! I—"*
>
> *"Shh! Quiet!"*

He used the key ring -- slowly. When the door was open he moved inside and lifted her quickly into his arms in a fierce embrace. Every inch of him begged to cling to her right there, to never let her go. Each of them drank the other's fragrance, as if they'd been parched.

He had to let go. Sure enough, she was still in her gown, and he could tell that the single blanket was poor cover in the cold of the cell block. She'd been shivering.

"Here. Put these on. Hurry!"

Maria opened the bag and pulled out the clothes. In seconds she was out of the gown, wearing only a stupendously low cut bra and a G-string he'd never seen before. The effect, even in the darkness and cold was stunning.

"My God, you're beautiful!" he whispered.

She looked up briefly and took in his wide-eyed gaze. He was not making eye contact.

"Get me out of here and you can have all of it. You don't look so bad to me either, cowboy!"

She was dressed in seconds, grateful for the warmth of the two layers of cotton and wool. The shoes were a half-size too small, but that was scant discomfort.

"I'm ready. Lead on studbiscuit!"

"That's muffin!" he said, almost laughing out loud.

"You Americans and your slanguistics. What is the difference between a biscuit and a muffin if both are studs?"

Jim put one finger to his lips, signaling her to tread softly. Both of them padded out of the cell, then down the stairs and past the lower block of cells. One prisoner stirred and mumbled something in Georgian, but they ignored him and were past his cell by the time he opened his eyes enough to see in the dark.

Then through the open cellblock door and down the corridor toward the guard desk. Jim was going to have to use the electronic device to open the main gates to get out into the rest of the building. He hesitated, not wanting to wake the sleeping guard with the sound of the gates opening, but there was no choice. He pressed the button. The doors slid open, but with considerable rumble and when they were part way open, a single metallic screech.

The guard stirred and started to rise. Jim had positioned himself well. He swung once and delivered a right cross to the man's temple with all the force he had. It did the trick. It also gave Jim a searing jolt of pain from his knuckles all the way up his arm. He hoped he hadn't broken his hand.

The two went quickly out into a broad corridor and searched for a stairway. It was about 50 feet ahead, and it had no door. They went down quickly, stopping briefly on the building's second floor.

"Follow me, and say nothing. Just stay with me and don't let anything or anyone get between us, OK?"

She nodded, now in her own adrenalin rush.

He hit the bottom of the stairs and walked very rapidly out into the corridor, retracing the 50 feet he'd come on the upper floor to find the stairs. At that point the corridor branched to the right and left, while straight ahead was the building's massive lobby. Sure enough, outside the main doors were the two guards, one smoking, both looking outward toward the broad avenue.

To his right was the desk of the interior guard, and again, as luck would have it, his back was to Jim.

This time Jim made no effort to be silent, instead walking as fast as he could, as if he were on an important errand, in some kind of emergency, but not running, as if he were fleeing.

When he was perhaps 15 feet from the man's desk, he turned around in his swivel chair. Jim raised an arm in a half-greeting, half-salute.

"Sir, I need some directions to the train station immediately. Can you help me?"

The guard was suddenly both galvanized and confused. Something was obviously wrong, with a man and woman rushing up to him at this hour, coming from heaven knows where *inside the building.* But in addition, the man spoke English, or American, or one of those, and the guard spoke only Georgian and Russian and a smattering of German. He had no idea what the man wanted, but he obviously wanted something!

He stood and raised both arms in a gesture for the hurrying man to stop, but Jim didn't even slow down. In a flash he was in the guard's personal space, and his sore fist struck once more.

This time he missed the temple and struck the cheekbone, which sent another torrent of pain up his arm, causing him to groan once through gritted teeth as he delivered his next shot, a hard left uppercut that got cleanly between the man's two raised arms and smashed his jaw. There was a sickening crunch of teeth breaking, and the guard collapsed in a heap. Unfortunately, as he fell, he knocked a telephone off the desk, smacking the floor loudly.

Jim barely broke stride, moving past the collapsed guard and down the hall toward the double glass doors in the building's west wall. They were a little further away than he'd estimated, and now he was at a dead run, Maria close behind him.

One of the two guards outside the lobby turned at the sound of the phone falling. At first he imagined the inside guard had had some kind of seizure and collapsed from it, but then he saw the blood pouring out of the man's mouth. He shouted to his partner and both yanked the doors open and ran inside. It was only when they got to the collapsed guard's body that they heard Jim and Maria's last running steps to the west doors. The first guard raised his Uzi and shouted for them to stop. They didn't, of course, and he shouted a second time, which was a mistake. He should have fired.

When they were half-way through the doors he squeezed off a round of six shots, all of which clattered and whined off the steel, but none of which hit their targets. For about the fourth time, Jim felt strangely, almost unbelievably lucky.

The guard who had fired his Uzi now turned to his partner and said *"Look after this one. I'm going after those two. Call for help!"*

The other one looked up, a frown on his face. *"I'll call, but who are we looking for?"*

"I don't know. A man and a woman. I didn't get a good look at them."

As he started to run down the corridor toward the west doors, he heard a shout from the stairway down the central corridor. The voice shouted *"Wait!"*

He stopped. Another mistake. The prison guard running down the corridor was shouting almost incoherently, as if the world had come to an end.

"It's the woman, the woman. The one who shot Viprotin! He's taken her. For God's sake, we can't let them get away. It's the one who shot Viprotin!"

The guard in the west hallway now realized how great his mistake had been. Winter was very early this year, and the cold was bone-chilling, the night as still as a graveyard. Though his ears strained as if they could listen harder with an effort of the muscles in the man's head, they heard nothing.

Finally, he heard the faint sound of shattering glass or plastic, once, then twice, then of a motor starting. He ran in that direction as fast as he could. When he had turned the corner of the next block, the Subaru was already moving at more than 40 mph and was three blocks away, its tail lights broken and dark. He raised his Uzi and fired another volley. One or two of the rounds may have hit the car, but though he prayed fervently, none ruptured the gas tank or shredded a tire. The car sped away, gaining speed remarkably quickly.

He cursed loudly, and ran back to the City Building. Inside the lobby the guard with the broken teeth and jaw was moaning and mumbling. The one who'd come down from the jail was waving his arms wildly, arguing with his partner. They were still trying to sort the situation out.

The four of them were of radically different minds about what to do, but all agreed, they had better come up with something intelligent, or their careers, and quite possibly their lives would be over before dawn. They had let the woman who had tried to kill General Viprotin to escape from their jail.

His partner seemed to be thinking most clearly, and finally convinced the others that they had to report the escape to Viprotin's aide, wherever he was. It was now 0152 hours, and unless there had been some miracle, Viprotin was still alive and in the City Hospital. Balnavia would almost certainly be still there.

"Perhaps the General is with the angels by now," his partner suggested hopefully.

"You mean roasting in flames, you idiot! That would be too much to hope for," the Uzi carrier replied. *"Dial the number. I'll speak to him."*

When the hospital answered the call and routed it to the General's suite, "Uzi" spoke rapidly.

"Ahh, Colonel Balnavia, how is uhh, how is the General?...Oh, I am sorry, this is Corporal Grigor Miashvili at the City Building, and of course it is none of my business! I am...we are only calling because if the General is awake we must report to him a recent incident here in the building....yes, of course I will wait."

As he might have predicted, he felt the sharp angina of a moderate heart attack the moment he revealed her escape, but even though the General had reamed him a new orifice right through the telephone, he would later swear that there was something truly strange about the General's tone, a kind of subtle "amusement" beneath the fury.

Nonetheless, a nationwide APB would be transmitted and both police and army forces throughout Georgia would be alerted to find the couple. The APB, however, would be delayed, strangely, for two hours, "*so that the General's own team of Special Operations officers could track them down -- both quietly and competently.*"

The other two men listened to Grigor's report of the conversation, and all three men breathed more regularly, for nowhere in the conversation was there word of punishment details.

Chapter Thirty-Five
The Road to Batumi

November 10, 0051 Hours
Into the West

When Jim had reached the Subaru, his thoughts were racing, a frantic effort to attend to every detail of a plan that was frightening him to death – primarily because it wasn't *his* plan. In fact it was an insane plan, a terrible plan, but what was almost literally driving him crazy was that he could find no alternative.

Still, he worked feverishly to anticipate as many details as he could. Before jumping into the car, he grabbed its tire iron from the trunk and smashed both of the tail lights, including their bulbs, in an effort to reduce the car's visibility from behind. Once behind the wheel, Jim drove the Subaru at the very edge of recklessness. The temperature was below freezing, but the roads were mostly dry, as the season's first snow had been light, a fine powder that blew in the winds rather than adhering to the roads, leaving only the occasional black ice patch here and there. The car's all-wheel drive certainly helped, but Maria still found it necessary to ride with her eyes mostly closed.

"My darling, I was so frightened before you came for me. I must admit, my joy at seeing you has already given way to new fear that neither of us will survive this trip the way you drive."

Jim smiled. *"Nonsense! The drive is nothing compared to what's coming."*

There was still that wonderful lightness in her voice when she exclaimed:

"My God! What can that be?"

"Your escape from Georgia. You're going on a sea cruise."

"Wonderful! Will we have a posh suite or only a lowly inside cabin? Is there a pool and hot tub?"

"None of the above, and we will have nothing, together, I'm afraid. You're going solo."

The warmth and humor were suddenly gone. In their place was fear and panic.

"No, sir Mr. Marine! I won't go without my rescuer! That's crazy! They will certainly be looking for you as a criminal for breaking me out of that terrible jail. You must come with me!"

He reached over and took her hand, holding it tightly. Truth be told, he wanted nothing more that. Sending her away alone was almost more than he could stomach.

"You forget that I'm here on a mission. I'll get you on board, but then I've got to get back to the Embassy before whoever is looking for me finds me.

Once I'm in the Embassy, I'm on US turf. I've got to finish my job, Maria. No questions about that."

"Listen to me, for God's sake! Your fine Mr. Ambrose <u>let</u> them take me! Why wouldn't he let them take you as well? Viprotin is probably enraged that you stole me away from him, if he's still breathing. You must get out as well, you must!"

"There's still my job. And besides, I have to trust the Ambassador. He and Akers put this entire plan together to get you out, and I have to admit it's more than I could have come up with in the little time we had."

She withdrew her hand and folded her arms. Now she was frightened to the core, and about more than just his driving. She felt a sudden sense of dread, almost a premonition.

"So tell me, my fine trusting husband. What is this 'entire, wonderful plan' your heroes have put together?"

"It's complicated, and it's a real challenge -- for you more than for me, but..." he lapsed into thought again, working his way through the entire plan, looking for flaws, for unanticipated risks, for easier alternatives. He was already out of the city and speeding along a main road heading west, so far with no pursuers that he could see. There had to be another way...

"...but I think it will work. Besides, there are no alternatives. We have to <u>make</u> it work."

The sense of dread deepened. She thought for a moment that she could actually smell a faint wisp of an odor, but couldn't say whether it was the scent of betrayal or the sour smell of her own fear.

He glanced over at her, arms folded, the angry pout of a spoiled teenager. She was all of a piece, except for the single tear that overflowed the corner of her eye and wandered down her left cheek. She made no effort to wipe it away. Jim felt his throat tighten, then his chest. "Shit."

When she spoke again, it was in a very small voice, no hint of artifice or even any attitude except honest fear.

"What do I have to do?"

It was a question he wanted never to have to answer, but Akers and Ambrose had convinced him. There was no other way.

"You have to do something very brave, and very bold. Something that will frighten you to the core, but I will help you with an injection that will calm your fear and let you complete the task quickly and confidently."

She shut her eyes tightly, squeezing out another tear.

"My God, my God, will you stop with assurances and preambles and tell me what I must <u>do</u>?"

He took a deep breath, softening his own voice, slowing his words.

"When we get to Batumi, I can't get you through the two security checks between the port road and the

dock where your ship is anchored. The only way to get you past the security and down to the ship is to have you crawl down a water pipe, about 1800 feet. I'll get past the security, meet you at the bottom, and get you out."

She had been holding her breath. When he stopped, she inhaled, deeply.

"Is it a big pipe?" She asked.

"Akers tells me its 40 centimeters in diameter, but its old, so perhaps a bit smaller inside with corrosion."

She breathed again, suddenly relieved.

She hadn't listened carefully enough. "That's not so hard! What is so difficult about straddling a pipe that big and sliding down hill? After all, I believe I have straddled an entire U.S. Marine!"

Jim smiled briefly, but then closed his own eyes. It hurt. It just hurt.

"You must slide down <u>inside</u> the pipe, Maria."

It was a tidal wave. She was belted into her passenger seat and the car was racing along a straight, flat road, but the words hit her so hard she wanted to scream. The acid bubbled in her stomach, a huge ball that wanted to force its way up her esophagus and out. She very nearly vomited at the thought. The sound that came from her throat was awful, a panicked animal sound, not human.

*"No. No. No. No. No. I cannot. I cannot. I
cannot! Shoot me! Kill me! Just leave me on a street in
Batumi. I'll find my own way out. Only not this!. I beg
you. Please, Jim! Please, please, please Jim. Not this!"*

She was sobbing. No longer a pouting teenager,
or spoiled princess. She was now 5 or 6, a thoroughly,
panicked child.

He hit the brakes hard, much harder than
necessary, and brought the car to a violent halt, anti-lock
brakes notwithstanding. With the car standing still in the
middle of the road, he turned and faced her, his voice
shaking her like thunder.

*"Stop it! I don't want to hear another word about
'please Jim not this.' This is the only way. There is no
other. You can do it. I told you, there is a drug that will
calm your fear. I'll give it to you now if you wish, or
later. But you will do this, and you will succeed. I will
not lose you to some evil bastard like Viprotin. I will not
lose you to your own fears either. You will do this. We
will get through. Period. Understood?"*

She would not look at him. She wanted to be
angry, but couldn't summon it up. She was suddenly
exhausted, more tired than she had ever been in her life --
still, silent, empty. Way, way inside, as if at the end of
some long, long tunnel, a tiny voice wanted to say "--
whatever!" But it was a voice she could barely hear, and
Jim heard nothing at all.

He put the car in gear and drove on down the road
west. Fifteen, twenty minutes later he looked over at her
very briefly. Her eyes were closed, tears still falling. Her

hands were clasped in her lap, and her lips were moving. Small motions, no sound. When he understood, he wanted to cry himself. She was praying.

Chapter Thirty-Six
The Water Pipe

November 10
0354 Hours.

They reached the outskirts of Batumi and left the highway. There were still two hours before the eastern sky could go from black to grey. The streets were dark and still, its few fishermen the only locals heading down toward the wider thoroughfares near the harbor. The ancient city had its share of natural beauty, steep hills rising above the water's edge, palm trees along the shore, a few of the older buildings restored to colorful baroque dignity by the Russian overlords before the breakup of the Soviet Union. The sooty industrial port area was rather small, with pier space for only eight ocean-going freighters, tankers, and the occasional cruise ship...tiny enclaves of prosperity spread to the north on the bluffs 200 feet and more above the water. The temperature here was a good bit higher than in Tbilisi, but still chilly, its effect heightened considerably by their fear.

As they neared the port area, Jim found the road he needed, one that ran north and south along a high hill above the complex of docks, warehouses, and freight loading cranes. Below was the series of concrete and stone piers and jetties, some occupied by tankers and freighters, some empty.

Here, there was activity, though it was hardly hectic. He drove slowly, searching for "her" ship, the

Caspian Queen, registered in Liberia and owned by a distant nephew of Stavros Niarchos. It would depart for Athens, Sicily, and Barcelona at 0630, carrying a crew of 28, a full load of coke from a Georgian mine 60 miles northeast of Batumi and God willing, one passenger.

To his left was a large field of long grass, littered with the detritus of a poorly civilized tribe. He pulled the little car off the road and onto the field, stopping about 40 feet from the road, so that casual passersby might not notice it in the dark.

0358 Hours.

"It's time. I'll give you the injection. We'll wait five minutes for it to take effect, then we get out. The water main can't be far, because Akers said it falls almost directly down to the pier where the ship is docked, with only two turns in the pipe, one 90 degrees, near the top. It should only take you ten, maybe twelve minutes to get down, but you have to move as fast as you can.

"I should get back to the car and get down through the security checkpoints faster than that. They are looking for you more than for me."

Jim reached behind his seat and pulled out the heavy adjustable wrench and the piece of lead pipe that fit over the wrench handle to improve its leverage.

"When I get to the water main, there is a cap with eight bolts. I will remove them with these. I need to have you out and the cap replaced by 0500 so they can turn on the water to supply the ship. It's done by the clock. I

have this wrench from Akers and if any are rusted, I have this. He's thought of everything..."

He held up a pint can of WD-40. Maria stared at it blankly, no idea what it was. Nor did she care. She was no longer exactly numb or dead. She was living through a nightmare. She had prayed for escape, but knew there was none. She didn't know if one could actually die of fright. If it were possible, she would very likely do so, but before then, she would do what she had to do.

Slowly, she pulled her left arm out of the sleeve of the bulky sweater and cotton turtleneck under it, revealing her bare skin. Jim reached into the pocket in the driver's door and pulled up the case containing the syringe. Carefully he took it out, checked the level of fluid, and gently pressed the plunger until a couple of drops came out, then inserted it in her upper arm and slowly pressed the plunger again.

"So," she said softly. *"Now I am Superwoman. Where is my cape?"*

He laughed a little, and it helped. He took her in his arms and held her tightly, his face pressed against hers.

"Believe me, sweetheart. Believe me, if there was another way...."

"Shut up. Drugs or no, I am only so brave. I have no idea when or if I will see you again after I get on that damned ship. It's no small thing for me."

She pulled back from his embrace to gaze into his face so directly and deeply it almost hurt to look back at her.

"Loving you is suddenly terribly expensive. Had I known how expensive a few months ago, I might have enjoyed one night with you, but I never would have let myself love you. Not like I love you now. Believe me, I am almost sorry I do."

He started to reply, though he had no idea what to say, but it didn't matter. She pulled away and put her hand gently over his lips.

"No more words. Let's go."

0407 Hours.

They left the car and headed back to the road and across it. Moving further south not more than 80 yards, he spotted the water main to their right. It was as Akers had described. He wondered briefly how the man had known so much, but flung the question from his mind.

It was a complex of utilities, electric lines, smaller pipes, and the larger central water main. As it came out of the ground, it made a sharp 45 degree turn and then a second 45 degree turn to the horizontal before heading off down the hill. About 200 feet further down it made another turn, not quite 90 degrees, and continued diagonally down to the dock at which the Caspian Queen was tethered.

In the short space of perhaps four feet after the first turn right in front of them, there was a heavy steel cap, with a spring-loaded handle which could be pulled (hard) and released, a heavy rubber gasket sealing the cap against the polished edge of the pipe itself. *("Why couldn't the same kind of cap be at the bottom?)* he wondered.

He grasped the thick rod handle above the pipe and pulled. The spring mechanism made it heavy indeed. He moved it an inch, maybe two, but not far enough to release the spring tension and pull it free.

He picked up the four-foot length of pipe and used it as a lever on his second pull, giving it everything he had, and after a moment at the top of the curved arc of the handle's travel, it finally gave, and the handle practically snapped open the rest of the way, with a loud clank.

Quickly, they both looked around to see whether any passersby might have been distracted by it. There was no one.

Maria closed her eyes one final time. She fought back one more urge to vomit.

"Here." Jim said, holding a thin, lightweight flashlight. *"Hold it in one hand, with both arms in front of you as you go in, or in your teeth. It'll help."*

"Holy Mother of God!" she whispered.

She thought for a moment about the two alternatives, and decided to hold it in her teeth. It had the advantage of encouraging her to breathe through her mouth, which reduced her ability tosmell anything in the pipe that really would make her wretch. Still, holding it there came close to arousing her gag reflex. Several times she had to fight to keep from spitting it out and vomiting. Only her fear of the dark in such a tight place was stronger than the urge to do just that.

Putting her arms over her head, she leaned over and inserted them into the pipe, allowing Jim to lift her up and help her slide in. Half way in, she spit out the flashlight, caught it with one hand, and cried out.

"No, wait, pull me out! Pull me out!"

He did, but the look on his face wasn't happy. When she was standing on solid ground again, she removed the heavy sweater, leaving only the cotton pullover, which fit rather snugly over her shoulders and chest.

"It was too tight. I would have shredded it and it would have slowed me down. When you get me in, for God's sake, hurry, will you?"

"I will! I will!"

0413 Hours.

He took the sweater from her and again lifted her in. When she was fully into the pipe, flashlight in her teeth, arms straight over her head, with no room to pull them down to her sides, she suddenly wished for nothing but darkness--the darkness of death.

She wanted to scream again for him to pull her out. There was no calm, no courage, only panic.

Opening her eyes and looking ahead down the pipe, the weak beam of light ended a few feet ahead, so that felt as if it were already shrinking around her, holding her in place. She felt she couldn't move. She spat out the flashlight again and opened her mouth to scream, but was stopped by the heavy thud of the cap being put in place behind her, its rubber gasket softening the clang. She closed her eyes and cried like a baby.

The air inside the pipe was fetid. Its walls were wet, with jagged shell-like calcium deposits seemingly growing along its surface in an oddly symmetrical pattern, as the water only flowed in one direction. The edges of each deposit nearest her were smooth, and tightly attached to the iron pipe. The downstream edge of each deposit protruded from the pipe by 1/4 to 1/2 inch, its edges jagged and sharp. Once she started to move forward, there would be no way to go back.

She didn't know how long she lay there crying. It could have been seconds, or precious minutes. Finally, some lost and gone adult portion of her panicked brain kicked into gear, and she sniffled once, almost choked on her own saliva and tears, and spat it out. She had to move.

There was too little room for crawling. She had to push with her feet, suddenly grateful for the running shoes' cushioned soles, although immediately fearful that they would be shredded long before she reached the bottom. That thought alone almost started her crying again, but she fought it off and pushed with both feet, feeling gently for pieces of calcium she could actually grab onto to pull with her fingers as well.

That task was occasionally successful, often not. In minutes, her fingers were bleeding -- all of them. The pain in her shoulders from having her arms forced so straight over her head quickly became excruciating.

0420 Hours.

"You have to move, you simple dolt. Move!"

She did. Each kick was an effort. Some moved her a couple of inches, some actually started a slide of a foot or more. Despite the beam of light held in her teeth, arching her head back far enough to shine the light directly down the pipe was almost too painful, so she decided to keep her eyes closed, at one point almost laughing at the lunacy of it.

Progress seemed infinitesimal, but she continued. The pain in her hyperextended shoulders was now a fire that threatened to snap her arms free of the rest of her body. She fervently wished they could be amputated on a nice sharp piece of calcium.

"How much easier life would be!"

Just then she pushed once more with her feet and suddenly felt the slope increase, and with it, sudden acceleration.

"OhmyGodohmyGodohmyGod! No, no, no, no, no, nooooo!"

The slide was only perhaps 100 feet, but it felt like free fall. She pushed hard against the sides of the pipe with her bloodied hands, and then finally, stopped as suddenly as she had begun.

Unfortunately the stop was faster than her reflexes, and she pushed back hard _after_ she'd already stopped, causing one of the calcium shells to rip through her shirt and bra under one breast. The flow of blood was immediate, warm and sticky, its sweet/sour odor half sickening, half fascinating. A peculiar series of emotions flooded her consciousness.

There was anger at her stupidity and clumsiness, followed by a wave of new fear, then a bigger wave of remorse and guilt. She knew how much her husband loved her body, especially her breasts. To damage one, perhaps permanently, was a terrible thing. She almost started to cry again, but stopped herself, laughing bitterly at her own vanity.

"Thy name is woman!" she said out loud, though her diction was garbled by the tip of the flashlight still held between her teeth.

Jim had raced back to the car and turned the key. The Subaru kicked over and he spun all four tires on the dew-wet grass before the tires bit and sprayed dirt and gravel as he lurched backward.

He headed south, making a right at the next corner, 300 yards further down. This road wound right and left down the steep slope toward the waterfront, reminding him of the street about 1000 advertising agencies used in San Francisco to advertise everything from new cars to sexy fashions and perfume.

About 1/3 of the way to the pier he reached the first security checkpoint, his heart already racing. The two guards standing behind the wooden arm that blocked his progress had rifles slung, rather than pointed at him. (*"Good news; they haven't gotten any bulletins about us yet."*)

He showed his diplomatic license, passport, and his special embassy identity card. The lead guard's examination of these took longer to read than any self-respecting first grader, as Jim fought to keep his breathing under control.

Then he was through, and only one more checkpoint before the pier.

0422 Hours.

This time three guards, two of whom had unslung their Kalashnikovs and were pointing them directly into his windshield. The lead guard was at least 6'6" and 125 kilos. He had a swagger the others didn't, and probably the rank to make the swagger official, though Jim didn't recognize the symbols on his epaulets.

"So Mr. American Yankee Sergeant, to what do we owe this visit, an inspection of our fine port facilities to witness pre-dawn industrial efficiency?"

Jim tried to smile through clenched teeth.

"No indeed! I could surely see your efficiency better about 6 hours from now, eh? No. Something much more humble. One of our senior officials desires to send a package to a lover in Athens via his friend, the Captain of the Caspian Queen."

"Ohh? What kind of package?"

*"I am not told. Feels like a love letter, and perhaps a trinket. Official embassy mailings must get logged in and the logs are subject to our Freedom of Information Act. He worries his wife may someday discover her right to snoop on his **un**official correspondence and catch him in the act!*

To prove his explanation, Jim held up a large manila envelope addressed to a certain Wilhelmina Romagna, at a hotel in Piraeus.

The guard took the envelope, turned it over several times in his hands, smiled once, then lifted it up to his nose, grinning more broadly.

"Your official is faggot? This is perfumed like cheap whore!"

"Not a faggot, but definitely strange. He thinks she likes this stuff. But then, you should see her!"

His hand gesture made the shape of someone more bovine than human.

The guard laughed heartily, but then remembered his job. He scanned the car carefully, and then grabbed a mirror on a pole, bending to search beneath.

"No foreign bodies, I see.   Go ahead with such great important task, Yankee Sergeant.   You will make the world safe for democracy tonight, no?"

"Safe for lovers, anyway! Thank you very much."

Jim smiled warmly as he retrieved the envelope and shook the guard's hand.   *"I'll tell your General Viprotin of your thoroughness <u>and</u> your kindness! "*

It was the guard's turn to smile.   *"You do that? Serious to do that?"*

"Sure! Gotta go!"

"Be good thing.   Must be, how you say?   Make certain to use name -- Corporal Shinanevai.   Must be conwincing, yes?"

"Absolutely! Really gotta go!"

0429 Hours.

Jim waved once as he nudged the accelerator and moved on toward the pier. His heart was now a triphammer and he found himself inhaling deeply as if he'd been holding his breath while playing "calm and cool" with the Georgian guard.

Less than a minute later he was at the pier. Dead ahead was the dockside terminus of the water supply pipe. The few crewmen and dockworkers on duty were focused on their tasks, and so took little note of his arrival.

———————

Inside the pipe, Maria had come to the end. There was sudden elation, the animal thrill of having conquered a demon within that might have paralyzed her, leaving only a whimpering child.

The elation didn't last long, however, gone in seconds. The demon wasn't dead after all. For the view in front of her was no longer an endless tunnel. Now it was mere inches. The demon now played with her eyes, shrinking the inches around her, until the pipe began to squeeze the very breath from her heaving lungs.

She closed her eyes tightly, wondering what had become of the courage drug Jim had just injected in her arm, for there was none. She felt her whole body shake with dead panic..

She wanted to scream, but as the pipe squeezed and squeezed, there was not enough air. she could only mew little sobs, a trapped kitten crying for its mother. The demon whispered, delighted at her panic.

"Go ahead, woman. Try to inhale. Suck with all your might. See what it gets you! Nothing!!!"

Perhaps 20 seconds later another piece of her brain clicked into gear, a recognition that she'd been lying there in panic for a third of a minute. Perhaps it was the cold wetness causing her to shiver violently. It wasn't enough, but it was a finger-hold on the edge of a cliff.

In possession of that finger-hold, she had just enough sense to spit out the flashlight, grab it with one hand and start banging it, as hard as she could with one screaming shoulder and arm, on the inside of the pipe.

"I'm here, Jim. I'm here! I've made it! I've made it all the way, Jim! I've done it! Be proud, my love, I've done my part! Now hurry, please God hurry! Get me out!

"Pleasepleasepleasepleasepleaseplease...."

––––––––––––––––––

0432 Hours

Jim hopped out of the car and ran toward the pipe end, the steel wrench given him by Akers in his right hand. He knew he'd gotten there in plenty of time -- his watch read almost told him he'd have more than 25 minutes to open the hatch, get her out, and replace it. It would be enough. Eight bolts and she'd be out. A minute later, maybe two, and she'd be on board. Five minutes more and he'd be heading back to Tbilisi, or maybe he should re-think, and stay aboard with Maria....

At 0432:28 he reached the pipe end, where it was connected to an eight-inch reinforced rubber line that extended into a port in the ship's hull.

He bent to put his wrench to the first bolt, and stopped, eyes wide, not breathing, staring dumbly at the cap below.

There were not eight bolts. There were twelve.
They could not be opened with the wrench in his hand in
a hundred years. Their outer surface was not hexagonal,
but round, each having a hexagonal hole in the top, to be
opened using an entirely different tool, a giant allen
wrench.

His brain exploded in panic. He screamed in
animal agony, and ran toward the ship looking for
someone, anyone.

The ship's gangway had been pulled up, its
bottom thirty feet above him. There was no one on the
pier. He yelled with all his might, frantic. No one
answered.

Desperate, he ran back to the pipe. He heard
tapping from inside the pipe. She had made it!

"I'm here, Maria! I'm here! Just a minute—just
a minute-just a—Oh God, no!!"

He froze. The entire world crashed around him as
he listened to Maria's frantic tapping again and again. In
a rush all the little odd, seeds of doubt, the little
discordant details about Ambrose, Akers, and this "plan"
suddenly came together like pieces of a puzzle. When
they did, and recognition dawned, he screamed again,
suddenly, thoroughly insane.

He ran up and down the pier, screaming for help.
None came. He yelled until he was hoarse.

Finally, he ran back to the pipe and wrapped his
arms around it. Every fiber of his body drenched with

adrenalin, he yanked at it, clawed at the thick iron of the bolted cap, tearing his fingernails. Nothing moved.

From inside the pipe, came the tapping again. She was there, just beneath his bleeding fingertips, barely an inch away and he couldn't reach her in a thousand years. He began to cry.

"I'm here, Maria. I'm here. I'm so…God forgive me. Dear God, forgive me!"

Just then someone somewhere in the port complex hit a button and a high pressure flood of water began rushing downhill to supply the Caspian Queen. Maria felt it as a sudden breeze, and wondered how it could be. Then came the roaring sound, and she knew. *"Holy Mary, Mother of God…"* she began, but got no further It was nowhere near 0500 hours yet.

Outside the pipe, Jim heard the sudden hiss of air being forced out of a small valve under the pipe. Seconds later, the tap-tap of the flashlight stopped. The soft rushing sound of water within the pipe was preceded by a tiny fragment of sound that lasted less than a second. Cut short by the water's rush, he knew instantly it was Maria's scream.

Chapter Thirty-Seven
Charleston, South Carolina

November 15
The Brig

The Charleston Naval Base houses one of several military prisons. Fort Leavenworth, in Kansas, is the largest. Charleston's facility is older than Leavenworth, and though it is much smaller, its age and architecture make it as miserable and painful to its Naval and Marine inmates as Ft. Leavenworth.

The USMC Personnel System contains a "book" on Captain James Darden that now includes a summary record of a court martial conducted in our base in Wiesbaden, Germany, resulting in a conviction on a charge of interference with the criminal justice system of a foreign state, illegal flight to avoid prosecution, and manslaughter in causing the death of one Maria Elena Contreras da Silva Darden. The single judge (a three-judge panel would have been normal) handed down a sentence of 30 to 40 years in the Charleston Naval Prison.

That record resides in the computer files and while it is classified well beyond top secret, and can be accessed by very few persons in or out of the Pentagon, no one in the Charleston Naval Base has ever seen or heard of Captain James Darden.

Lawrence Claymore saw to that. It was his one addition to the plan hatched by Ambrose and Akers, which he had found surprisingly adequate, if a bit melodramatic.

"Fine, fine. I'll take care of the court martial – we'll do it in Germany, and in light of the damage to a strategic relationship with the State of Georgia, we'll prosecute the good Captain with all possible speed."

Claymore also shared with Ambrose that when his conviction was in hand, Darden would never see the inside of a stateside military prison, or in fact any place inside the US of A.

Instead, he made a phone call to the newly appointed Director of the CIA at Langley -- an appointee whose confirmation process he had personally shepherded through the Senate. He loved making the call, loved giving the orders to the Director, and loved that they were carried out precisely and immediately. It had been one of the very special chores that made Claymore feel what he had dreamed of feeling even as a Political Science undergrad when he'd done research on the Chief of Staff position in a seminar on the US Presidency.

Today he could do things like this. Things that were way outside any official authority conferred upon his position. More important still, things that were 100% silent, secret, with no paper trail. That was power, real power. And it was his.

At the order of the CIA Director, four members of the US Army Delta Force were dispatched to Wiesbaden,

Germany to accept responsibility for transporting one Captain James Darden, USMC, from the Military Tribunal to a waiting C3 transport plane and then to the Charleston Naval Prison in South Carolina. At the last possible moment, the crew of the C3 would be reassigned to fly a Congressional delegation from Wiesbaden to Paris.

Two of the four Delta Force team members who were also skilled and certified pilots would then take the Captain to Charleston in a much smaller civilian plane -- a Gulfstream twin jet outfitted for trans-Atlantic flights.

Only they wouldn't set course for Charleston at all, but for a secret American compound in the ice-covered steppes of northern Finland, where they would hold the Marine defector and spy until they had learned each and every military secret they were told he had sold to the Russians while on duty in Georgia, and then execute him.

Jim was blindfolded as he was transferred to the four Delta Force "couriers," so he never saw any of their faces. He arrived at the facility at 0220 hours on the morning of Tuesday, March 6, only 12 days after going "berserk" on a wharf in Batumi.

Escorted by his four guards up two short flights of stone stairs that had been shut off from the rest of the century-old hunting shelter for decades, he was locked into a 6'x10' cell without a single person laying eyes on him.

Sgt. Claude Gribbner and Lt. Dick Urquit began the interrogation almost immediately after a flight in which not a single word was spoken to Jim.

In fact both Gribbner and Urquit were highly motivated. Each fashioned himself a thorough American patriot, and each had been briefed on Darden's treachery, even that throughout his entire legal proceeding, he had uttered not a word, even to his own attorneys.

"The guy's got to be cold..." they agreed. *"...cold as ice!"*

Gribbner dressed in the uniform of an Army Colonel and Urquit wore the braid of a Navy Captain, but only on "official" days at a Stateside military base. Today they wore olive-drab tee shirts and eight-pocket cammie pants. Their boots were not the sand-colored desert boots worn in Iraq and Afghanistan, but the older black leather models with stiff soles and steel toes.

Both men entered his cell together. Urquit shouted "Ten Hut!" and Jim, now free of his blindfold, leapt to his best imitation of 'attention' with his hands cuffed behind him. The "Colonel" came forward and with no warning, hit him three times in quick succession with wicked blows to the solar plexus and each cheekbone. Jim could not raise an arm in defense. He hadn't noticed the gloves the man wore, thin leather with steel plates covering the knuckles and backs of each finger. He felt them, as he fell into merciful unconsciousness.

It didn't last long, and when he began to come back, the pain was huge. He found himself being lifted to his feet. Gribbner had moved swiftly around both the others and now supported him from behind. Six more blows cracked two, perhaps three ribs. Now the act of inhaling was nearly impossible, each attempt bringing stabs of new pain. He heard himself making whimpering sounds that were entirely involuntary.

"Good morning Captain Darden. We'd like to know a little bit about you for our files," Urquit sang in a weird sotto voce.

Gribbner chimed in, using his best imitation of Tony Soprano. *"Yeah, and if you think you might not wanna share wid us the little gems you been sellin' to the fuckin' Russians, well, fuggedabouddit!"* followed by a surgically aimed blow to his left kidney, then his right. After the second blow, Gribbner let go, letting him fall to the stone floor, hitting his forehead with a sick wet smack that was happily the last thing he heard or saw for hours.

When he next opened his eyes, many hours later, he was lying on a steel-framed bed, a thin hard mattress under him, a single blanket providing at least a measure of protection from the cold. As he awoke, the pain returned with each attempt to inhale, combined with massive aches from what felt like a face three times its normal size. Had he seen his reflection in a mirror, he might not have recognized himself.

Two men sat on folding chairs by the side of his bed. Both wore military buzz cuts, both were clean shaven, and both wore camouflage-print field service uniforms, with officer insignia on their shoulders.

"Good afternoon, Captain Darden. I'm Major Hoover," said left-chair, *"and this is Colonel Strallick. We want to apologize for the greeting you received from the other members of our team. It was excessive, to say the least. After all, until recently, we thought we were all on the same team, including you."*

"I don't...I don't...understand." Jim felt every facial muscle cry out with the smallest effort to speak, the words coming out in a fog of pain that sounded as if he'd been drinking for a serious long time.

"Of course you don't, with a greeting like that, no warning and all," said right-chair Strallick.

"It's really pretty straight-forward, Captain," said Hoover. *"You've been convicted of selling military secrets to the Russians, and we need to learn what secrets those were. The sooner we know what you shared with them, the sooner this unpleasantness can be over and you can be -- well, relieved."*

"I've...what? No! You don't ...there's...mistake!"

Strallick shook his head sadly. *"Now there, you see? Even with the greeting he got from our team greeters, here he is telling us we're mistaken. And we thought they'd been too rough on him. Tsk, tsk."*

With that Hoover and Strallick simply rose from their chairs and headed for the door, which opened to admit Gribbner and Urquit.

Pain.

An entire, exhaustive, and exhausting menu of pain. More kinds than he had ever known, more than he ever imagined, even in the most brutal of his special forces training.

There was the sharp stiletto stab that came with each breath as his lungs pressed against cracked ribs with each tiny effort to inhale.

An exquisitely deep, intense flame of heat each time he moved even an inch, in the soft tissue of his back where his kidneys wore deep bruises from expertly aimed blows.

A frightening fragile soreness about his face, which threatened to fall to pieces if it hadn't already. The steel-lined gloves had cracked his cheekbones and loosened several teeth. There were pungent reminders in his nostrils and on his tongue as he awoke to taste his own blood, now congealed and drying as he could only breathe through his mouth, even in unconsciousness, his nose filled with mucous and blood from other blows.

The loss-of-circulation pain combined with growing numbness in his wrists and hands from having lain on his handcuffs for who knows how many hours. His brain sent urgent alarm messages to move off the mattress just to relieve the pressure on his hands, lest they die before the rest of him did.

A comparatively dull, but awesomely loud ache throughout his head, as if his brain had swollen within the skull and now sought to relieve the pressure by pouring out through his ears, a terrible feeling spiked by even the smallest movement of his head.

Finally, as he lay on the stone floor, unable to move, there had been two vicious kicks to his crotch, a soaring scream of pain that dwarfed the others, and made him wretch once on his way to unconsciousness

Each of these distinct and separate pains worked with the others to make a thundering wall of "sound," a screaming crescendo with each effort to move even an eyelid. It took every ounce of his strength to force the wall of pain music back, while he struggled for minutes on end to roll over, then draw his knees under him and finally to stand, and breathe.

After several more minutes he took a few steps, then slowly lowered himself to sit on the bed, the wall of "pain music" began to subside, or perhaps his brain function began to kick in enough to push back against it.

He slowly lowered himself onto the bed, the shrieking cacophony slowly residing as he closed his eyes, desperate for silence.

He couldn't be certain whether it was sleep or mere unconsciousness, and he had no idea how long it lasted, but when it ended, it was another sound that shattered it, more devastating than any of the pains.

It was a small, frantic, metallic tap-tap, tap-tap. When he heard it, he wanted more than anything to cover his ears with his hands, but of course couldn't. Instead, he just lay there and cried aloud, a battle-trained, 30-year old Marine sobbing like a two-year old, trying desperately to drown out the tap-tap, tap-tap -- from inside the pipe.

He had not slept a single night without waking to it. It was the thought, and vision that had filled his mind for weeks.

"I've killed Maria."

That nightmare had haunted him in every sleep since. He heard again and again the tapping of her flashlight from inside the pipe. Saw again that the wrench Akers had given him was useless, screamed again for help, but no one appeared on the dock, until after the water had begun to surge through the pipe. Suddenly there were people everywhere, mostly security guards. The rage he had felt returned in each sleep, but even that was overwhelmed by a perfect storm of futility. Suddenly, the whole sequence of events took on the shape of a demonic symphony, a hellish stage play in which he had played the part of the village idiot.

That forced his beaten brain to trace through more thoughts.

"I've failed my mission."

"I fell for Akers' plan – I was so lost, so panicked, so damned stupid!"

"I've been court-martialed...convicted."

"I'm in prison...somewhere. I don't know where. It's cold."

"They think I've done something else. Spy? Me?"

"Why?"

"Why?"

"Wh—"

The question remained unanswered as the key squealed in the lock and the cell door opened.

Gribbner and Urquit entered…smiling.

Chapter Thirty-Eight
Washington, DC

November 19
The Embassy of Spain

Don Alberto wore a wrinkled brow, a distracted frown, and a surly temper as if they had been an old sweater. He was definitely in one of his "brown studies," a mood during which few colleagues sought his attention and even fewer his agreement.

He had not heard from his beloved daughter in over a month, and none of his calls had found her. That had never happened before.

He was at his desk after an interminable luncheon with an assortment of American importers and wholesalers who had harangued him about pressuring Spanish vintners to lower their prices in order to capture more of the burgeoning U.S. wine market.

The afternoon was blessedly quiet, no appointments, no conference calls, no reports due. The peace might have been enjoyable, but for his growing concern.

When his desk phone rang at 2:13, every fiber of his body tightened. Somehow, the very electricity within him knew before the phone stopped ringing, who was calling.

"Si?"

"Don Alberto, it is Juan Gonsalvo, in Madrid."

"How are you, my friend? Have you found the train bombers?"

"Some. Not all. Everything in its time, Don Alberto. That is not the reason for my call."

"Your voice has already told me that, Juan. The small hairs in my ears and nose tell me it is about my Maria Elena. Si?"

"Si."

"You know where she is?"

"Si. (A sigh and a troubled pause told him before the words came.) *"She is with the angels, Don Alberto. I am more sorry than I can say."*

Da Silva felt the temperature of his body drop several degrees in seconds. He gripped the phone so hard all the blood drained from his fingers so that they were stiff when he released the pressure minutes later.

"How?"

"You know, Excellency, that I owe you my life and my career, more than I can ever repay. But at this moment I fear that the details would serve no good purpose but only to increase your pain. I would save you from that if you will let me."

"Then it was not an accident."

"In a small way, yes, it was, but in the larger truth, No, Don Alberto. It was not."

When da Silva spoke again his voice was calm, a measured monotone.

"So, my friend, I must request everything you know, and everything you can learn. It will cancel all debts between us. I mean everything. No detail is too small, or too terrible for my ears. Do this for me, Juan. It is the last thing I will ever ask."

"So, as I predicted. I will not use a telephone for this information, Don Alberto. I have only a few of the details now. I will be in Washington in two, perhaps three days. We will share the terrible details face to face."

"As soon as possible, my friend. Where is her...body?"

"I cannot say. When I see you, I will know."

"One more question, Juan. If you can tell me, how did she come to find the young Darden in Tbilisi?

"A position in our Embassy there was arranged for her, Don Alberto. By your man there in Washington."

"My man?"

"Si.. Bottegas."

Don Alberto closed his eyes, suddenly rigid, barely breathing. Bottegas. Slime. The perfect paragon of corruption, greed, and manipulation. He would deal with Bottegas.

When he hung up the phone, he felt a sudden deep pain throughout his body. For a moment he was certain he would lose his lunch before he could get to the bathroom down the hall, but with effort, the wave of nausea passed. A rush of perspiration dotted his forehead. He blotted it with a fine cotton handkerchief and reached for a pen and pad. Suddenly, there was a great deal of work to do.

He quickly reached for the phone again and dialed a Colonel in the British Special Forces serving in Britain's embassy on Massachusetts Avenue.

A short conversation relayed a request which was honored without question or delay. Three hours later, he answered the return call.

"Signor da Silva, your request, unusual as it was, has produced some bloody strange information, which I hope will make sense to you, for it doesn't to us.

"The Personnel Office in the Pentagon considered our request routine and the Major queried the Marine Corps' data base, but whatever the system's response, his tone changed rather abruptly. He told us he was not permitted to give out any information on Captain Darden, which is most unusual.

*"We followed up with some personal friends,
however, and were able to learn a good bit more.
It seems Captain Darden is rather close to General
Markham, the Commandant. We shared a pint with
Colonels Tirada and Hackman, who apparently knew
something about Darden's current assignment, but when
they queried the personnel system, what it told them made
no sense to them either, so they went directly to General
Markham."*

"Yes, and so?"

*"And so, Signor da Silva, it seems that Captain
Darden has been court martialed and is serving a
sentence of 30-40 years in the Charleston Combined
Naval Brig for removing his wife from a Georgian prison
and then killing her, sir."*

"What!?"

*"We agree, sir, it sounds bizarre. What is
stranger still, is that Captain Darden's entire case has
been classified. Even the Commandant didn't have
access to it until we raised the issue."*

Da Silva's vision began to swirl. This could not
be true. Not possible. Could it?

*"Thank you, very much, Colonel. You have gone
to even more trouble than I imagined. I am in your debt,
and at your service to return the favor at the first
opportunity. Good day to y--."*

*"--Signor? Signor? I'm sorry, sir, but that's not
quite all. You see, I also called an American attorney in*

Charleston who has handled a rather delicate matter for us recently. He called the brig to seek an interview with Captain Darden. It seems he's not there, never has been.

The Warrant Officer who handles the prison's records division swears he never arrived three weeks ago as the list indicates and when he himself inquired about Darden's whereabouts to the Pentagon, his orders were to keep the Darden file on record, but to make no further inquiries."

November 21

Two days later, Don Alberto sat on a bench near the Jefferson Memorial. It was just after 7:00am, and the suddenly frigid weather meant no tourists and only the hardiest of joggers going by. He waited patiently for his old friend, his overcoat collar turned up, but otherwise oblivious of the cold and wind whipping the few dead leaves and litter past his feet. As focused as he was on the subject of the conversation he was about to have, he wondered what kind of defect must exist in human DNA to cause otherwise responsible people to leave rivers, even oceans of litter in their paths through life. It was a mystery he would not unravel anytime soon.

A few minutes later he was joined by Gonsalvo, fresh off a flight from Madrid.

"So, my friend. Help me unravel this thing, in which my son-in-law has murdered his wife and my beloved Maria. This cannot be true."

"Indeed, Don Alberto. In one sense, it is indeed true. But that is barely the beginning."

———————————

When the two men finished their conversation almost 90 minutes later, they stood, embraced, and left their bench, walking quickly in opposite directions. By noon, Gonsalvo was climbing to 35,000 feet on his way back to Madrid. Da Silva was in his office, composing his resignation letter.

A marvel of brevity, it contained only two sentences, respectful in tone, but silent on any and all details. He was careful to deliver it to the new Ambassador personally, with a short statement of gratitude for his opportunity to serve his King and nation, but again, no clue to his immediate plans.

Three hours later, at the big desk in his home, he had made several more phone calls. With what he knew now, he would waste no time. The anger that flared as he sat on the park bench and listened to Gonsalvo's story now burned with the fine blue flame of a welder's torch. He would control the anger, master it with what was for him, an ancient and honored creed.

Justice. Always justice. Systems of laws and their enforcement are there to maintain it. Use them while we may, but when they fail, we move outside the system. Death by evil ones must be met by death *of* evil ones, whether by the system or by individuals.

("In this case, the system has not worked -- will not work. They took my child, the most precious thing I have created in this life. They must pay...with interest.")

Now, tempered by that focused flame of blue heat, Don Alberto Contreras da Silva would balance the scales, and restore the status quo ante.

Step One would be the recovery of James Darden. In this, he would need help, first just to find his son-in-law.

November 22

A short cab ride down Connecticut Avenue deposited Don Alberto in front of The Palm Restaurant. There would be no rib eye or prime rib dinner tonight, but in a back booth in the bar he shared his new information with General Markham over a single glass of Pando, one of his country's dryer sherries. The aging Spaniard recited his story, his English cadences cold and spare, only slightly softened by the rhythms and lisps of his Castilian upbringing. The General listened with increasing alarm, then with increasing anger.

"Jim Darden is a fine young man, one of our best. If what you say is true, he's been railroaded, probably by the people we sent him out there to identify. What's clear is that this came from the very top of the command structure – else I'd have heard about it, and would have had to approve it. I didn't..

"You can rest assured we won't leave him out on his own. We don't do that in the Corps...period."

That said, the Commandant of the United States Marine Corps made his own phone calls, the first two from right there in the back booth. Though Markham kept his voice low, Don Alberto knew he would not want to have been on the other end of those orders and suffer the consequences of any delay in carrying them out.

Executing the General's orders took more than a day. Nonetheless, 27 hours later, it was done.

The Corps has its own cadre of Special Forces, men and women who have much more than special training. They also have special access, special sources of information, special ways of shining small beams of light into the darkest of secret places.

Eighteen hours into their search, one of those sources produced an interesting piece of information.

A recently retired Marine Special Ops officer who lived in McLean, Virginia, had a neighbor, a mid-level technical functionary in one of the defense contractors who had always wanted to be a CIA field agent, but who had been rejected five times in 16 years by the Agency's personnel people, despite what he believed were admirable qualifications.

Frustrated for years, Alexander Soltzer did the next best thing. He surrounded himself with friends, neighbors, and acquaintances who really did work in the world of espionage and secret skullduggery.

He bragged to his "civilian" friends that he even had two close buddies who were "wet ops" agents, whose job was to "take out" enemies and enemy agents around the world. But his very favorite activity was sharing bits and bites of his vast array of "top secret" stuff with active duty and retired military types, stuff even *they* didn't know, and thus impress them as a "deep insider."

Soltzer was obnoxious to many of his claimed "buddies." He suffered immensely from "small man syndrome," saying and doing anything he could to appear bigger, tougher, more important than he was. Virtually all his neighborhood friends believed (or hoped) at least 50% of his so-called "inside dope" was imaginary.

Nonetheless, from Soltzer, retired USMC Col. Anthony Calcavecchia learned that another of the man's neighbors, Army Delta Force Col. John Strallick had just been given an assignment – he would leave the following morning for Germany to grab "a wayward Marine who'd been spying for the Soviets" from Wiesbaden, take him to a secret CIA "detention house" in Northern Europe, and there to "strain him and drain him."

Soltzer was particularly proud of himself for extracting this gem from Strallick. It had taken him an entire evening of fawning and probing, plus a full bottle of Louis XIII cognac, which had set him back $375. He was certain that shared with the right active duty types, this gem would raise his "stock" among them, and expand his access.

Calcavecchia really was impressed. So much so that he immediately contacted Major Allen Hershfeld, a key man on General Markham's personal staff.

Hershfeld was a master at connecting seemingly unrelated dots, and given his order to help locate Captain Jim Darden, he began doing just that. The coincidence about the "wayward Marine" was too much to be a coincidence.

It was less difficult to obtain a list of the seven secret prisons and interrogation "holes" the CIA had been using in Europe, since September 12, 2001. Four were in Northern Europe. The question was which one?

Flight Plans filed by all US aircraft leaving Wiesbaden over the past three weeks were also accessible. Two had listed Charleston, SC as their destinations, both on the same day. The larger plane, a C3 transport, had revised its route and destination 20 minutes prior to scheduled take-off, and instead carried a short passenger list of Congressmen and staffers to Paris.

The second, a civilian twin-jet had filed for Charleston, but apparently never arrived.

Hershfeld was in charge of the Commandant's research team. His team did its homework, vacuuming every scrap of data they could find. Their cramped "war room" in the second Pentagon basement was littered with six computers and hundreds of scraps of paper, to say nothing of coffee cups, Krispy Kreme bags, and one lonely but fragrant wrapper from a Subway 12-inch BMT sub.

Hershfeld was meditating on the Gulfstream take-off that never reached Charleston. The others on the team recognized the Major's body language, leaning way back in his chair, and his glazed-eye expression and knew not to interrupt his thoughts.

("The Gulfstream 450 has a range of 4,350 miles at mach 0.8, with a payload of what, 1,600 pounds with a full load of fuel? That's barely enough to get to Charleston from Wiesbaden without extra fuel...no margin for weather or winds....")

After perhaps 12 or 13 minutes locked in that stance, he suddenly sat bolt upright.

"Billy! Get on the horn to Wiesbaden tower control. See if they can get hold of the fuel truck log for departure day."

Staff Sgt. Billy Crudup understood immediately, probably because he was only a tick or two behind Hershfeld in his own meditative powers. Ten minutes later he had the data Hershfeld was looking for.

The plane had taken on fuel sufficient for about 3,400 miles. Quickly Crudup drew to two circles on his computer map, both centered at Wiesbaden, one with a radius of 3,400 miles, one with half that.

If its actual plan was a one-way trip of 3,400 miles, there was no CIA facility within 100 miles of an adequate landing field. If it was a round trip, however, one facility lay 1606 miles from Wiesbaden -- and only 6 miles from an old Soviet military airport -- in Northern Finland.

———————————

Jim Darden had known pain. He had known uncertainty. He had known the great fear that he was inadequate to answer the call, the challenge that confronted him. He had, however, never experienced the fatigue of long suffering…the slow drip, drip of his strength and resolve as skillful people drained him of his every resource. This was new, and it was both frightening and depressing.

What drained more of his inner being than anything else, however, was none of the above. It was confusion, ignorance, an almost childlike innocence.

He didn't know what these people were after. He had never sold the secrets of his country, never even imagined doing such a thing. He knew, perhaps better than most, that his country was far from perfect. He remembered Churchill's description of democracy -- the very worst form of government -- until one compares it with its alternatives.

He'd listened to a recording of Janice Joplin singing "freedom's just another word for nothing left to lose," and he'd related, though her star rose and fell before his time.

But now he knew the deadly combination of pain, fatigue, and fear, and like many before him who had been driven to the edge of that edge, he was ready to agree -- to agree with almost anything, just to stop the punishment and get some sleep.

Despite the fear of being at the very end of his limits, the cold shivering certainty that he was just about ready to give up anything and everything he had believed in, there was a darker place in the deep pit of his soul that haunted him when everything his torturers had done to him was over.

It was only then, in the silence of solitude, alone in his cell, no sounds, no motion, no slightest movement of the frigid air to distract him, that it returned.

The beatings…their sound deafening, though their decibel count was small; frantic, to be sure, but fragile. Their rhythm increasing with the panic behind it, first the beatings alone, then the in the silences between them, the small, muffled, barely audible cries between the taps of the flashlight against the rotted iron pipe. Inches from his face, inches from his clutching, tearing, impotent grasp. Then the whistle of the escape valve, as the onrushing water forced all the air from the pipe.

"Maria-a-a-a-a-a!!!!"

If only he had known.

His four interrogators sat around a plastic table, four coffee mugs half-drained, and a globe-trotting box of Entennman's chocolate-covered donuts half-devoured.

Their mood was somber, a kind of seriousness that bordered on sorrow. None of the four liked taking apart a fellow American, even one who had sold America out to an enemy. None of them could accept or forgive a traitor, but none of them was anxious to delve too deeply into a traitor's motivations, especially if they'd been based in disagreement with his own country's government. They had enough disagreements themselves.

There was a lull in the conversation, a silence that served only to deepen the pall over their mission. Hoover finally broke the silence, and later the others would agree that while he'd given voice to it, all had been thinking the same thing.

"Gentlemen, forgive me for injecting a note of doubt in this assignment, but facts, hunches, and my own integrity require it. I'm beginning to believe the jarhead might be telling the truth."

Gribbner looked hard at his team mate, using his enormous powers of assessment. He'd grown to trust Hoover's judgment on a long list of previous assignments. But then, he and Hoover had never disagreed before.

"What makes you believe that, Steve?"

"The first questions. They're give-aways. A single degree of tonal misfire and we know he's an asshole, one who's sold our country down the river.

"But with Darden, all I got from his tone was innocence."

"Innocence?" Both Hoover and Strallick asked, almost in unison, while Urquit kept his own counsel.

"Not innocence like he's some vestal virgin, for God's sake! Innocence like he was really confused, really thought he'd fallen down some time tube or...or..."

"Yeah, or the rabbit hole..." said both together.

"Right. I believe he was really confused... ...disoriented, and frankly frightened. But not exactly frightened of us -- more like he was in some kind of bad dream where he couldn't relate, you know what I mean? In fact...I'll bet on it."

"OK, friends," Urquit chimed in. *"Suppose our soft-hearted buddy here is right. What does that mean to us? Our mission here? And what do we do about it?"*

An hour later, Steve Hoover led his three team members into Darden's cell. Jim raised his head an inch and almost allowed himself to groan once, but immediately he sensed something was different.

Instead of picking him up and starting the "softening up round," the four men brought in folding chairs and sat down facing his bed. Gribbner released Jim's hands from the handcuffs, and all four watched as he brought his arms forward and rubbed gently, tentatively at his bloody wrists, his stumbling movements those of a man twice his age.

Hoover began, his voice softer than usual, though still somewhat detached and cool.

"Captain Darden, let's say for grins you didn't sell secrets to the Russians. Why do you suppose you're here?"

Jim felt the question go off like artillery inside his head. He was amazed to find himself almost immediately crying like a baby, out loud. He felt the heat of embarrassment, but it was nothing like the searing flame of the question as its flames licked his heart. He cried so hard his first answering words came out one at a time, among sobs and snuffles.

"I'm...here...for...here for...killing...my...wi-wife...Ma...Maria."

"You <u>what?</u>" Gribbner and Urquit asked together.

Slowly, haltingly, he began to recount the horror at the Batumi pier...

...but was interrupted three minutes later, by a rapid knock at the door by one of the eight facility guards, who opened it from outside.

"Sorry gentlemen. We have visitors!"

"Shit!" Gribbner said, and the four men left Jim's cell.

The Commandant had rousted 36 members of 1st and 3rd FAST Companies. Within two hours they were deployed from Naval Air Station Norfolk, ferried first by jets to Keflavik, then by three Navy MH-53E Sea Dragon helicopters fitted with extra internal fuel tanks to Finland.

At this moment two of them made awesomely loud landings within feet of the front door while the third remained stationary perhaps 100 feet above, its weaponry trained on the same front door.

Twenty-four armed marines jumped from the copters on the ground, and took up positions surrounding the building, weapons at the ready. At their center was Craig Minter, a no-nonsense officer with Captain's eagles on his shoulders. When he spoke, the guards blocking their entry into the old concrete horsebarn were impressed -- and nervous.

"Gentlemen, you are holding a United States Marine who has been wrongly convicted of a crime, though not the crime you are holding him for. His conviction has been overturned, and all charges against him have been dismissed. I am holding orders signed by the Commandant to relieve you of your custody of Marine Captain James Darden, which I offer for your inspection. We want him, and we want him now. You will stand down, and take us to him, or within 10 seconds we will stand you down."

Only about five of those seconds ticked away before the first of the four guards lowered his weapon and executed a left face to assume an escort position. The others quickly followed suit, none of them finding it necessary to study the Captain's papers -- or use up the full ten seconds.

At the Captain's orders, the Marines immediately located all interrogators and guards. Within seconds they were gathered into a single room and lined up, spread-eagled against one wall. Each was searched extremely thoroughly. A whispered order was relayed to three other members of the General's team, and resulted in quick action.

Most weapons, but more particularly, all communication devices were confiscated immediately. A thorough search of the entire facility removed all cell phones, computers, radios. There were no land-line phones. They'd have taken matches had they feared smoke signals.

When the search was completed, the Captain turned to Gribbner and Hoover, the two interrogators nearest him.

"We'll be taking the Captain. You men and your security guards will be our guests here for awhile. No duress, no questioning, no hardship duty or punishment detail of any kind. Just a little vacation from the world for two weeks, maybe three, then you can go home.

"Hope you have a few decks of cards, boys. It'll probably seem longer."

With that, he turned on his heel and left in two of the copters, while twelve FAST Team members remained behind.

Chapter Thirty-Nine
La Gomera, Canary Islands

November 25
San Sebastian

The tiny island off the coast of Morocco has been one of the world's never-ending geopolitical contests. Spain and Morocco have argued over it since the 15th century, when Christopher Columbus stopped here on his way to America to have the Pinta repaired.

San Sebastian, its capital, faces east, toward Tenerife, and receives visitors on the ferry from Los Cristianos. The volcanic island is small, and mountainous, its few beaches rather narrow and giving way immediately to deep Atlantic waters. San Sebastian has seen few cruise ships docking at the small port village of 7000 souls for decades, none in the past 20 years. Tourists have to really want to get there.

On the Calle Lomo del Claro, just north and high above the village, is a lovely villa owned by Signor Don Alberto da Silva and his father and grandfather before him. It is a very private retreat offering sweeping views of the sea but more important, absolute peace and privacy.

The Padrone and his son-in-law had arrived very late last night on one of Tenerife's private water taxis.

Both men had been exhausted, and had made no conversation while traveling.

"Tomorrow morning will be soon enough," Don Alberto had said, and Jim had been grateful for the silence.

In fact, the next day, and three more days came and went before he next saw da Silva. A doctor had arrived to tend to his wounds and offer him a supply of pain killers. He spoke gently, telling Jim that had he not been in the best physical condition prior to his "interrogations," his injuries might have been much worse. As it was, he could anticipate a complete recovery – in time.

Other than that, his only contact was with Esperanza, a house servant at least 70 whose English was halting, but whose authority was not.

"You will rest. Breathe. Eat. Sleep,with hope for no dreams. Notice only that each morning is today -- and you are alive in it. Nothing more, si?"

For three days and nights he had tried to do precisely that. He could not prevent the dreams, but each night when they awoke him, he cried again, then fought them, pushed them back, and slept again.

Now the two men sat on the stone veranda overlooking the village and the sea beyond. The morning was crystalline, the blues of water and sky, the air so warm and sweet it might have been perfume. The lush greens of palms and pines and the white stucco of buildings, the red of their roofs, all made a sparkling palette, a little paradise.

Despite the beauty, the new freedom, the ebbing of the pain from his beatings, and the delicious breakfast he'd just finished, there was little happiness in either man's heart. In fact, so far the two had exchanged few words.

Esperanza silently recovered the breakfast dishes and refilled their coffee mugs from an insulated pot.

"Gracias, Esperanza. You may leave the pot. We won't be needing you for several hours, so you can go down to the village while the market is full. Some fish for this evening, some good bread, a few Sevilla oranges, si?"

"Si, Don Alberto, pronto."

When she had gone, he turned slowly to face Jim, both hands gently encircling his coffee mug. He looked deeply into Jim's eyes while Jim at first avoided the gaze.

"You have been to Hell."

Jim nodded silently, swallowing painfully. There was no way he was going to be able to have this conversation without revisiting that Hell. Still...

"I have learned a good deal about what happened," Don Alberto said, gently, *"... perhaps more than even you know. You can fill in my gaps, I can fill in yours. I know it will be difficult."*

Three hours later, both men had been to Hell's deepest pits -- and back. Don Alberto had long since shed his tears for his lost daughter, but today, Jim cried aloud as he listened to what his father-in-law had learned about Maria's death. As his story drew to a close, he sighed and paused, as if to digest what was so very indigestible.

"There was little left of her body. The pressure of the water drowned her quickly enough, but it also pulled much of her blood and flesh off her body and into the ship's storage tank. What was recovered from the pipe was barely recognizable as human."

Jim covered his face with his hands.

"I failed her," he said softly. *"I failed so many ways...in my mission... and I killed her."*

Don Alberto moved suddenly across the table, grabbing Jim's left wrist and pulling it from his eyes, the two men's faces inches apart.

"Make that the last time you will ever say that -- to me or to anyone. Do you understand?"

He didn't wait for Jim to respond.

"She was murdered by others, who planned the entire sequence of events. Planned them, arranged them, scheduled them, provided the props, everything. You were merely their pawn, an accomplice. Witless, perhaps, at least for the moment.

" As to your mission, your reports to your Commandant were not everything he needed, but neither were they useless. He continues to make progress, despite your absence…

"…Finally, as to your career as a Marine, I have spoken at length with your Commandant. He decided, and I agreed, that his best course of action was to arrange an immediate discharge, honorable, of course. You are no longer a United States Marine."

Don Alberto stopped for a moment, letting those last words hang in the air between them. Jim felt their stab penetrate his heart. When he replied, it was as if he hadn't heard the last statement at all.

("I was such a damned fool. Witless? Not exactly, but maybe something worse. I knew Major Akers was a complete asshole, and that he had a chip on his shoulder the size of an anvil – toward me. But I believed, when the chips are down, any man who wears the uniform of the United States would put his country, and his fellow citizens first. Witless? I might as well have been…and every time I think about it, I want to hurl.")

"…For that…" Don Alberto continued, softly, sadly, *"… you may well be ashamed, and even suffer that shame for the rest of your life. I cannot change that, though I do not blame you for what they did. You did everything you could do to save her from the consequences of her own passion for you and of her own foolishness. You loved her with honesty and truth. That is my belief and I will carry it to my grave.*

Don Alberto stopped, letting those last words sink in. When he resumed, he did so in a different tone, the hard edge of commitment and purpose evident in histones and cadences.

Today, James Darden, we have work to do, work that will require your skills and your anger, but not your shame or sorrow."

Jim pulled his wrist free from Don Alberto's grip, and the older man returned to his chair. In a span of perhaps 10 seconds Jim forced the heat of his guilt to disappear, replaced by a chilled silence where there had been whirling emotion.

Don Alberto watched the transformation with satisfaction. Reaching under the table, he found a folder at his feet and brought it up, opened it, and passed a trio of pages across the glass to Jim.

"For what we must do, you will need this…"

They were discharge papers. An honorable discharge from the United States Marine Corps, signed by General Markham himself, along with a personal note. They had been drawn up in response to a very passionate, very personal request from Don Alberto to the Commandant.

Jim felt shock, but only for a moment, as the idea sank in. He was free. Not that he had sought freedom from the Corps, or even imagined it for at least another year, perhaps two or more. Still, here it was. He was suddenly just Jim Darden, American. It was stunning.

The note explained the discharge, praised his service, and assured him of his country's undying gratitude.   It invited him to visit at the General's home in Virginia *"...when time and circumstance permit.. Semper fi."*

Jim studied the pages, then locked eyes again with Don Alberto.

"Yes sir. I <u>do</u> have work to do."

"No, Signor James. You do not. <u>We</u> have work to do. We shall do it separately or together. I would prefer together, though I cannot force you to work with me."

Jim started to shake his head, but Don Alberto continued.

"You will find that I have resources beyond your own. These may prove invaluable, even indispensable. As to my motivation, it is as strong as your own...if not stronger."

Jim raised an eyebrow, which the old man understood.

"Granted, she was your wife, but she was my only child. If you were already a father, you might understand."

This was no time to argue fine points of motivation. Jim lowered his head for a moment, a sign of mute assent.

"When do we begin?" he asked.

The older man leaned forward in his chair, placing both hands on the table.

"We have already begun."

"Oh? But there are several of them. Who is first?"

Don Alberto shook his head.

"Dealing with them one at a time would be difficult, if not impossible. The news of one's dispatch would alert the others -- they would go to ground and we would have to chase them -- perhaps around the world. They have resources too. No... I have another plan, and as I said, while you were imprisoned, I have put the wheels in motion. We shall meet them all in the same building, deal with them in the same room."

"What?!" Jim didn't hide his surprise.. *"How?"*

"Greed. Avarice. Lust. Covetousness. Corruption. Traits they all share, traits that will draw them together."

Jim's open hands curled into fists, white-knuckled, then relaxed.

"Whatever. I want them all. How doesn't matter."

Da Silva didn't move a muscle. When he spoke, it was with a quiet intensity barely above a whisper, but Jim heard every word, every syllable.

"It matters to me. It matters a great deal, and I am not certain what you mean by having them 'brought in.' I mean for them to die. In fact, their death is little more than anticlimax. What happens on their way to death is crucial...to me."

Jim felt an involuntary shiver run up his spine. He felt the heat of the older man's intensity, found it truly frightening.

"What do you have in mind?"

Don Alberto pulled himself forward again, resting his elbows on the table, closing his eyes, as if to see the scene he had planned. He remained silent for a small eternity, then opened his eyes and stared into Jim's, a cold fire burning within.

"Viprotin. The embassy doctor. Roberts. The military man, Akers. And Ambrose. Each will die in the presence of the others, but each will die in a way that balances the wheel of his own evil, his own sins. And each will wish for death well before he finds it, my son, just as our Maria suffered before she went to God."

Jim sat very still and looked away. His eyes slowly scanned the beach and small port area below them, but focused on nothing. When he returned his gaze to the white-haired Spaniard, what echoed in his own ears were the words "my son," a phrase which he had not heard in years, and which did not escape his attention.

Finally, slowly, he reached his hand across the table, his eyes and Don Alberto's locked on each other's. The older man's grip was dry, steady, and strong.

"Together, then..." was all Jim said. It was enough.

Chapter Forty
Georgia

November 28
An Invitation

Peter Ambrose was in his office when the courier arrived. His new secretary interrupted his conversation with Roberts with a trio of short stabs at his intercom -- a signal that something was important.

He waved Roberts to silence and picked up the phone.

"Yes Angela?"

"Sir, there's a courier here with a something for you. He says it must be delivered personally – 'for your eyes only.'"

Ambrose sat up a little straighter. *"Has he been checked through security?"*

"Yessir, no problems."

"Well, send him in then..."

"Uh, well, sir, I'm not supposed to do that. He says he has to deliver the -- eh, the envelope to you alone, sir, with no one else present."

The Ambassador became quite thoroughly focused. He covered the phone mouthpiece and turned to Roberts.

"Something I have to handle, here. Let's resume our little talk later..." he checked his watch... *"...come back after 4:15, ok?"*

"Fine, sir," Roberts said, making a mental note to find out what he could about this interruption. It was definitely not business as usual.

As he left the Ambassador's office, however, nothing was out of place. Angela smiled at him as he left, her usual plastic smile, and there was no one else around, waiting to go in. (*"Oh, well, I guess I'll have to pay for it again. Damn!"*)

When he'd turned the corner and headed down the stairs to his own office, the courier came out of the men's room 30 feet down the hall, and walked quickly back to the Ambassador's office. Angela waved him on and he went straight through the closed door to deliver his envelope.

"Well, well..." said Ambrose. *"What have we here?"*

"Sorry sir. I have no idea. I'm just following instructions. I'm to ask you to open and read the contents while you are totally alone, and then burn the contents, to make totally certain no one else learns of their existence."

Ambrose was suddenly all ears. He smiled at the courier, a poor attempt at a Cheshire cat smile, but behind it was a tiny alarm bell, tinkling so softly only he could hear it.

"Please sign here, sir."

"I'm to sign for a message I've never received?"

"It may be unorthodox, sir, but my orders are to produce proof of delivery to you personally."

Peter studied the receipt form closely before signing it. It was simple enough -- just a receipt. He signed with an abbreviated squiggle, much more hurried and indecipherable than normal.

"Thank you sir. Have a good day."

"Yes, well..."

The courier smiled, the briefest, tiniest flash of teeth, and he was gone.

Ambrose looked the envelope over carefully, suddenly wondering if the courier had actually handled it...or...yes, of course he had. *("OK, there's no anthrax on the outside....")*

Still, he opened it slowly, carefully, even deciding not to inhale while he did so.

The contents were a single sheet of fine vellum, translucent, obviously expensive, very high quality stuff.

The ink was lovely, a deep black with a classy gloss, the letters hand drawn by an expert calligrapher.

THE RIGHT HONORABLE AMBASSADOR
PETER AMBROSE

THE HONOUR OF YOUR PRESENCE IS REQUESTED AT A GATHERING OF UNIQUELY RESPECTED LEADERS AT THE DIGA PALACE. WE SHALL CONVENE PROMPTLY AT 3:00 PM ON SATURDAY, DECEMBER 17.

YOU ARE ONE OF A SMALL, EXCLUSIVE GROUP INVITED TO PARTICIPATE IN A WEEKEND OF FAR-REACHING DELIBERATIONS ON THE ISSUES AND OPPORTUNITIES FACING THE WORLD TODAY – AS WELL AS SOCIAL ACTIVITIES BEFITTING THE STATURE AND SOPHISTICATION OF THE PARTICIPANTS.

THE NATURE OF THE GATHERING REQUIRES THAT IT BE ENTIRELY PRIVATE AND CONFIDENTIAL. ANY FOREKNOWLEDGE OF IT BY ANYONE ANYWHERE IN THE WORLD WHO IS NOT AN INVITED PARTICIPANT WILL RESULT IN ITS IMMEDIATE CANCELLATION. THANK YOU FOR YOUR COMPLETE DISCRETION.

HIS ROYAL HIGNESS, LION OF BASHIR, SERVANT OF ALLAH, KING KHALID IBN AKHBAR

"Damn! Son of a bitch!"

Ambrose was wide-eyed as he re-read the caligraphed invitation. He rubbed his fingers along the printed surface of the vellum, feeling the slightly raised letters, as if to certify their reality.

Not only was the invitation itself a wonder, but he literally tingled as he studied the signature at the bottom of the page.

"Akhbar is...is what? The richest man on the planet? The one man who can make the mucky- mucks at Exxon-Mobil and Shell dance a samba any time he pleases? And I'm invited? Damn!"

He sat back in his chair and let his eyes drift upward into a middle-distance fog. It was a complete surprise, to be sure, but immediately he began imagining that it shouldn't have been.

("In fact, you should have been expecting something very much like this for some time now, Peter. It's high time you were on the inside, instead of out here on the edge of nowhere. This, my good man, is the inside of the inside. And you're part of it!"

He carefully re-folded the vellum and returned it to its envelope, tucking it gently, almost reverently, into his jacket's breast pocket. Burn it, hell! He would keep it with him, next to his heart, until the 17th[st].

Nineteen days. He giggled as his fevered brain clicked on an old TV ad for Heinz ketchup, the red oozing out of the bottle with exquisite slowness.

"An-ti-ci-pa-a-a-tion!" the choir sang. The coming eleven days would be delicious indeed.

———————————

Different invitations for different folks. Akers' invitation came from a man wearing the uniform of a Colonel in the Georgian Army, ibn fact a Colonel who reported directly to Viprotin, and one whose uniform sprouted enough chest salad to make the American feel jealous, cheated.

Akers had never met the man before, but the two men had found themselves seated on adjoining barstools at the American Recreation Association. The Georgian had been there longer, and was at least a couple of rounds ahead when Akers arrived. The Georgian's English was excellent, a good thing for Akers' command of Georgian ended with "where is the men's room?"

Their conversation had wound on into the evening, growing warmer and more intimate as the vodka and bourbon loosened their reserves.

Akers was growing absolutely fond of the Colonel, a rare phenomenon, especially with one who outranked him. Pyotr Shalikashvili was not merely polite and friendly. He was also truly intelligent and wise beyond his years. The evidence? He agreed with damn near everything Akers thought and said. Not everything, of course, but a good 90% of Akers' statements brought a hearty agreement and praise.

Finally, 'Pete,' as John had taken to calling him, lowered his voice and leaned in.

"Listen, my friend. I have an idea. It is crazy, of course, how do you say, 'out of bound?,' but what are you doing on the 17th[t] of this month?"

"I'm not sure. Why?"

"Well, because there is a gathering. A very special gathering of men like us. Like you and me. Special gathering, special men."

"And you're inviting me?"

'Pete' leaned closer. *"I am. But with great caution."*

"Why great caution?"

"Because the gathering is entirely silent, entirely secret. It's a great gift to those invited, but if any word gets out, there could be trouble. Big trouble."

John Akers listened for nearly ten minutes, while 'Pete' whispered a detailed, delicious menu of activities and arrangements for a night of friendship, recreation and earthly delights among the truest warriors of Eastern Europe, and "a few of our brothers from across the ocean -- men like you."

John Akers hadn't often thought of himself as a "true warrior," but if Shalikashvili did, it was enough. An honor, even. And God knows there hadn't been enough of those in his lifetime.

For Viprotin, the enticement was still different. It was one of the Prime Minister's Executive Assistants, Gagne, a Georgian immigrant whose ancestors were

French and Prussian, and a man who had spurned the warrior culture for the subtler gears and mechanisms of diplomacy. He was a man educated in the ivied halls of Oxford and the Sorbonne, a student of Premananda and a host of other Buddhist and Hindu teachers. He had learned many lessons at their feet, though perhaps not their most urgent one, which was to raise himself to a position of no preferences, no judgments among alternative life paths.

Gagne still had preferences and judgments. One of his most ardent was his disdain for the history of war and warriors. It had not been difficult for the aged Spanish Consul to convince him that General Viprotin was nothing more than a violent animal, a threat to all that is civilized and peaceful.

His own reputation within the wheels of the Georgian government was that of the supreme intellect, the master of complex issues, the philosopher who saw beyond sight.

He appealed, softly, but directly to Viprotin's damaged and grieving sexual ego.

"It is time for the Bear of Georgia to show himself -- to reclaim his place as lead stallion among the great herd. And fortune smiles, as the Saudi Sheikh has created the perfect opportunity."

"Oh?" The General sounded a bit dubious, even hesitant.

"Indeed! He has invited a select group of military men to a secluded palace, for a weekend

meeting. Totally quiet, totally discreet, but very much a
scene requiring a lead stallion. You know this can only
be led by one man, General."

"Mmmm. There will be plenty of women there?
New ones?"

"As I understand it, women, girls, boys, virtually
anything one might desire! And General, you <u>are</u> quite,
eh, healed from your recent injuries, are you not?"

"Well, of course! What do you think? Though for
a time I might have feared that the bitch's aim was too
good. It was a rude shock, you understand?"

Gagne saw the need to change gears, which he
did effortlessly, seamlessly.

"Of course, General. Perhaps...it is too
soon...for your return to this...arena. After all, it's only
a couple of weeks away -- the 17st. You might need more
time, more practice, perhaps more treatments."

Except for Gagne's stature, Viprotin might have
struck him for that remark. He certainly felt the blood
rise. But even that was a kind of private encouragement.
He felt himself ready.

"Perhaps nothing, you imbecile! You forget
whom you are addressing!"

"Of course, sir! A thousand pardons!"

Chapter Forty-One
La Gomera

December 10
To Sleep...Per Chance to Dream...

Jim twisted himself into a new position. The La Gomera nights were warm, his pillow damp with sweat. He was not quite asleep, not quite awake, but in that dimlit netherplace that disturbs the peace of the night and leaves a slow pain the morning after.

His demi-dream had no images, no sights, only the soft sound of voices, both of them his own.

(*"Justice. I want it -- for Maria. Our system is supposed to provide it, but it has failed. It is up to me to make it happen. Five men must pay the price for what they've done. It is a worthy goal, and I need no higher purpose. Justice for Maria. For myself. For my career, my reputation, my mission."*)

With that, he awoke more fully, and thought of his mission. True, he had reported to General Markham what he had learned, on his way from Finland back to the States, and before joining his father-in-law on La Gomera. Markham had praised him and promised action would be taken. What spoiled his sleep, however, was the very clear awareness that he had not dug deep enough, had not provided the kind of solid information the Commandant had sought.

He rolled again, and fought his way back into semi-sleep, his face seeking, but not finding a dry place on the pillow. The sheet grew tighter around him, twisted into a cotton prison. The second voice spoke.

"Revenge is what you want. Admit it. Simple, blood revenge. You have taken an oath to uphold the Constitution and laws of the United States, and yours is still a country of laws, of civilization, checks and balances, safeguards for freedom known nowhere else in the world.

"You are not the system, but having judged the system a failure, you simply move outside the law and substitute your own ego, and your own personal violence for it. You flatter yourself with bullshit references to justice, when what you really want is nothing more than an eye for an eye -- a 'justice' that has failed for millennia."

His eyes closed tighter as he struggled with the sheet, groaning softly before surrendering to a new position of greater discomfort.

(*"Not true. Citizens must act to fight lawbreakers when the system fails. I support the system. It's what I've dedicated my life to, but no system is perfect. When it fails, of course we move outside -- to right the wrongs, to restore a balance, to assure the triumph of right over wrong, of decency over greed, lust, and murder."*)

The second voice grew more strident.

("What you are planning is nothing more than new murders. New killing to 'balance' old killing, when there is no such balance. The Israelis have tried this since 1948, and look where it's gotten them. Your scripture doesn't say 'thou shalt not kill most of the time.' It doesn't say 'thou shalt not kill except really bad guys.' It says 'thou shalt not kill.'")

His head began to throb, the pain nearly enough to awaken him, but not quite.

("Listen...) said the first voice, it too growing louder. *(...the whole world acknowledges the right of a nation to defend itself, to go to war to protect its citizens, to defeat threats to its sovereignty, its way of life. God knows I'm not a Quaker or a neo-hippy peace-nik or a coward. I'll put myself in harm's way if I have to, to defend my country and defeat its enemies!")*

Now the second voice was shouting.

("Bullshit! This isn't about protecting anybody! It's about taking out five men who made a fool of you, such a perfect fool you accidently killed your wife. It's about killing them to cover your own guilt, your own embarrassment! No amount of high-sounding rhetoric can paper over the fact that this is revenge, pure and simple. It has only the slimmest connection to your mission, which you have not completed. Above all, Captain Darden...above all...it is NOT worthy of you!")

The sweat, the throbbing, the discomfort of his tangled sheets weren't enough to fully wake him, but volume of the debate was.

He untangled himself from the mess he'd made of
the bed and headed for the bathroom where he dried his
sweat-soaked body and then wrapped the towel around
his middle and walked out on to the terrace overlooking
the harbor and town of San Sebastian below.

The night was sweet peace, a soft cooling breeze
barely rustling the palm fronds. He drank in the
fragrance of it, but its very sweetness brought tears to his
eyes. The echoes of a hundred pains in a hundred body
parts, and the yawning emptiness in his heart made the
very beauty of the place a mockery.

The stars were an infinity of pin-prick lights, yet
their numbers could not relieve the darkness of a new
moon night. The breeze died away, so that the air barely
moved, its stillness making the expanse of the island and
sea below him feel smaller, almost more fragile.

"What about Don Alberto?" he asked himself
softly. *"He's got no questions at all, no doubts. He
believes in this 100%. Why the hell should I be tortured
with doubts. Maria was my wife -- she was everything to
me. I killed her -- fell into their trap like a goddamn 12-
year old. I stood there on the pier crying like a baby
while she died, then let them grab me and railroad me,
mute and dumb as a post...."*

He looked up into the vastness, fixing on one star,
then another, before relaxing his focus to take in the sheer
immensity of the night.

In that immensity, his mind refocused, as if for
the first time, on the others. He saw each one parade
before him: Ambrose, Akers, Roberts, the Georgian

Bear, Viprotin, even the drunken Embassy doctor. Each one wore a smile. Each smile dripped with contempt – and satisfaction.

Finally, he closed his eyes and felt himself give way, surrender. He felt his body relax. The arguments that tortured his sleep fell away and shattered like thinnest glass on the tiles at his feet.

What rose in their place was a slow, formless tide, a darkness greater than the night. His eyes still closed, felt, more than watched, as the tide rose into a single great wave, coming out of a calm sea, a rogue, high enough to reach all the way up the hill. It came with a great roar, even to where he stood, and higher still. As it swept over him, all thought fled, all arguments swept away in the deafening rush of it. He felt himself go limp, powerless to resist it, yet powerful for the first time since he had stood on the pier sobbing for help as Maria died beneath his fingertips.

As suddenly as it came, it died, swept away as if by a single great hand. Jim opened his eyes, and saw the calm sea below him, fishing boats barely moving at anchor.

Yet there was something still here, left behind by the force of the wave and his surrender to it. He felt it grow within, a thick, bubbling caldron of heat. Pure sensation, it flowed up out of some deep pit of his core, syrupy smoking lava burning away any part of him that stood in its way.

Something within him began searching, suddenly frantic to understand what this burning thing was. He closed his eyes again and ran through mazes of underground tunnels filled with surging thick-heat lava. The walls of the tunnels were filled with graffiti, fragments of words appearing and disappearing as he rushed by, before the lava scoured and burned them away.

"What?" he cried as he ran. The walls of graffiti gave no answer, but only laughed at him.

"Ha-" one wall said. He ran on, but saw only shapes, fat curves and angles that only barely resembled letters. The only thing he recognized was heat.

"tre-" flew by on another wall, but it made no sense. In fact, nothing did. There was just the heat.

Suddenly he reached the flat, dead end of the tunnels, having run through what seemed like miles of them.

The crackling, burning rush of lava and the noise of his own panic were suddenly silenced, leaving only the intense heat.

There on the wall in front of him was the sixth letter, united with the first five. The word stood before him in letters four feet tall, blazing brightly for the briefest moment before they burned away entirely.

Hatred.

Jim Darden opened his eyes again, found himself still standing on the same terrace above the same town, looking down at the same sea beneath the same moonless night.

"I understand." He said softly.

"Not quite,." said a softer voice. *"Hatred it is. That you see. But know this. It is not some force from outside, some wave that overcomes you, makes you powerless to resist."*

"It comes from within your own being. It...and its consequences...are your choice...and your responsibility."

Jim was silent for several minutes. Thoughts started to form, stumbled, and then disappeared.

Then, in the stillness there on Don Alberto's hilltop terrace, it returned.

The beating. The frantic metallic taps. The muffled, barely audible cries. He shut his eyes and covered his ears with both hands.

Finally, after a long stretch in which the only thing he could hear was his own heartbeat, he simply opened his eyes and said aloud:

"So be it."

He turned and went back to bed – and slept in the blessed silence of simple sleep.

Chapter Forty-Two
Washington

December 12

There is no news in the statement that many, if not most of those who govern us, whether elected or appointed, believe they know what's best for us, even when we don't.

Nor is it a revelation that those who govern us often believe that at least some of the decisions they make must be kept silent…and secret.

Finally, it is no surprise that virtually no one in government acts or makes decisions alone. Virtually all "secret decisions" are thus "conspiracies," whether for good, or not so much.

Is secrecy necessary? While there are reasoned and passionate arguments on both sides of the question, the clear consensus of those in government would appear to be "yes, certainly, absolutely!"

The most popular way to justify the secrecy of any government decision or action is to cloak it in the sacred mantle of national security. The secrecy of goings on within Area 51 in the Nevada desert might be cloaked in the name of both national security and "domestic tranquility," depending….

The more timely question, however, is not whether secrecy is necessary, but whether it is even possible?

The arts and sciences of data storage, security, encryption, etc., are colliding ever more explosively with the competing arts and sciences of computer hacking, social networks, and global access to virtually everything that hackers care to share.

While our Government scrambles to prosecute Julian Assange, it simultaneously carries out recruitment expositions, hoping to attract the very Wikileaks hackers who penetrated our "Berlin Walls" of data security, offering them high salaries and sweet benefits rather than jail sentences, to strengthen the walls rather than tear them down.

In this increasingly volatile global environment, one thing is clear. When two or more "governors" conspire to do something secretly, they must rely on the oldest and perhaps simplest form of protection of their secret: the threat of immediate punishment for anyone who leaks the secret…

…not just capital punishment, either, but a whole family of punishments both cruel and unusual.

Inches from Glory

Jim Darden's sleep was tormented by the horror of his dreams. Presently, Larry Claymore was losing sleep too, having one of his "nervous for nothing" nights. He'd checked and re-checked every detail on a damn-near daily basis, but still lay badly on his pillow, his neck hurting, and his mood growing darker as the night hours crept forward.

Things were going well on all fronts. The President's plan to take silent ownership of the pipeline was nearly executed. He, Larry, would have his share, only a tiny percentage, but more dollars than he'd ever imagined having.

So far the plan's critical ingredient, total silence, was a miracle and a masterpiece, most of it his own doing. He looked forward to an extra bonus from the first American President who would retire from office with an instant multi-billion dollar fortune and a power base even greater than that of the Oval Office after sitting in it for eight long and powerful years!

Larry would be there when the fruit was ripe for the picking, when the new powers were taken up, including the greatest of all -- the power of silence.

Still, this was yet another in a growing string of sleepless nights, and Larry couldn't for the life of him figure out why.

He rose from his bed, padded down the hall to his study, and found his desk chair in the darkness, feeling for the power button on his computer monitor.

When it flashed on, he immediately punched in his password string, logged onto the White House network, and began the process for the hundredth time, checking every possibility.

The Georgians were in place. The important ones had received their fees, and were, for the moment, fat and happy. When the ownership was fully and finally executed, all twelve of them would die, suddenly and tragically. Seven in a plane crash and five in a bold Chechen terrorist attack.

The oil company executives were all in line, having demonstrated their loyalty to the President, (through Larry.)

They had met with Larry several times, very privately, and had contributed their ideas on the exercise of their new powers and prerogatives, once everything was in place and the President was safely out of the White House and a private citizen again.

That was Larry's master stroke. He had fed them an incredible tale, and had done it so skillfully that they had bought it all. They believed they would be "Members of the Board" endowed with both advisory *and* decision-making powers in a new "shadow government" Farr would create, not in Washington, but from several more idyllic spots around the world – spots they would own. Their belief was important -- for the present.

Once again, Larry had peeled back the onion several more layers than the others knew existed. At the heart of things, he would control about 90 percent of the decisions and actions "The Board" would take. The oil guys would be invited to deliberate on perhaps 10 percent of the less consequential issues.

What caused his current bout of sleeplessness wasn't the oil guys and it wasn't the Georgians. Larry knew perhaps better than anyone that the linchpin of the entire plan was silence. Complete silence. It was also the boldest, most fragile, and most magnificent achievement of the whole magilla.

That every single one of the participants should remain totally silent was miracle enough. That no one else in the entire government, or even outside it for that matter, should even suspect what was already nearing completion, was perhaps the greatest political miracle of modern times. He'd engineered it, crafted it, kept it together against a variety of leak threats and dangers, and protected it like a mother lion protected her cubs.

Yet now, as Larry punched the keys to check the details one more time, he felt a shiver run up his spine, causing him to shrug his shoulders almost violently. He could almost imagine himself as a lion, listening in the jungle night air for sounds of danger. The image made him chuckle aloud.

"If you were a lion, old son, you wouldn't be listening for danger, you'd be listening for the arrival of dinner!"

There had been no news on the Marine who'd been over-zealous in his security duties at the Embassy in Tbilisi. What was his name? Garden? No, Darden.

For the record, he'd been safely tucked away in the brig in South Carolina -- in solitary confinement, no visitors, no interaction with other prisoners. The paperwork on his court martial was in a code-restricted file on his hard drive. Still, Larry had taken the fail-safe step to guarantee Darden's silence, by sending in his CIA/NSA team to move the Marine further from any place from which he could be harmful. Where was it they'd taken him? Finland, for God's sake?

There'd been no word from Gribbner. Larry had taken the extra precaution of inventing Darden's treason story to assure that Gribbner and his team members would be properly motivated to finish Darden, quietly and completely.

Maybe he should check. He picked up his secure line phone as he punched the keys on his keyboard to locate the number.

He got no answer. Shit. He tried three other numbers, for the other members of his team. No answer. Damn!

"I knew it. I just fucking knew it!" Even as he grew frantic about what to do next, he felt a curious satisfaction in the realization that he never ever got nervous for nothing.

————————————

What Larry didn't know, was that the phone numbers he had dialed, and which gave him no answer, had indeed rung, in General Markham's office in the Pentagon. The Commandant's team noted the caller's number on each phone's video screen. Pieces of their puzzle were coming together.

Pursuers of the Pursuers

Claymore was at his desk at 6:15am, as usual. He'd scanned the President's morning briefings, updates, situation reports, and schedule, as usual. He wore a look that said "if you want to live beyond the next minute, get the fuck out of my way," -- as usual.

What was beneath the look and the performance however, was very unusual: genuine, honest-to-God, ice-cold fear.

("This is it. Right now. Today...") he thought. *("The day you hoped would never come. The day you've worked your ass off to prevent. The day this whole damn thing could come undone...")*

("...Unless...unless you can find this goddamn Marine and his asshole father-in-law -- and stop them cold.")

Truly, Larry had pulled out all the stops. He'd taken steps, steps he knew could blow up in his face, big time. He'd exceeded his authority by about twelve miles. He'd toughed out a fix that would either solve the problem or create a real international crisis, and he'd done it with over-the-top guts and leverage. Even as he sipped his third cup of coffee and scanned the President's e-mails, the wheels he'd set in motion were turning.

A call to Geoffrey Bowden in London had started the wheels. Catching Bowden at 1:55pm GMT, he'd blown a high hard one past him and after pressing him hard, had set him in motion. Claiming orders from POTUS himself, he literally ordered Bowden into action.

After some brief, but incoherent resistance, Bowden, Head of Britain's MI-5, had agreed to send a team of his wet ops specialists to Georgia, to hunt down four men. Bowden's resistance focused primarily on Don Alberto da Silva. Killing a senior Spanish diplomat with a long history of honorable service and no reputation whatsoever for dirty doings was a clear recipe for international chaos, to say nothing of a quick sacking by an enraged PM.

He had no particular problem with the others: Peter Ambrose, Maj. John Akers, US Army, and Captain James Darden, USMC, recently disguised as a Sergeant, recently assigned to Embassy Security Detail in Tbilisi, recently arrested, tried, and convicted of various crimes against the State of Georgia, recently a prison inmate, and now (Claymore felt sure,) on a dangerous rampage somewhere in Georgia. These he could take down quietly with little fear of the consequences.

All four, Claymore had told him, needed to disappear permanently, and quite urgently. There could be others, American and perhaps even Georgian, who might be found with the four primary targets, and if so, their disappearance was definitely desired collateral damage.

Claymore had leaned hard on Bowden to honor the "historic partnership with the President in matters of mutual interest and the global war against terrorism."

"This is a crucial moment in that ongoing war, Geoffrey. A moment when action must be immediate, and silence must be maintained above all. But then, Geoffrey, that is your particular value and gift to Britain, is it not?"

It was probably important that Claymore had caught him at this early hour. It may even have been important that Bowden had been sleeping off a long week of late nights covering the PM's hind quarters from Liberals and Labor devils who were sniping at him about the ongoing and hopeless messes in Iraq, Afghanistan, Eastern Europe, and Africa, and a long night last night of heavy gin and light tonic with the lads from Southwick, his primary school soccer team.

Whatever, Claymore had reached him at a particularly appropriate moment, one in which his mind was fuzzed, his resistance was weak, and his susceptibility to calls to patriotism was foolishly strong. Bowden had straightened his spine at the American's last reference to Britain, and agreed to send a crack team eastward immediately.

Dick Atwood would lead the team. A more hardened operative was nowhere in the British Commonwealth. As a Colonel in the Queen's Army, Atwood had ruthlessly destroyed several hundred under-prepared Argentines in Maggie Thatcher's holy war to save the Falklands. When he'd come home to her congratulations but no one else's, he left the Army and might have set the Guinness record for blood alcohol content over a period of a year, until Bowden had rescued him.

Atwood had selected three of his best men and after outfitting themselves with all manner of lethal weapons, night vision, surveillance, and related gear, had emplaned eastward from the British airbase near Swansea. Dressed in Savile Row suits, they would arrive in Tbilisi as new staff to the British Embassy, changing into mission outfits and gear once inside the Embassy compound. The plane even carried two Land Rover V8 SUVs for their transportation over and off Georgia's crumbling road system.

Within five hours of Claymore's call, their plane was circling the Tbilisi airport, awaiting permission to land. Their mission was to find out where Ambassador Peter Ambrose had gone off to, find him, and kill him, leaving no traces, no remains. Along with Ambrose, they were to find an aged Spanish diplomat, one Don Alberto da Silva, and a young US Marine, Jim Darden, and cause their eternal disappearance. It was highly likely that all three would be found together, possibly with one or more others. All were to disappear along with all bone, muscle, hair, and DNA. And no one, not one citizen of Planet Earth was to be the wiser.

Chapter Forty-Three
The Diga Palace

December 17
Smoke and Mirrors

The Diga Palace was built in 1762 by a Prussian General who lived for the glory of battle and the spoils to be won, which he considered entirely secondary to the glory.

Nonetheless, he was quite particular about his choice of architects, in this case the highly respected Rene Vallois, the designer whose estates were all the rage along the Loire in France.

Vallois was a brilliant man, well educated, and steeped in the classics, a man of exquisite tastes in all things, from music to food and wine, to women and art. In this commission, however, he accepted the challenge of stepping well out of his own highly developed tastes and ideas, to design a mansion for a client whom he came to describe as "barely out of mastodon loin cloths."

A case of hyperbole, to be sure, but numerous others could testify that Klaus Von Golsch was little more than a beast. He spent his entire life, from age six, killing animals of perhaps 60 species, when he wasn't killing men and occasionally women and children of alien tribes.

He dined on every lower species he killed, and the hoarier legends hold that he occasionally feasted on the roasted thigh and heart of lesser human warriors. What remained today was a set of fine French cutlery, heavy knives and two-pronged forks with handles fashioned of carved and polished bone from Russians and Slovaks subdued by him personally.

Today, the Diga Palace is one of Georgia's historic treasures, but it remains hidden, a thoroughly embarrassing and entirely un-PC national artifact. The character of the place is one reason -- it is a museum of a particular brand of Neanderthal brutality. Secondly, of course, it was built by a foreigner for a foreigner, neither adding a whit to the heritage of the Georgian people.

The building has four stories above ground, surmounted by three towers, and three stories below the surrounding lawns and fields. The ground floor's ceilings rise eighteen feet, its great hall stretching 40x80 feet, festooned with huge chandeliers and guilded mirrors in gold frames, tapestries from earlier centuries than the eighteenth, and finally with the expertly stuffed heads and other parts of more than 90 animals.

Don Alberto had arranged everything to the last detail. As the five "guests of honor" were announced, a crowd of perhaps fifty men and women greeted them with polite applause. Champagne was being distributed by servants in white coats, and the gathering seemed festive and positively normal. Viprotin even noticed with satisfaction the scents of several cigars, pipes, and cigarettes perfuming the room.

In short order, the "Sheikh" played convincingly by a tall, black-bearded Israeli in flowing robes and kefiyah approached each of the special guests and greeted him warmly, asking each to accompany him to another part of the palace for "some special entertainments we have arranged just for you."

General Viprotin was escorted away first, as Don Alberto saw him as the least trusting of the five. As soon as he was out of the hall, a servant carrying a jeroboam of champagne "accidently" bumped into him and quite expertly reached around and jabbed him with a needle filled with a powerful horse tranquilizer.

Viprotin was instantly enraged. He reached for the man's coat and lifted his other arm to smash him, but the servant quickly lifted the heavy bottle and jammed it into the General's face, breaking his nose, and causing his eyes to water heavily, momentarily blinding him. It was enough. After one roar of pain, happily drowned out by the music in the great hall, he slowly slumped against the wall of the hallway and slid down to a sitting position. It took four men to lift his limp form and carry it two levels down to a somewhat darker, but still quite impressive room.

Each time the "Sheikh" returned, his smile was wider, his charm more abundant. One by one he greeted Ambassador Ambrose, John Akers, Roberts, and the Embassy doctor, each time leading them from the great hall for "more appropriate diversions." The same clumsy waiter executed his ineptness four more times, albeit with lesser doses of the tranquilizer.

Each of the five men thus entered the Prussian's private retreat unconscious, and so they remained until all were present, seated in heavy chairs bolted to the floor, bound hand and foot with thick iron bands.

Don Alberto and Jim sat in somewhat more comfortable chairs, facing the five men. The door through which the five men had entered was now locked and barred. A second door behind Darden and Don Alberto would serve as their exit, an underground tunnel winding in a snake-like route extending almost a half-mile to an opening in a tall rock formation near the unused, snow-covered road at the rear of the palace .

Akers was the first to awaken, and the expression on his face reflected bewilderment, then shock, then intense fear, all passing across his eyes in a matter of seconds. He was, perhaps wisely, speechless.

Jim could barely sit still. The sight of the five men before him, bound and defenseless, was almost more than he could bear. He felt an intense heat of pure rage, his knuckles white from gripping the arms of his chair with barely enough force to keep him in it.

He looked across at his father-in-law. Don Alberto da Silva was everything he was not. Stony. Utterly silent. Cold as ice. He would wait.

It was several more minutes before the other captives regained consciousness. Viprotin was the last, having evidently taken even more of the tranquilizer than necessary. As he awakened he felt the square arms of his heavy wooden chair and manacles binding him to it, hand and leg. There was something else, though at first he couldn't say what it was. Something foreign around his still tender genitals. When he opened his eyes, he looked around, recognizing Ambrose, Akers, and Roberts, though not the American Embassy doctor. Then he stared at the two men in front of him, recognizing the younger man, though he had only seen him once before.

Still, he understood his situation, and laughed aloud.

"So, I see that I have been stupid while others have been clever. Congratulations!"

He gazed at the two men seated before him, first one, then the other.

"You must be the bitch's father. She has already taken a piece of me. You want another?"

Don Alberto stared at the General -- a hot fire suddenly burning behind the icy blue of his eyes. He spoke slowly, softly, whether because his own effort to control his rage was as difficult as Jim's or because he was taking every ounce of pleasure possible from this moment.

"Oh, my, yes, General. I will have another piece of you. The biggest piece. I will have your suffering and your death."

At this, the others reacted simultaneously. Ambrose, Akers, and Roberts all spoke at once, almost shouting, while the doctor closed his eyes and fainted.

Da Silva simply allowed their cacophony to run its course and die out, without uttering a word in response. In fact he ignored them entirely, focusing on the General, who sat very still, somehow calm, even defiant.

"So you have me. Proceed...only tell me, is there some victory for you in this?"

Don Alberto leaned forward in his chair, the hatred in his eyes blazing. He spoke even more softly.

"No victory for me, General. Only defeat for evil, for you. Only justice. It is enough."

Viprotin spat onto the floor at Don Alberto's feet.

"Justice, is it!? Whose justice, eh Spaniard? The justice of your tribe over mine? Of your God over mine? Of your power over mine? Of your '<u>moment</u>' over mine?"

Don Alberto rose half out of his chair. Without thinking, Jim reached out to grip his arm, stopping him. Without acknowledging Jim's intervention, his father-in-law sat.

"Somewhere in your soul, Viprotin, you recognize that there is good and evil, decency and brutality, right and wrong. What you and these men did to my daughter led to her suffering and death. The wheels of justice must turn to balance the evil men do, or civilization stops and we all become Godless beasts. It matters little to me what you call it."

Viprotin gave the manacles a huge wrench, letting out a roar of sheer effort, their steel edges cutting into the flesh of his forearms. They held, and finally he relaxed.

"Then do what you will, old man. I have no apologies for my life, not to the likes of you. Go ahead. Shoot me."

Don Alberto's face grew a shade darker, though as Jim watched, there was something else, a veil of sadness across the old man's eyes?

"Shoot you? I think not. My daughter suffered unspeakably before her death. To end your life without suffering requires more mercy than I have. No, General, you will die, but before you do you will know something of her suffering."

He reached down to his left to begin, but as he did, Jim gripped his right arm again.

"Wait, Don Alberto. I have some questions for the General."

Turning to Viprotin, he felt his own rage beginning to dissipate as he remembered his mission, and his obedience to it and to the orders that had sent him to Georgia.

"General. You may be able to help us, help me to end another injustice, one against your own country and countrymen. Tell me what you know about the oil pipeline being built across Georgia."

Viprotin sat back in his heavy chair as blood dripped from his arms and legs where the manacles hat cut into him. He looked at Jim for the first time, and smiled as if he'd just finished a glass of good bourbon.

"I would be delighted, __Sergeant__. Only do tell me, what is in it for me if I do? The old man here seems to confuse vengeance with his notion of 'justice,' and my suffering and death are his keys to both. So which do I forego if I tell you what you want? Suffering or death?"

"I would have to say that would depend on what you can tell me."

To the General's left, Ambrose squirmed again, lowered his eyes and stared at his own manacles.

("How has it come to this? Where did things go wrong? How in hell did this man get out of a military prison and get back into Georgia? Everything I've worked for, for so damn long! Gone! Jesus Christ!")

When he uttered those last words silently, he grew desperate. His mind raced, bouncing off this post and that cushion, a pinball gone mad. Nothing worked, nothing made sense, but somehow there must be a way out of this, some way to salvage...

The smile was gone from Viprotin's face. In its place was utter disdain.

"Here is what I can tell you, __Sergeant__."

He spat again, now at Jim's feet.

Jim released his grip on Don Alberto's arm. The old man reached down again to his left and moved a lever.

Electricity surged through wires under the General's chair and up through a copper loop around his testicles. It was enough to vibrate his entire body as if it were a rag doll. An inhuman sound came from his throat, as if he was choking on his own tongue. The surge lasted ten long, excruciating seconds. The doctor fainted again.

Don Alberto replaced the lever, stopping the current.

The General slumped in his chair, smoke rising from his privates, every fiber of his body shaken loose from its adjoining fiber. He had never felt such pain.

His voice still soft, and now definitely tinged with sadness, Don Alberto turned to Jim.

"How long would you say my Maria suffered in that pipe before she died?"

Jim's mind was suddenly awash with every piece of suffering and death that he had witnessed or caused with his own hands in his deployments as a Marine. Each was a still photo, a slide show running past his eyes, almost, but not quite too fast to focus on each one for a searing moment.

He closed his eyes tightly and shook his head to clear it.

"Thirty, perhaps more."

Don Alberto looked back at Viprotin, as the General raised his wet eyes and returned his stare.

"More, then. Perhaps forty," said Don Alberto softly. It was the only mercy Viprotin would get.

Chapter Forty-Four
US Embassy, Tbilisi

December 17, 3:56pm Local Time

Dick Atwood and his number two, Harry Ramsey, had been passed through security to the Ambassador's Office, having shown both proper identity papers and an "official" cable from the British Prime Minister. Their pinstripe suits were impeccable, and they were every bit the proper Brit foreign service types.

Ramsey was in charge of pressing (and charming) the Ambassador's secretary. Atwood stood by, slowly, imperceptibly, and ultimately invisibly fading into the background (actually sliding off behind the secretary and into the Ambassador's office.

Virginia Kieffer, who was serving as Ambrose's secretary while his permanent assistant was on home leave, was one of perhaps ninety million American women who believe without question that British men are automatically handsome, charming, and incapable of telling a lie, especially when they're being handsome and charming.

Ramsey was all of the above, possessed of an extraordinary charisma that consisted entirely of making other people feel terribly important to him. It was a talent he could turn on and off in an instant, and he used it with devastating success everywhere he went, except at home, where his wife of eighteen years would have none of it.

"Well Virginia, you don't know how glad we are to get here! It's always an honor and a great pleasure whenever my orders take me to your country or even just to work with Americans on our side of the pond."

"Really, Mr. Uhh...?"

"-- Ramsey, my dear. Harold. Please, call me Harry. I must say, Virginia, I've always had the utmost respect for American women's recent achievements in government and diplomacy, but I'm especially awed by one who rises to your level with the additional challenges you face."

"Additional challenges, Harold, er, Harry?"

"Well, you'll have to pardon me for being so forward, but a woman of your attractiveness in such a demanding position might well wish for less beauty. It is, after all, a distraction for the men who have business with you -- almost what your legal system refers to as "an attractive nuisance," one might say."

Virginia blushed, smiled, then suddenly erased the smile, a tiny terror crossing her brow. *("Oh God, I just finished that Greek salad for lunch. I'll bet I've got grape leaves stuck in my teeth!")*

Ramsey continued.

"But where was I? See, I'm distracted already!"

(Virginia licked her teeth as discreetly as possible, but could not help but smile again.)

"We're here on urgent business, actually quite a major dustup, and it's terribly important that we see Ambassador Ambrose as soon as humanly possible. May we count on your help in locating him? The Prime Minister, and. I understand, your own President would be awfully grateful."

"Oh dear, well, I'm not certain I can be much help. You see the Ambassador left the Embassy last evening, and usually he lets me know his every move, but this time he was gone, without a trace!"

"Damn!" said Ramsey. *"That's bloody awful."* (American women expected "damns" and "bloodies" as manifestations of English passion -- it was ridiculous, but those two words were obligatory, he'd learned, in every seduction.)

He lowered his voice and leaned in, conspiratorially.

"But Virginia, work with me a moment. Maybe there is a trace, some little detail that escapes your attention at the moment, busy as you are."

Virginia put on a frown of conspiratorial concentration, thinking as hard as ever she could.

"You know, Harry, you're right, there was something, but I have no idea what it means!"

Ramsey flashed a $16,000 smile, newly refurbished and sparkling, his breath faintly redolent of spearmint.

"Bloody good, Virginia! What is it?"

"Well, a few days ago a courier arrived with an envelope for Mr. Ambrose. Very hush hush, to be opened by Mr. Ambrose himself, no one else, and no one was to be in the room with him when he opened it."

"Awesome, Virginia! That's excellent! As I expected, you'd be a smash in Scotland Yard! Do you happen to have this secret document?"

"Well no, silly. It was top secret. Top top secret! Mr. Ambrose only!"

"Of course! Stupid of me. Did he speak to you of it then?"

Now she was really upset, having to disappoint this charming Brit twice in succession.

"N-no, he didn't. Sorry!"

Their conspiracy went on for several more minutes, Harry becoming so engaged that Virginia noticed nothing whatsoever of Atwood's disappearance or re-appearance from the Ambassador's inner office.

"Let's off then, Harry."

"Right, Dick. Listen, Virginia our thanks and those of the PM and the Queen. If you should hear

*anything at all that would help us locate His Excellency,
use this private number, won't you? Night or day.
Thanks ever so much."*

*"You're welcome, Harry. I'll call as soon as I
hear anything!"*

As soon as they were gone, Virginia whipped out
her compact, slapped it open and checked her teeth. Sure
enough. Two tiny specks of dark green between her
upper bicuspids. ("Damn! Damn! Damn!")

Not a minute later, Enriqueta Villona-Camaron
was at her desk. "Riki" was an assistant to the Embassy
financial officer, and one of the friendliest and best loved
people in the complex, especially the women, with whom
she shared more gossip than anyone else. Not shared,
exactly, but mostly gathered, rewarding her sources with
huge sighs and "Oh My's."

*"Madre de Dios, Virginia, who was the handsome
one who was so taken with you?"*

*"Oh, him? Just, well -- did you think he was
'taken' with me?"*

*"Are you kidding, sister? He was all over you
like a dog in heat!"*

*"Really? Well, I must say. He was one of those
British Foreign Service types, looking for Peter.
Something urgent, but I couldn't help him. Apparently
the English are scouring the country for Peter. Must be
something big. You haven't heard anything about where
he's gone off to, have you?"*

"Not a thing, but wherever he is, it might not be a bad thing for you if your Englishman has to come back and meet you again in his search, eh?"

"Damn!" Virginia pouted. *"No chance of that! You know I smiled at the man, not once, but twice."*

"So?"

"So I had stupid grape leaves caught in my teeth both times. I must have looked like some hick from the holler! He'll never be back!"

"Listen to Mama, Gringo! I watched him from behind the corner here. He was leaning over you and looking down your blouse every chance he got, and you <u>know</u> he liked what he saw there!"

Virginia looked down at her blouse, noticed that an extra button had come undone, and suddenly felt encouraged.

Riki said a quick "see you later, chickadee. You better practice up on the Queen's English!"

Minutes later, back in her own office, her door tightly closed, she dialed the number of an international cell phone. It rang in the basement of the Diga Palace.

Don Alberto answered the second ring, but had trouble hearing the voice on the other end. He had to excuse himself to climb the stairs to the main floor where the "party" was in full swing. Taking no chances, he walked quickly through the great hall and out onto the slate patio at the rear of the building.

"Si, Enriqueta… Atwood? Himself? How long ago?"

"Did he get any help at the Embassy?"

Don Alberto listened patiently.

"Thank you. Call me again, immediately, if you hear more."

He felt a sudden wave of concern. He had known of Atwood's work in the Falklands, as had all Argentines and diplomats the world over. *("He is a well-known killing machine, one who is sent on the toughest, and most expensive missions.")*

Don Alberto's mind shifted into another gear. Whoever had arranged for Darden's imprisonment and torture in Finland had also meant for him to die there. Clearly, they had learned of his escape, and needed to complete their earlier mission, now even more urgently, if they were willing to involve the British Government. He made the sign of the Cross.

("Holy Father, there is no time to lose. Be with us now. You know three more men must die if we are to have your justice. There is no question there. But we must complete our work and make certain that the evidence of it is gone, then I must be sure that my son is also safely gone. I cannot allow him to be trapped and imprisoned again. He is all I have left.")

Chapter Forty-Five
The Diga Palace

The Smoking Room

The smell of burnt flesh was enough to horrify and sicken everyone in the room. All except one. It sent the Embassy doctor into his third fainting spell. Having shut down the current for the fourth and final time, Don Alberto rose from his chair to check the General's arm for a pulse. There was none.

He turned to John Akers. *"You, Major Akers, are the one who, I understand, devised the ingenious plan for my daughter's destruction...her suffering, her death. It is now..."*

"-- Hold, Don Alberto!" Jim rose from his chair.

"Let's deal with two others first. I have my reasons, and they are important. We'll get to Major Akers in a few minutes."

Don Alberto looked hard into his son-in- law's eyes, studied them, then sat down.

Jim turned to the Embassy doctor, who was just coming out of his third swoon.

"Doctor, you gave the Major a syringe for me to use, to help Maria deal with her claustrophobia while in the pipe."

*"Oh my God, yes, but pleasepleaseplease understand I had no idea I was helping him to – to -- I had no idea what I was doing! I thought I was **helping**, I swear. He told me he needed something to help someone calm their fears of small places. I started to provide the drug, but he stopped me and made me give him only a syringe of water. I thought surely it was nothing more than a practical joke, I swear to God! I had no idea it was for your wife! You've <u>got</u> to believe me!"*

Jim heard the words, saw the abject terror in the trembling and tearful eyes, and tried to push them from his mind. He couldn't.

"Don Alberto, please step outside with me."

The old man's face suddenly wore a look of apprehension. This was not the way things were supposed to go. Slowly, he rose from his chair and followed Jim through the door behind them and into a darkened tunnel.

The two men stood silently in the dark for a moment, their eyes adjusting to it.

"If what he says is true, we have no cause to kill him."

The Spaniard thought for a moment. "<u>If</u> what he says is true. If it is <u>not</u>?"

"Then he dies, but I wasn't there. We can't be certain that he is lying."

Don Alberto was silent for a length of time. Jim waited, sure that both of them were thinking the same thoughts.

"There is no way to let him live, my son. What we are doing here is too important. It is hard to say, but if a merely corrupt man must die so that guilty ones pay the price, so be it."

It was Jim's turn to be silent, chewing on Don Alberto's words, including his sudden, unanticipated use of *"my son."*

"I have done my country's bidding. For two years I fought the Afghan tribesmen. I killed several, face to face, two after interrogations. I believed that my mission was more important than my feelings, even my personal beliefs about killing. In this case I am suddenly not so sure. This is not my country's mission. It is mine."

The old man understood, and suddenly felt a wave of sadness so strong he actually shuddered, though Jim couldn't see it in the dark.

"Listen to me, James. We cannot stop now. If we let the Doctor live. What becomes of us? What becomes of the justice that we bring to the others? I would gladly lose my life in the taking of theirs, in battle, but I would not sacrifice yours to a government or a legal system that allows them to go free after such an evil murder of the woman you loved. It may be hard, but the Doctor must

die, if for no other reason than that he is here, witnessing what befalls those around him who have truly earned their own suffering and death."

It was the way the old man had said "James." He couldn't stand it. His mind raced, searching, searching for somewhere to stand, some principle that was tall enough, strong enough to turn them aside from what he knew they had to do, not because it was right, but because it was necessary.

His plans didn't cover what he might do beyond killing Maria's killers. To him there was no honor in killing the doctor. No rightness. But then, he had to admit he hadn't even thought about it.

"Shit!" he said, and turned to open the door.

The old man spoke softly.

"I will handle it. You talk to him. Tell him it is difficult, but you believe him. Tell him you forgive him."

The two men walked back into the room and faced the semi-circle of five chairs. While they had been gone, it was clear that Ambrose, Roberts, and Akers had been talking, but at their entrance the voices stopped in mid-sentence.

The doctor seemed to have shriveled, a size or two smaller than he had been. Despite what might have been the hopeful sign of his captors' caucus, he was still terrified.

Jim took his chair and faced the doctor, while Don Alberto continued walking around behind the semi-circle. Ambrose and Akers craned their necks to follow his movement, but the doctor was riveted on Jim.

"Well I must say that your words gave me some doubts. I'm inclined to believe you, Doctor, and I'm inclined to believe it would be wrong to kill you here..."

"-- Oh, my God, my sweet God, thankyouthankyou thankyou! I swear I had nothing to –"

The report of the pistol was muffled by its silencer, but the quick crunch of bone and the spattering of blood and brain was followed milliseconds later by the clatter of the bullet against the stone wall and finally the floor behind Jim. As it tore through his skull, the doctor gave out a final terrified squeak, not unlike a small dog, or even a rodent. It was an enormously pitiful sound.

———————

Jim turned to Roberts, who seemed to have avoided the panic that surrounded him.

"Listen. You are a Marine. You know that people in and out of uniform are sent on missions every day, well, damn near every week anyway, to take somebody out. Usually some foreigner. We were doing our job, nothing more. I'm sorry it involved you and your wife. I share your sorrow, even your anger at that, but we're all on the same team here. We're Americans, doing jobs for America. You've already taken out the

*Georgian Bear and the doc. Why not call it a day and
stop the bloodshed?"*

*"This has nothing to do with my mission, Major.
It's personal."*

*"Bullshit. You know you were sent over here to
dig up dirt about Mr. Ambrose -- to spy on your own
countrymen. And you know damn well why your wife got
roped into it -- to stop you. This thing is so much bigger
than you and me. We're both pawns in a global chess
game. Be honest -- you recognized that a long time ago.
It's a crappy chess game at that, but it goes up so much
higher than a Marine Captain and an Assistant Nothing
in Tbilisi, Georgia."*

*"Really? Why don't you educate me? Just how
high does this – 'chess game' go?"*

Ambrose was now sweating profusely, even
though the temperature in the dimly lit room was
decidedly cool. He twisted his neck to glare at Roberts.

*"Shut the fuck up you twit! Do you actually think
you're going to talk your way out of this? These people
are nuts. Crazy. Can't you see it in his eyes? Look at
what they did to the fucking doc?*

"On the other hand..." he looked back at Jim,
taking a more respectful tone.

*"...I can assure you that Roberts had no real part
in anything that was done to you or your wife. He's
right. He's an Assistant Nothing. Let him go. I'm sure
you will have his eternal gratitude and silence."*

Don Alberto ended the conversation with a second muffled blast from his pistol. This shot was to (and through) Roberts' right temple, the bullet making a much bigger exit hole than entry, spilling blood and pink brain tissue on the already dead doctor.

"I am sorry to be so abrupt, Jim, but time is of the essence."

Only Akers and Ambrose left.

"I understand, Don Alberto, but these two require a bit more time. A single shot to the head is too little for these two."

Don Alberto simply nodded, as both Ambrose and Akers started shouting at once, rambling with hysteria.

"You can't do this! It's not fair! You can't just grab people and torture them for -- I never meant to hurt your wife! It was your mistake, not mine! I thought I gave you the right wrench, I swear I did! I've got a wife and children, for God's sake! Pleasepleaseplease don't!"

Jim waited patiently, sitting perfectly still until they both finally fell silent, exhausted. He gazed at them, first one, then the other, his eyes finally coming to rest on Akers.

"John, it takes everything in me to put aside the fact that you're an arrogant shit with no basis for your arrogance. I wouldn't be surprised if you were a grade school bully, picking on kids smaller and weaker than

*you. I don't know what you have against the Corps, and
I don't care.*

*"What will kill you in the next few minutes is what
you did to me and to Maria. How creative it was, how
masterful. You were the man with the net and tweezers. I
was the insect. You pulled my wings and half my legs off
and made me run for shelter, probably laughing as I
struggled. You didn't kill Maria. You made me do it,
knowing that saving her was everything I was working,
even dying, to do.*

*"You probably enjoyed every minute of it. Just as
I'm going to enjoy the next few minutes."*

Akers was suddenly face to face with ultimate
defeat. There were no words he could say to change that.
He glared back at Jim, the corners of his mouth curling in
a sneer.

*"Go ahead, then, Mr. Big Shot Jarhead. You
guys are all alike -- buying all the horeshit they feed you
at boot camp about being better than mere soldiers and
seamen, God's fucking gift to warfare. The Few, the
Proud, the Bullshit!*

*"You're damn right I took you down, boy-o! And
I laughed my ass off at the thought of you down there on
that wharf, crying 'oh dear, the wrench doesn't fit,
whatever will I do? I don't know how the hell you got out
of the brig, and found your way back here, but it couldn't
have been on your own nickel. You couldn't find your ass
with both hands. And as for your big-tit bimbo..."*

This time it was Jim's revolver, also silenced. The muffled pop was drowned out by Akers' roar of pain. The bullet had shattered his right kneecap, small fragments of bone flying out of his shredded pant leg in several directions.

He continued to groan and cry loudly, suddenly inhaling in tiny, shallow panting breaths, as if his lung had been punctured rather than his knee. As he struggled with the suddenly wrenching task of drawing breath, he finally accepted the reality of his situation. He looked up at Darden with an entirely new expression, one Jim had never seen before. He was suddenly 10 or 12, crying like a baby.

"For God's sake! Have some fucking mercy!"

Jim's fury was a hot wind that circled around his brain, rushing blood to his eyes, a throbbing of his racing heart in his own ears. It was all he could do to get the words out through clenched teeth.

"God may have mercy on you. I have none."

The second shot shattered the other kneecap. More screams of pain. The third shot blew away his left elbow, the fourth his right. He waited until the screams died away, leaving only ragged panting and animal whimpering. Akers lost consciousness, but only for a few moments.

Jim reached down to a panel to the right of his chair and pushed a button. The manacles binding Akers' arms and legs snapped open.

"Get up John."

"Nonononono pleasepleasepleaseno. You know I can't move. For God's...sake!"

"You have no God, John Akers! Get the hell up! Now! Or the next one takes out your balls!"

Akers lurched forward, but what was left of his legs crumpled under him like straw. He fell forward, with another scream, but when his forearms hit the stone floor they collapsed as well. The sounds he was making now were pitiful squeaks, then even those stopped as his agony finally overwhelmed his consciousness.

The storm of rage was a consuming holocaust behind Jim's eyes, a mushroom cloud of hot wind that roared in his ears and overwhelmed everything in him that was human. He watched Akers' shattered body quiver several times at his feet, but still he watched through a blood curtain of his own fury. He looked around quickly, searching for something, anything, to wake the man up so he could continue.

Don Alberto caught Jim's glances around the room, sensed their purpose, and, stepped between the two men, pointed his pistol downward and put a hole in the back of Akers' skull. No more movement. No more screams.

Peter Ambrose couldn't take any more of the smell of warm blood and tissue that littered the space between him and his captors. He leaned as far forward as he could and wretched, doing his best to miss his trousers, but failing miserably. The smell of his own

vomit now combined with the others' to make him
wretch even more violently for several minutes.

Don Alberto turned to his son-in-law, reached out
to hold Jim by both shoulders, looking deeply into his
eyes.

*"I can take care of the rest of this. We need to
clean up and get out. Others are coming for us. People
more ruthless, more violent than either of us. You go, out
the back to the car. Let me finish."*

Jim shook his head. *"No! We do this together.
We finish it and we leave together. We have an
agreement. Besides, this last one is important for more
than the justice we seek."*

There was much yet to do.

———————

Dick Atwood sat in the State Travel Office in
downtown Tbilisi with Ramsey and Reggie Wills, a
veteran of Afghanistan and Iraq. Together they peppered
the harried clerk with question after question.

*"Any hunting or fishing cabins away from other
people, other distractions?"*

The clerk scratched his head, then shook it.

*"We fish in our rivers and a few lakes, but it
would be hard to say they are far from anywhere. We are
not a large country."*

"Show me."

The clerk swiveled in his chair and picked up half a dozen black and white brochures from a rack behind his desk. Atwood took them and scanned them, rejecting one after another.

"No good, I'm afraid. We need something else."

"Resort hotels? Big ones that are empty or near empty right now?"

Head scratch. Slow head shake.

"The best hotels are probably right here in Tbilisi or over on the Black Sea. Once again, we are a small country, mostly poor, though things began improving recently when we escaped the heel of the Russian boot...although we have been hearing sounds of boots again – even here in the Capital."

Atwood shook his own head, quite a bit more rapidly. He was getting frustrated, and that was an emotion he didn't bear well.

"Listen. I'm looking for seven men who've disappeared -- all at the same time. Apparently five of them were invited somewhere, and they went, so the invitation had to be pretty attractive, pretty impressive. So stop scratching your bloody head and give me some ideas on where this attractive, impressive soiree is going on."

The clerk automatically reached up to scratch again, but stopped his hand half-way to his scalp, suddenly embarrassed. The look of bewilderment gave his bald head, bulbous nose, and tiny eyes the appearance of a man with serious mental limitations.

Suddenly the tiny eyes widened, followed by a smile of very bad teeth.

"Well, it could be the Diga Palace! Quite a fine place, if you like dead animals and gold leaf, and it is as far from anything as one might find in Georgia!"

Atwood reached over and patted the man on the cheek as if he was a three-year old. *"Now, that's encouraging. Where the hell is the Diga Palace?"*

"It is, let me see, perhaps an hour from here, perhaps a little more -- to the north. I can get you a brochure -- and a map!"

Wills chucked Atwood on the shoulder, nodding his head in encouragement while the clerk rose from his chair and went into a file room behind him. He came back with even wider eyes and his massively ugly smile.

"As a matter of fact our records show it was recently reserved for some sort of event!"

Atwood snapped to attention. *"Who reserved it, for when, and for what?"*

The clerk dismissed his smile, suddenly remembering his official status as a State Travel Office Chief Clerk.

"Well, gentlemen, I am not at all certain I am permitted to reveal such information to a foreigner. After all, we are no longer a Communist colony and we have certain rights in this country, such as privacy!"

Atwood reached halfway across the Chief Clerk's desk and this time patted the back of the man's hand softly, smiling his own sweet smile of warmth and understanding. Suddenly, however, he grabbed the man's third finger and twisted it backward, snapping the knuckle where the finger joined the palm. The Clerk gave a high pitched squeal of a tortured farm animal and nearly fainted with the pain -- but not quite. For in the next second, Atwood had his own fingers wrapped around the Clerk's ring finger and was ready to dislocate it as well.

"Oh God, no more no more, I beg you! I'm terribly sorry. It was rented by the firm of Caballos y Cervantes, for a large party this weekend. The firm requested total privacy, no publicity of any kind. Please no more, I beg you!"

Atwood looked at him with a mixture of surprise, horror, and tender mercy.

"Dear, dear, did I do that? How awful of me! It must have been the excitement of the moment. Here, let me fix it."

With that he grabbed the limp third finger and popped it back into place with a loud crack. The Clerk squealed again, even louder, and fainted dead away. When he awakened, he was overcome with relief, not only because he was alone, but also because the third finger of his left hand was actually functional. Terribly sore, but functional.

Atwood and his team were miles away, heading north, traveling very fast, despite the snowy roads.

Peter Ambrose was drowning -- in a violent, sucking whirlpool of utter defeat. Everything he had worked for, every advantage he had sought, every stratagem he had concocted, now counted for nothing.

No fortune. No influence. No membership in the club of powerful people, no chance to wield his own sword in the great fencing match of political games people play in capital cities around the world.

And now, no more sight. No sound, no touch, no joy of victory, only the agony of one final, crushing defeat.

Unless...

"Captain Darden. You must be feeling quite powerful right now. Quite in control, and in fact you are. Congratulations. You have won the battle, sir, and you deserve the commendation of your superiors."

Jim was already tired of this. He picked up the revolver and stared down at it.

"*No, no wait, please! Let me speak. I have something you want -- if I'm right, you want it perhaps more than you want me dead.*"

Jim looked up again, one eyebrow a little higher than the other.

"*That's right. I realize why you might want it more than my death. Because beneath your anger and your passion to avenge your wife, and I don't blame you for that at all, is your dedication to the Marine Corps and to your country. You are first of all a patriot, a man who puts country first.*"

The eyebrow began to drop, the stare became a glare.

"*No, please, don't get even more angry with me. I'm being as sincere as I can possibly be -- fuck, I'm staring at the barrel of your damned gun and I'm bound here, utterly, utterly powerless, and four other men around me are dead! I've got my own puke all over myself. Jesus!*"
(*"No, no, calm down, this isn't going right at all. Get yourself together!"*)

Peter took a deep breath.

"*Jim. For God's sake listen to me. I have what you came here for. Your mission, Jim, your reason for leaving... (what the fuck was her name? Oh, yes!)... Maria behind just after your wedding. I have the plan for sub-rosa ownership of the oil pipeline. I have the names. I can give it all to you. I can give you the achievement*

*you came here for. I can -- I can restore your career,
your reputation, your soul for all I know."*

Jim raised the gun, pointed it directly at the center
of Peter Ambrose's face. As he did, he watched the face
disintegrate. From the obvious look of intelligence, it
worked frantically to the look of a frightened, defeated
adolescent, a child even. Peter Ambrose began to cry, his
eyes and nose running, mucus running down into his
mouth, unable to raise a hand to stop it,

*"For the love of heaven, Jim, I'm begging you.
Let me give you what you want. Just let me live. I
realize...I realize...what it means, as I never did before.
I've been chasing a stupid, hollow dream for...for as long
as...oh, God, Jim, just let me live."*

Captain James Darden, USMC, raised his weapon
and fired three rapid rounds. The muted detonations and
the clatter of bullets against stone walls quieted perhaps
four seconds later.

In those four seconds, Peter Ambrose wet his
trousers with more than vomit. He did, however,
continue to breathe for a few moments longer, until a
final bullet from Don Alberto's gun put an end to that.

Twenty minutes later the room was empty. A
large raised square of marble in the center of the floor
had been opened electrically, and five bodies had been
pushed into the deep pit below, including the room's
furniture. There an intensely hot, gas-fed fire incinerated
everything to a fine ash. Above, Jim used a high-pressure
hose of boiling water to wash down the entire room,
happily relieving it of its olfactory horrors.

Chapter Forty-Six
Washington, DC

December 18, 9:17am
The Oval Office

"The Tragedy of life is not that man loses, but that he almost wins." (Heywood Broun, 1922)

Larry Claymore was sitting with the President. The Oval Office, in fact the entire West Wing had been overwhelmed with Christmas decorations. Strings of greeting cards from all over the world were taped up on every vertical surface, flowers and little lit trees everywhere, even to the plates of variously iced butter cookies and the steaming pots of cinnamon-and-clove scented cider near every coffee maker.

They had worked through the twelve things on Coleman Farr's agenda extensively, so thoroughly in fact, that Claymore was sick of it, especially as distracted as he was.

Finally, the President had relaxed his snide, hard-ass, belittling barrage of questions and admitted that Larry had done everything he could, (and damn-well should have done.)

Though he hadn't heard from Dick Atwood and his team yet, Claymore was confident that the MI-5 squad was just what the doctor ordered. He expected word any minute.

The knock on the door was way too firm to be the President's secretary, too rapid to be casual business. As it opened, three secret service suits entered followed by the Commandant of the US Marine Corps, the Vice President, four other four-star generals, one Admiral, and the god-damn Chief Justice of the Supreme Court. It was he who spoke, his sonorous voice deep and clear, less pompous than when at a speaker's rostrum, or behind the bench, but somehow even more serious. There were no holiday greetings.

"Mr. President, I regret to inform you sir, that charges have been filed against Mr. Claymore and several others. A special prosecutor will be named shortly, and he will have numerous questions for you personally.

"Serious charges are pending that will result in immediate indictments and if this situation involves you, moves to impeach. We would ask Mr. Claymore to leave the White House now and go with these men, and that you sir, consider surrendering your powers to the Vice President immediately and obtaining counsel."

For perhaps the first time in his adult life, Coleman Farr was (practically) speechless. He could only look at Lawrence Claymore in disbelief.

"What have you done to me, Larry? What in God's name have you done?"

Larry didn't return the President's questioning gaze. He kept his eyes on the floor as he was led out of the Oval Office.

("I was so close, so damn close, you sonofabitch! I could have bought you and sold you a hundred times before breakfast!")

When they were outside the Oval Office, General Markham stopped the procession, grabbing Claymore by the elbow.

"Before we go anywhere, Mr. Claymore, you have a job to do, right now."

Claymore shot him a surprised look. *"Oh?"*

"Get back on your cell phone and call off your MI-5 dogs...right now, or I'll personally have your ass."

Claymore was thunderstruck. All this time, he had been so sure of silence, of secrecy. Suddenly he wondered whether he'd been traced through all of it. The world around him was collapsing with stunning effect.

Slowly, he reached for his belt clip and drew up his cell phone and punched the buttons.

"Geoffrey? This is Claymore in Washington. No, no. Nothing more. In fact I'm calling to tell you to call Atwood's team off. The mission is over. Cancelled. (A long pause.) Listen. I understand, but do what you can to call them off, Geoffrey. Now. This minute."

He hung up, handing the phone to General Markham.

"Mr. Claymore, you'd better damn well hope you were in time. Adding murder to the charges against you won't do your lifespan a bit of good."

As he left the White House for the last time, Lawrence Claymore was actually dizzy. His entire world, so carefully constructed, now whirling like bathwater going down the drain.

Still, he broke a small smile – as Plan "B" began to take shape in his disappointed mind. He would go down for what he had done, and he would go down hard. But he would take the man who had made his life so miserable for almost eight years with him. The smile grew wider.

Chapter Forty-Seven
La Gomera

December 24, 6:17pm

It was Christmas Eve. The terrace overlooking San Sebastian was as captivating as ever, perhaps more so. Esperanza had decorated it with a large and elaborate crèche in one corner and dozens of brilliant red poinsettias surrounding it. In the town below, decorations were everywhere, and last-minute shoppers picked among the season's offerings, not so much for toys or other gifts, as for special treats for family Christmas meals.

Don Alberto was full of smiles, the joy of the season reflected in his eyes as he took in the beauty Esperanza and the people of San Sebastian had assembled.

Jim should have been happy, but he wasn't. He should have been at peace, but he wasn't. He should have felt vindicated, satisfied, but he didn't. Carols, even in Spanish, and joyous Christmas greetings wishing "peace on earth to men of good will" felt like nothing more than a jagged bone stuck in his throat.

His was drawn, tired to the point of exhaustion, but more than that, his face wore a look of sorrow so deep it might never fade from the once smooth cheeks with quick brown eyes and ready smile.

Don Alberto studied the lines of his son-in-law's face, and saw the suffering within. Knew that with time, it might fade. With new love, new missions, it might fade further, but this suffering might never disappear totally. Nonetheless, he would try everything to bring some relief. This was not his son, and in truth he had only known him a short time, but with his wife gone these many years, and Maria, his only child now in heaven with his beloved Carmelita, Jim Darden had become as much his son as anything else.

"You are grieving. Would you like to be alone?"

It took a long time for Jim to answer. Don Alberto waited patiently.

"I suppose I am. But not just for the loss of Maria. I did that in the cell in Finland when they left me alone. I guess I'm grieving for something else. Something more."

"Surely it cannot be for the death of evil men...men who stole your Maria and mine."

"Not for them, precisely. The doctor, perhaps, didn't deserve to die. It could be he was telling the truth. We killed him because we were afraid to let him go."

"Listen, my son. I was the one who pulled the –"

"-- Don Alberto, please, there is no distinction between us. What we did, we did together. I won't divide the responsibility. We killed those men."

He was silent then, and Don Alberto could think of nothing to add. After a time, Jim continued.

"I grieve for my soul and yours. Something died in me in that room with all the anger and rage and desire to punish those men. In the moment, there was a blood rush, something in me that was as much animal as human. As vivid and powerful as it was, I can't be proud of it. When they died, the killing brought no satisfaction, or peace, or vindication of any kind.

"Ambrose spoke about restoring my reputation, my career, my soul. Nothing is restored, Don Alberto. Instead something in me died."

A flame flickered near the older man's heart, a flame of something like sudden anger.

"Is this remorse I am hearing? Guilt? Are you seeking absolution for destroying evil men?"

For another long silence the two men stared hard at each other, then both looked away, far off into the Atlantic. Jim finally continued.

"We did what we did with full intention, with full planning and preparation, and we played out our script, almost to the end. We eliminated the evidence, and evaded the Brits until they were called off. We were successful....

"...Absolution? No, Don Alberto, I seek no absolution...because I don't believe there is one. In fact I would think less of my God if he were to forgive me so easily.

"We killed five men. We avenged Maria. What pains me most now is that she is still gone, and the death of those men leaves me not satisfied, not peaceful, but hollow, exhausted more deeply than I could imagine."

Don Alberto found himself struggling all the harder to find some way to relieve these feelings, to make things better.

"James, even your General Markham bears no such doubts. He has done something truly extraordinary, in wrapping this entire chain of events in a cloak of silence. How long it lasts is anyone's guess, but for the moment we need fear no charges, no punishments. Yet he knows full well why you and I went back to Georgia."

Jim actually smiled at that, but it was a small, fleeting smile.

"True enough. It was more than I could have hoped for."

Don Alberto tried not to laugh, but failed.

"Let's just agree," Jim said. *"We did something I would not want to do again. We fought evil with evil. Killing with more killing. I am certainly not a happier man today, and in my heart, I'm pretty sure you aren't either."*

Don Alberto's face filled with a cloud of sorrow.

"You have not been listening, my son. I don't have your doubts..or your regrets. I believe we have been given the intelligence needed to discriminate

between good and evil. Some men merely do evil – they should be punished – and then forgiven. Others actually <u>become</u> evil. They must be stopped. Their evil must be defeated. Justice demands it"

Jim did't answer at first, but first looked into Don Alberto's eyes, and then far out to sea.

"That is too easy. I certainly don't regret the desire to find justice, to balance the wheels of evil. In that room under the Palace, the fire in me wanted more than any 'justice.' More than any 'balance.' Now that it's over, from this side of the ledger, I don't believe an eye for an eye balances the wheels. I'm not sure what it is, but there must be a better way."

The old man turned his face to the sea breeze, and was lost in thought. The sky began to darken as the sun set across the Atlantic. In the growing dusk, he finally spoke, his voice firm and strong.

"Then we agree to disagree, for in my heart, I believe you are wrong. Your doubts are a burden I don't carry. For me, justice can be primitive, direct, swift, and absolute. Those men took one life, and nearly another. Why? to serve their own lust for money and power, their own greed and corruption. They not only took a life, but took it with a wanton cruelty that finds no sympathy, no milk of human understanding in me. Justice required their suffering and death. Period.

"As to the doctor, perhaps there were mitigating circumstances, and there, I too will harbor some sorrow.

"For the others, no. As to their deaths, I have no doubts. The contest between good and evil will go on until the day of our Judgement. When that day comes, we must all be ready to face God and His accounting of our actions. Until then, I will sleep peacefully.

"In fact, you might say I sleep the sleep of the dead."

About the Author

Lou Briganti has been a management consultant serving federal agencies and private sector clients for more than 30 years in and around Washington, DC. His varied career includes classified military research and development, disaster preparedness, nuclear facilities vulnerability to terrorist attacks, and a wide range of related disciplines.

Born and raised in metropolitan New York, he graduated from Georgetown University and pursued law studies at the Georgetown Law Center before changing to Business Administration at American University. He has conducted numerous management and leadership seminars over the years and in 2005, wrote a self-help book on communication skills for business people, entitled "Right Side Up!"

He suffers both deep depression and eternal hope for his adopted baseball team, the once awesome and now awful Baltimore Orioles. He is married to Jacqueline Billings Briganti, who causes him no depression at all. They live in the beautiful Shenandoah Valley, in Fairfield, Virginia, and have two grown daughters and five grandchildren.